CLAN WOODSMEN

BOOK 1:
THE GENERAL'S REFUGE

BY: A.C. GILLIES

My Thank-You's:

I want to thank my family for always believing in me.
I love you guys.

I also want to thank my editing companions.
You guys are awesome.

Thanks, Michele for all the grammar lessons.
You made things much easier for me.
You are the best.

This book is dedicated to all the women who love
Alpha-Males:
The Hunter, The Cowboy, The Conqueror,
and last but not least,
The Soldier

PROLOGUE

On a moonless night, just outside of Morocco, the arid wind blew fiercely. Special Forces Captain Luc Trembley sat on his cot wiping the desert grit from his face. He took a deep breath as his piercing almond shaped eyes scanned his surroundings. His adrenaline was just getting under control. He was sitting in the dark fuming; he was angry at his cousin Marcus.

"Captain Trembley."

Luc stood up. He immediately jumped to attention and saluted his commanding officer.

After returning the salute, the commander spoke to him, "Captain Marcus Allard is causing too much trouble lately. We are busting him back down to Lieutenant. He's been reassigned to your platoon, he's your problem now. See if you can straighten his ass out."

What else could he say, "Yes, Sir."

"Luc, on a better note, I just got word. They liked how your platoon handled the mess this afternoon. A high value target was terminated. Tonight, you're going to bed a Captain, tomorrow you'll wake up a Major. Good job son."

"Thank you, sir."

"Unfortunately, your promotion comes with a price. They are shipping your platoon back to America. A treaty was signed between our country, the U.S., and Mexico. Canada will still have its own military branch, however, we will all be considered one united country. It became official today. We are at war with Russia and South America. Marcus will rendezvous with your platoon before you reach your new post. May God protect you, Captain Trembley."

"Thank you, sir."

CHAPTER 1

Elise closed her eyes. She tried to make sense of this life she was now leading. It was early spring and still cold outside. She was chilled to the bone despite the warmth of her garments. This time five years ago she had quit her job and was going back to college to finish what she had started a decade before. At 35 she still had a young face. She was no ordinary beauty, with her long brown hair and green eyes, she was stunning to look at.

The stench of the body odor surrounding her brought her back to reality, and the realization that life had changed, and would forever be altered. War had brought down society and turned its survivors into warring clans and tribes. She had been caught unaware of the men on horses surrounding her as she had been hunting, or more like scavenging for food. Her hands and feet were bound and yet she was unhurt. She had not fought the soldiers. She had surrendered like a coward, or perhaps, like a smart woman who knew she had been defeated.

It seemed like days since she had been in the prisoner wagon. There was one other woman and two men. She imagined that they would be treated fairly, since no one had mistreated them thus far. They had been fed, not a lot, but enough not to be ravenous. The prisoners were a dirty group; they smelled atrocious. No one spoke or even looked at one another.

Elise was awoken with a shove, she was disoriented and stumbled from the wagon. It was twilight, dark, but light enough to see her surroundings. A man pushed her and the other prisoners forward to show it was time to start moving. The men and women were separated. Elise looked at the wall of the outer building she was standing next to. It was a great sturdy rock wall with limited windows.

The men stayed in the large open area outside the building, a form of courtyard, and the women were shown to a large room with many candles burning, and multiple cots. The man from the wagon told the women that they were to stand and wait. They were informed that they would be able to bathe and eat, before being allowed to sleep. It felt like hours until someone, a servant it seemed, showed up to cut them free. She escorted them to a bathing chamber.

Elise washed her hair, scrubbed her face and body. She donned a light cotton robe that had been provided for her. She felt like a million dollars. It was ages since she had a proper bath. Funny how a day can seem like forever, and a month an eternity. The women were escorted back to the room they first entered. Food was waiting for them, more than enough had been provided. Full and clean, Elise felt a calming in her soul. She sensed everything was going to be okay. She may be a prisoner or future servant of this clan, but she perceived that life was going to be less stressful. No more being cold, hungry, or afraid. She had never had an issue with hard work, she would accept this fate, and this clan.

She wasn't sure how long she had been sleeping when she was gently shaken awake. A man standing over her told her to come with him. Shy and disoriented she followed. He led her through several hallways and into a large, dimly lit room. The furnishings were expensive, the room clean. There was a large bed in the center of the room, and a fire burning in a fireplace. The man handed her a small cloth and asked her to sit on the bed and put it on. He explained to her briefly why she was there. He told her not to worry or be frightened, that no harm would come to her.

How could she not be afraid, when suddenly, it was clear. She felt like a coward, she didn't fight, she didn't argue, or question. She didn't cry, Elise did what was asked of her. She sat on the bed, put on the blindfold, and waited. The door creaked only once as the man left. She absently sat there running her fingers through her long, now dry hair. Blind to the room, a man's voice made her jump. His voice was soft, kind and sexy.

"What is your name?"

She just sat there in a daze, unsure. He said something soft almost purringly in what she suspected was French, or a dialect of French. She could smell him. He was close. She felt his fingers touch her hair, and it sent shivers down her back.

He asked her again in a soft whisper, his voice a masculine seductive timbre. "What is your name, Ma Chérie?"

She replied softly "Elise".

"Ah, Elise, stand up and let me look at you." His voice was soft. He whispered to her, like this was a secret rendezvous between two lovers.

She made no move, so he reached for her shoulders pulling her up. She stood before him half afraid, half excited. He kissed her neck and sent shivers down her back. He kissed her mouth. She did not kiss him back. He whispered something in French in her ear, then kissed her neck. She was excited, turned on. He could be anyone, she could be anyone. It had been a long time since she felt the touch of a man. He was being gentle and patient. He could be a soldier, a warrior; he could take what he wanted and be brutal and fast. Instead, he pulled off her robe and picked her up.

She let him. He kissed her mouth, and she kissed him back. It may have been wrong, but she'd worry about that in the morning. He kissed her and caressed her until her body was on fire. He entered her slowly, and she moved with him. He made love to her, took his time, enjoyed her. The blindfold had been erotic. She could be passionate and not be afraid. She felt uninhibited. She matched his passion until they were both satisfied. She climaxed and he was finally happy to surrender, he had waited until she had been satisfied. He wanted her content. They laid on the bed silent for a few moments enjoying the warmth of each other. The bed was soft, it smelled fresh and masculine. The smell of sex hung in the air. Finally, he covered her with a blanket and kissed her back.

He whispered in her ear "Until next time Ma Chérie, wait a few moments before you remove your blindfold. Sleep well."

Elise did as she was asked. She waited a few moments, removed the blindfold, and she was alone. It was amazing how erotic that moment had been, a pure fantasy. She wondered if he would love her again. She had enjoyed the passion he had instantly found in her; she would welcome his touch should he come to her again. She fell asleep and slept long and hard for the first time in many months.

Elise woke the next morning when the girl she met the night before opened the shutters.

"Good morning, my name is Bridgette. You're going to like it here. Life is not hard."

Sleepily she replied to her, "I'm Elise." She blinked the sleep from her eyes and adjusted herself to the light.

Bridgette smiled at Elise. "I've got fresh things for you, get dressed and bring your robe with you, I'll be waiting in the next room". Elise nodded that she understood.

When she entered the room, she remembered passing through it the night before. Bridgette explained to Elise, that she would be with her on the General's side of the house. Bridgette was brief about the General. "He is the head of the clan. His cousin Marcus is second in command, they are kind men, but do not cross them. Especially the General, he has a fine temper. Do what you're asked, keep your head down, you will be fine."

Elise thought Bridgette was lovely to look at, she studied her features while she was talking to her. Elise wondered what had happened to the other people that had been brought here with her. Elise liked Bridgette and was relieved to be staying with her. Bridgette showed Elise around. She took her to the bunk house where she would be sleeping, she showed Elise the kitchen, where she saw one of the women prisoners. Bridgette finally took Elise to the back of the compound. She informed her that today she would do laundry, but that she might get moved around a bit depending on what was needed.

Elise was deep in thought when she heard two men with deep booming voices behind her.

"Look at what we found." The voice came from a man with a sing-song French accent. A hand grabbed her and swung her around.

Two of the biggest men she'd ever seen were looming over her. One was a rugged, burly brute. The other tall but not wide shouldered like his partner.

"New here, are you?" the same rugged man asked in his French accent.

Elise shoved the man's hand off her shoulder. "Don't touch me," she told him without fear.

The man slapped Elise across the face. It wasn't hard yet stung enough to receive the message that had been sent.

"What's going on here?" The two men jumped at the sound of the new voice. It was masculine, harsh, with authority in every word. "I said, what's going on here."

"Nothing General, we've just found a new dove," replied the brute.

Elise turned to the voice. He was handsome and tall. He had black hair and dangerous black eyes. His hair wasn't short, but long enough to reach his collar. He sported a full beard and moustache. Elise noticed something in his eyes, surprise maybe. "This brute hit me because I told him not to touch me."

The General laughed. The men looked unsure. "Go back to the yard. If you don't have anything to do, I will find you something."

The men both nodded and said "Yes, General," simultaneously. The men turned and left.

The General walked closer to Elise. "And you are?"

"Elise," she replied quietly, surprised at herself for her most recent bravado.

He nodded. He reached out and grabbed her hair with his hands. His expression changed from the smiling man, to an almost hostile nature. His tone was harsh, "Bun your hair. I don't want to see it again."

Elise cocked her head sideways at him, showing she did not understand.

"Men see your hair and they will want to ravish you. Bun your hair or be raped by my men. Your choice Elise."

Elise lowered her face to the ground, "Yes, General," she said meekly. He turned and walked away.

Elise finished the laundry. The day had gone quickly. The sun was going down, and there was an ache in her back. She wondered about the events of the afternoon. She hoped she had not made an enemy, whoever the brute may be. Elise went in search of Bridgette and found her in the kitchen. Elise informed Bridgette that the laundry was complete and asked if anything more was needed from her.

Bridgette said to Elise, "Usually we only take care of the General, his cousin, and a few men at a time, so after we get them dinner we may retire. However, tonight they are having a feast. Something big was killed for food and we all may enjoy it."

"Well, what do I do now?" Elise asked her.

"Come with me to the storeroom and help me get something for the men to drink." Bridgette led her through the large dining hall. It was filled with six or so men laughing and talking. Elise noticed the General right away. He had been laughing at something, but his expression had changed the moment he noticed the two women. Elise wondered what he was thinking about. She did not notice that he followed them out of the room with his eyes.

He had been laughing at his cousin's joke, but he couldn't stop thinking about those green eyes. He noticed that she had bunned her hair. Good. Maybe she will avoid trouble yet. When she walked in, he couldn't help himself but look at her. This displeased him because he had more self-control than that. As Elise walked away, their eyes met, and held for a fraction of time.

She could understand why he was the man in charge. She felt electricity run through her veins. She could see from his eyes, his expression, and his attitude, that he was a virile and sexy conqueror.

Bridgette and Elise carried multiple bottles of wine and beer to the dining room. Elise poured the wine for the men, starting with the General. He did not look at her; he maintained his conversation with one of his men.

She had gotten to the third man and he spoke to her, "Thank you, Ma Chérie."

Elise unconsciously looked up and smiled. Could this be the man from last night? He smiled at her. He was handsome and had a boyish charm.

"Marcus, she has other cups to fill, stop hogging the woman," the General said with much irritation.

Elise immediately knew her mistake. His voice sounded angry. She looked at him and felt sorry. If they had been alone, she was certain he would have beaten her.

His eyes alone could describe his mood. She moved on to the next man, then the next. The last to fill was the brutes. She kept her eyes down, never making eye contact. He laughed at her and made some joke in French that all the men laughed at, all except the General. "Elise, go grab more wine, and be quick." A muscle in his jaw twitched.

"Yes, General." He was definitely angry at her for some reason.

Elise's back was turned to the door; she did not hear the man come up behind her.

He whispered in her ear, "Ma Chérie, close your eyes."

Instinctively she obeyed. She had wondered if she would know his touch again and relished in the knowledge that it may be soon.

He whispered in his seductive timbre, "I want you again, let me come to you."

"No, I am not alone," she told him.

"I will find you alone soon. I was jealous when I saw your smile to Marcus. I want your smile all to myself." He kissed her neck sending shivers down her back. "Is that wrong? I must go. Wait a moment for me to go, then you can open your eyes. Until next time, Ma Chérie." He kissed her neck in a one last parting gesture. His voice had been sensual and seductive in such a soft whisper. Her body had already begun to respond to him.

"Elise," the General's voice nearly shouted at her causing her to jump and turn. "What is taking you so long? When I ask you to do something, do it quickly."

She stood there stunned, unsure how much time had passed between the kiss and the shout, but it was like ice cold water being dumped on her.

"Well?" he asked her.

"Uh, I'm sorry," she replied, feeling foolish.

"Grab two bottles and be quick," he practically growled at her.

She quickly did as he asked, then followed him back to the dining hall. She started her rounds over, some men needed more, while others passed. She made no eye contact. She spoke to no one. Remembering Bridgette's advice, she kept her head down.

The men spoke in English and French, some both, others only one or the other. The general got up and talked quietly to Bridgette, then followed her out of the hall.

Elise was just finishing her last round. The bottles were empty when the General sat back down. He engaged in conversation with Marcus in French. Bridgette returned to the hall carrying a tray to take plates and used or unused items back to the kitchen.

The General beckoned Elise and Bridgette to him. He spoke to both women, "You may retire for the evening; the other women can finish tonight." The women nodded in understanding and with that he dismissed them by turning his head and starting a new conversation.

The two women headed towards the bunk room. "Elise, I'm so excited." Elise turned to look at her, unsure of what was going on. "Now that there are so many new women here to help, they have made two new rooms so that we don't have to share the bunk room.

"I don't understand," Elise told her.

"Well, there are too many of us now for one bunk room. You and I get a new arrangement. Let's go look."

They stopped and Bridgette pointed down the hall, "Those are General's rooms. This is mine," she pointed to a door in front her, "and this is yours."

It was down the hall from Bridgette's room. Elise opened the door to her room. It was small, perhaps a closet converted to a bedroom. It was clean with a small bed, a stool as a nightstand, and a small two-drawer dresser.

"Your robe is in the top drawer and a spare set of clothing in the bottom. Come with me; I'll show you our bathing chambers."

It was smaller than the one from the night before. This one was tidy and obviously for a smaller group. Elise hung her robe on an empty hook and took a clean towel from the open pantry. Bridgette told her that this was her bathing chamber as well and she was welcome to anything. It was for them to share. Bridgette explained that her first night was going to be easy, after that all bets were off. Bridgette excused herself from Elise, knowing that Elise would want some time to herself.

Elise wondered about her days to come as she soaked in the tub. If this was an easy day, she wondered what a hard one would look like. She was tired, but the water was soothing. She thought about the General. He was constantly getting angry at her, and this was only her first day. She didn't heed Bridgette's advice very well and keep her head down. She was definitely not invisible or keeping low. He was a handsome man. She couldn't help but be attracted to him. Even when he was angry, he was sexy. He exuded raw masculine power. She wondered what kind of lover he might be.

She finished her bath, she felt better, but even more tired. Clean and ready for bed, she made her way back to her room. A small candle had been left for her on her bedside table. She was grateful for Bridgette, small things like this reminded her of home. Her robe was thin and soft; she left it on as she climbed into bed. She fell asleep, exhausted from her day.

The small candle still burned as he found her in bed. Her long dark hair spilling onto the pillows, her dark lashes touching her cheeks. His loins stirred instantly just by the sight of her. He stood there a moment taking in every inch of her that he could see. He needed her, he wanted her, and soon he would see if she wanted him. He blew out the candle, thankful of the darkness.

CHAPTER 2

She felt soft, smooth hands caressing her face. She was dreaming, half awake, half asleep. The hands touched her throat, shoulders, and then her breasts. Her soft peaks rose to the fiery touch being placed upon them. The kiss on her chest is what finally woke her. She was startled, but calmed as he whispered, "Ma Chérie, I've wanted this all day."

The room was pitch black, so no blindfold was needed. There was no need to close her eyes or worry. He kissed her long and hard. She kissed him back with equal passion. The kisses told each other they were needed, and they both had longed for a lover to ease the burden of this world. They both touched and explored, uninhibited in the darkness, loving every kiss, touch, and caress. They made love for hours, finally climaxing together in ecstasy. He rolled off her and pulled her into his arms. Elise fell asleep cradled in his arms. She hoped that one day soon, they could be together openly, not just in secrecy.

Elise woke the next morning to banging on her door. "Yes?" she asked sleepily. The door opened, and she sat up.

"For God's sake, Elise, cover yourself," the General growled at her.

She had forgotten her nakedness and immediately covered her body with her blanket.

He yelled for Bridgette.

Bridgette was in her own room making her bed when she heard the General calling for her. She stopped what she was doing and went towards the sound of his voice.

"Yes, General?"

"Get her up and dressed and in my room in 5 minutes." He walked away and she scrambled to get ready.

He was irritated as he walked to his room. He wanted her now; he couldn't help himself. She looked sexy, her breast barely showing above the blanket, her hair wild and seducing. He wanted to take her right then, but he didn't dare. She would be frightened of him, and that he did not want.

Elise knocked on his door and he called for her to come in. "Elise, I've brought you in here because starting now your duties are solely about me. You are going to clean my room, do my laundry, prepare my bath, layout my attire, etc. Do you understand?"

She nodded, "Yes, like a personal assistant."

"Yes, kind of, but you are still going to help with dinner. Unfortunately, that is still needed. However, other than that, only my things are going to be your priority." She nodded her agreement and understanding. "You may start by cleaning my room. If you need anything, just ask Bridgette or you may find me in the yard."

"Yes, General." He smiled at her. Elise smiled back at him. The instant she did, his smile faded. He looked angry at her.

"Elise, you may be wise to understand early that men mistake smiles and kind words for attraction. You should think twice before smiling at my men."

She understood and just nodded. She wasn't stupid, she understood that. Her smile to him had been a reflex, not a seduction.

She started picking up his room and made his bed. Looking around she was getting to know him intimately on a private level. She hadn't noticed anything when she had entered earlier, only his eyes, those beautiful piercing black eyes. She wondered if he slept alone or slept at all. Some men barely sleep. The stress and constant need for protection keeps the soldier in men alert and ready. She smelled his pillow; it was rich with masculine aromas, familiar, and pleasing. He had a rocking chair in front of a fireplace, a dresser, a table and a set of chairs by a window. The room was uncluttered and relatively clean. She found his laundry and got busy.

She spent her day wondering about the General, her mystery man, and her new life. It was happening so fast, but everything after the last big war seemed to be that way. She finished early and decided to seek out Bridgette.

Bridgette was happy for the help. She told Elise that dinner was almost ready and asked her to go and grab multiple bottles of wine. She told her that tonight's dinner was special because tomorrow the men were going hunting, or raiding, she wasn't sure which.

Elise poured wine like the night before, careful not to make eye contact, or notice any of the men. She especially avoided the General. He had occupied her time far too often that day, and that didn't sit well with her. It was more than curious wonderings, and she wasn't about to set herself up for heartache. The men laughed and joked, some in English, some in a mixture of French and English. Bridgette and Elise were dismissed early for the evening.

Bridgette followed Elise to the bathing chamber, and they bathed simultaneously. They chatted and laughed about their day. Bridgette told her about something funny that happened in the kitchen. She also explained to Elise that if their hunt or raid were successful, there would be a feast when they returned. Sometimes they might be gone for days at a time. Finally, the two women finished their baths and said goodnight.

Elise was lying in her bed when her door opened. "Why are you not waiting for me in my room?"

"I'm sorry, I don't understand?" she replied somewhat timidly.

"Did I not tell you this morning that you would take care of my personal things, like my bath?"

"Oh, I'm sorry. I'll be right there, General."

He stormed off leaving her door open. She jumped out of bed and ran after him. Someone had lit his fireplace and brought the bathwater. She tested the water and realized that it was perfect. She was thankful for small favors. She was grateful these tasks had been taken care of because he could have been angrier at her. She couldn't believe she had forgotten that part of their conversation. She would remember to thank Bridgette in the morning. She could hear him get into his tub and went to his wardrobe to search out a robe and towel. She found them and laid them out on his bed. She smoothed the robe's collar.

"Elise?"

"Yes?"

"Come here and bathe me." She stood there unsure if he was serious. "Come here."

She moved to where she could see him sitting in the tub. The rim was high, so his upper torso, shoulders, neck, and handsome face were all that were visible. She stared at him; he stared back. Her hair was down, a small strip running down her right shoulder and breast. She was half-naked, wearing only her robe.

"Come wash my hair, Elise."

She came closer and wet his hair with his pitcher and began lathering it. She started humming a song, not realizing she was even doing it. She washed and rinsed his hair. When she put the pitcher aside, he pointed to a cloth and soap. She understood that he literally wanted to be bathed. She got on her knees beside his tub. She began with his back and then his chest. She ran the cloth and then her fingers down his chest; lost in what she was doing. Elise was too passionate a person to be embarrassed.

He watched her, mesmerized by her eyes, her touch. He wanted her and tonight he was going to have her.

She washed his arms and then his legs staying focused on what she was doing. Finally, she looked him in the eyes and he smiled. She dared not smile this time. A test maybe? One she had yet to understand that she had already failed.

He smiled even bigger, then chuckled, "Alright, go into my room. I'll be there in a moment."

She turned her back and walked to his fireplace. She felt chilled, despite the warmth of the room. She sat in the rocking chair and stared into the fire. Elise had enjoyed touching him. She felt like a hussy, wanting two men. One she only knew his touch, the other, only his face. She could hear him behind her, putting on his robe.

"Come here, Elise."

She got up and walked towards him.

He had turned out all the candles, and the light from the fire was all that was left.

"Come here."

She walked until he could reach out and touch her. Her heart was pounding.

He lifted a lock of her hair; he smelled it and touched it to his face. Then he smiled at her. "I told you to bun your hair. I told you the consequences." He pulled her robe across her shoulders, not enough to completely uncover her, just enough to bare her skin.

She was unsure of what he was going to do. Was this a test? Would he be soft and sensitive like her unknown lover, or would he be brutal with her? Could she deny him? Did she want to? "I don't want this," Elise told him quietly.

The General looked shocked at first then quickly covered up his surprise. He was no fool. He could see the passion in her eyes, her desire. Why deny them both something they both needed? "I am your master, and you are my prisoner, my servant, mine." Elise looked down at her feet. "Look at me, Elise." He grabbed her chin with his thumb and index finger, forcing her to look up. She looked into his eyes, she did not see satisfaction, nor anger. She didn't understand what she saw, passion, mixed with something else perhaps. The General spoke in his commanding, no argument tone, all masculine and virile. "Do you understand? You are mine. And this is what I want."

He kissed her forcefully, crushing her body into his. He pulled her robe off then, kissed her neck and chest. Her body had already begun to respond to him. He was a handsome and rugged man with a commanding personality; she couldn't help but want him. She loved the tickle of his facial hair on her skin. He could see in her eyes that he had already won this battle. He picked her up and laid her across his bed. He pulled off his robe and let it drop in his haste to get to her. He wasted no time and climbed on top of her.

"Elise, I want you." His voice had changed to a seductive timbre. Passion resonating off his very soul. She would have noticed the familiarity; had she not been so caught up in her own lust and need for this man between her legs. He kissed her hard in his hunger, as he entered her quickly. He did not take his time. He seemed rushed and fevered, as if she would disappear and he would never be able to have her. He wrapped his hands in her hair and kissed her forcefully over and over. He took tiny moments to taste other parts of her.

Elise was overcome with his passion. He was forceful, strong, and yet he did not hurt her. She reveled in his lovemaking and matched his movements. The more she enjoyed him, the more passionate he became. He rolled over bringing her on top of him. His hands were on her hips as she rode him over and over until they both climaxed with amazing force. They lay there a moment, she on top of him, her head on his chest, both spent.

The General did not move; he did not make a sound. Elise rose on her palms, looking at him. Tired, naked, and physically spent, she moved to roll off the bed. He caught her elbow and forced her to stop and look at him. "No, I want you to stay."

Elise was surprised. He pulled her to him and covered them up. He kissed her shoulder and told her that she was amazing. She was warm and content. She slept hard in the comfort of his arms. She was safe and dreamed of good things to come.

The next morning, Elise was awakened by the General. He placed a kiss on her cheek and told her good morning. "I'll be going with the hunting party today and I may not be back tonight. I want you here, where I can find you." Elise nodded, but said nothing. He turned and walked out of the room.

CHAPTER 3

The General and his men were gone for four days. Elise went about her chores. She helped Bridgette often, and was thankful for her. They were becoming friends. They laughed and chatted. They seemed more like childhood friends than strangers who had barely met. Elise remembered to thank Bridgette for preparing the General's bath. Brigette explained that it had not been her. Elise realized that The General must have done it himself. He had not been angry with her, making her wonder if his bark was worse than his bite.

On the morning of the third day, Elise realized she needed something else to occupy her time. With the General, and a lot of his men being gone, she had more time on her hands. She was spending far too much time thinking about the General and the past. She thought about her family and had become melancholy. Thinking about the past only hurt, it wasn't good for anything. She wondered where her brothers might be. She thought about her daughter.

Elise had gone searching for Bridgette and found her in the bathing chamber. She was doing inventory. She asked Elise if she would like to learn how to make candles and soap. Elise was intrigued, she very much wanted and needed that kind of distraction.

"Do you like to read?" Bridgette asked Elise.

"Very much so."

Bridgette smiled, "Good, after I finish inventory in here, I will show you the library. We are all allowed in there, we can borrow and read anything we like."

"Sure, that would be great." Elise picked up a soap and smelled it. It smelled like the General. Clean, yet woodsy and masculine.

"What do you think? Do you like it here so far?"

Elise thought a moment before she replied sincerely, "I'm not sure what to think yet, but, yes, I believe I will be happy here."

Bridgette told her about the compound, and how the cousins had come to find it. She told her how they had built the clan. She told Elise how she, herself had come to be there.

"General, Marcus, and a few men from their regiment, found this place abandoned. It was already half stocked. Weapons, food, and there were vehicles hidden in barns. It was odd, someone had built this place for survival and never came to reclaim it. They had a few horses, but traded for more, and found wild abandoned ones in the woods. Now there are many." Elise was intrigued, she listened intently, not wanting to interrupt her, she held her questions. "They use the horses to hunt, and they use the vehicles only to raid or scavenge. You won't see the vehicles often, they are hidden and used only for supplies."

Elise finally asked, "Did they go hunting or raiding?"

Bridgette informed her, "They took the horses, so hunting. They never return without, but this is the longest they have been gone since I've been here."

"How long is that?" Elise was curious to know.

"I've been here two years now. I was frightened to death when they took me and brought me here. I have not been mistreated. We may be called servants, or prisoners, but I am not sorry I am here. We are well fed, clothed, taken care of. I do not consider myself unfortunate. I was found with my brother; the cousins took us both. Thinking the worst, we were afraid. Now my brother is one of the men, he fights, he contributes, he is considered free."

"Are you bothered by the men?" Elise asked her cautiously.

"Yes, occasionally, but only by one man. These men are selfish and do not like to share. If one man claims you, no other will touch you. He is handsome, I do not mind." Elise wondered whom it might be, she did not ask, and was not told. She would know eventually.

Elise changed the subject, "Do you know how to sew, stitch, maybe knit?"

Bridgette smiled, "Yes I do, actually. Would you like to learn? We will do candles tomorrow, soap the next day. Today we will sew, yes?"

Elise returned Bridgette's smile, "Yes, I'd love that."

CLAN WOODSMEN: THE GENERAL'S REFUGE   A.C. GILLIES

They finished the inventory and walked to the library. Elise was amazed at the collection. There were books along every wall of the room. They were stacked five shelves high and dust free. This room was well taken care of. There were two small love seats, plush and inviting, in the heart of the room. The room was cozy, and Elise felt thrilled. She loved books, had always loved to read, even as a child she had craved knowledge. She had been able to survive in the woods for months. Mostly because of her brothers, and her knowledge of what to eat or stay clear of, knowledge she had learned from books.

Bridgette waited silently while Elise picked two books. One was about candles, the other farming. Elise brought her books with her to their next destination. It was a small room with three different tables, all containing different materials, and colors of fabric. There were two rocking chairs next to a fireplace. Bridget started a fire while Elise wandered from table to table, admiring and touching the different textures. She touched several pieces of soft cotton and picked up multiple shades of blue yarn.

"What would you like to make?" Bridgette asked her as she was standing up, dusting off her hands.

"Anything really. I know next to nothing about any of it, so I need the basics."

"Don't worry," Bridgette assured her, "You will pick it up in no time, I promise."

Elise smiled. "Well, how about some cozy socks, my feet are always cold?"

Bridgette returned her smile, "That we can do."

The men rode over the hill, the compound in the near distance, bringing with them three bucks and several small game. They were a dirty, tired crew with little sleep and yet they were all happy in their own way.

The General was sipping his canteen, happy, for food would be plenty in the coming weeks. They would cook some and jerky the rest. The fur alone would be nice this winter. He would make something nice for Elise. She occupied his thoughts day and night, he felt that he had become too distracted since she had come to be with them. He had almost missed the buck, his thoughts taking him from his hiding place and transporting him into her arms. He missed her face and couldn't wait to see her.

Marcus pulled his palomino up to his cousin, the General, "This was a good hunt. The fur alone will be much needed come winter." The General nodded in reply. "So, Cuz, thinking about your woman?"

The General looked sideways at his cousin for the remark. He could lie, but no one knew him like Marcus.

He smiled. "Maybe."

"You had best make it known to the other men." Marcus warned him, then kicked his horse into a gallop.

Yes, I guess I had better, he thought to himself.

He thought about that first night he had taken Elise. He hadn't had a woman in a while. He needed that release. The soldiers had come in that night bragging about the luck they had finding so many in the woods; about one in particular. A woman with long dark hair and beautiful eyes, even filthy they knew they had found a prize. He couldn't resist, he wanted to see her for himself. He hadn't wanted her to be frightened, so Marcus suggested the blindfold in jest. His plan was only to look at her. From the start, he couldn't resist her. Just like every time he'd seen her since.

He will tell her the truth, soon. He had been angry at himself for losing his self-control where she was concerned. He had been jealous of Marcus; and he was never like that with Marcus. He wanted her smile all to himself. He didn't understand this control she had on him. He seemed to be snapping at her at every turn. He wasn't that guy. Not really. He made a mental note to be more patient with her. Elise wants me, but she wants him more. He needed to stop thinking of himself as him.

He decided he would not go to her in secrecy again. He wanted to get to know her and let her know him. The real him. It was time he let someone new in, and she wasn't just anyone. He realized it the moment he saw her eyes. She had been angry at Robert for manhandling her; she had called him a brute. That had made him laugh. He smiled now thinking about it. There had been static in the air, he had seen the passion in her eyes. She had been a great lover, exciting, fantastic, but he had zinged the moment their eyes had met.

The great hall was buzzing with excitement, the men had returned. This was no ordinary hunt; it would be a great feast. This was the most they had brought home from a hunt. Never had they caught so much at once. Elise had been reading by the fire when she heard all the commotion outside. She practically ran to the window to see what the fuss was all about. The same wagon that had brought her here was now covered and piled high with animal after animal, ranging in color and size. She saw many men, she didn't recognize, to come and help. She didn't realize how many people belonged to this clan. For the first time she saw children. She had only seen some of the compound and realized it was much larger than she had suspected.

She knew the General would want a bath, and fresh clothing. It was chilly today, so she had kept a fire going. She quickly added a log to the fire, then rushed to prepare his bath. She rushed through his garments, picking a dark shirt and military style BDU pants. She had seen him wear those often and figured he would have chosen them for himself.

The General was beyond happy to be home, however, he was surprised and somewhat hurt that Elise had not come to greet them, and welcome them home when they had returned. He had seen her in the window and knew she was aware of their return. He entered the great hall to find multiple people, but no Elise.

Elise had water brought into his room. She had everything prepared for him. She missed the not so distant past when running water was taken for granted. She sat in the rocking chair and started to read, when he opened the door and walked in. Her heart skipped a beat. He was so rugged and handsome.

Elise wasn't sure she had missed him, but she was glad he was back. She smiled at him.

"Welcome back, General, congratulations on a great hunt."

His voice was strong, masculine and blunt, "Thank you Elise. I'm surprised to find you here."

She looked around confused. She had misunderstood him, what a fool. She stood up from the rocker, "I'm sorry General, I misunderstood you. I thought you had told me to stay here, so that you would be able to find me."

She walked past him and out of his room. Elise made her way to the kitchen to help. She explained to Bridgette about the bath and she told Elise not to worry. Bridgette explained to her that it was early, and the men still needed to prep the meat.

"The General is hands on. He would never ask his men to do something, he himself was not willing to do. He will not bathe right away. Skinning and deboning is dirty business."

Elise felt stupid for not realizing this in the first place, she had witnessed her brothers doing that exact thing. She put the incident from her mind and got busy.

The General was irritated at himself. He had in fact told her to stay where he could find her. She had prepared a bath for him and pulled out fresh clothing. She had kept a fire burning, and how did he treat her? He had once again hurt her with his inability to control himself around her. He knew deep down that it was this secret between them. He needed to resolve the issue, and he imagined his reactions and mood would change automatically.

Elise was tired and the day only half over. She and Bridgette got up early to make candles. It was easy enough, but time consuming. The two women had enjoyed themselves, laughing and chatting about nothing and everything. Now with the men back and the feast being prepared she realized she should have napped instead of reading her book. She went to the storeroom to grab a few items that Bridgette had requested. When she got back to the kitchen, Bridgette informed her that she was wanted in the yard, and that the General was looking for her.

He was easy to spot, he was taller than most men; only Marcus topped his height. She noticed the animals had been removed and the wagon gone. He smiled at her. She did not return his sentiment.

"Walk with me, I want to show you something, I want to show you how fine a hunt we had."

She was somewhat surprised. She didn't think he had the time to deal with her. He walked beside her like an equal, not in front of her, he used his hands to gesture the direction in which they would be going. A large barn with a corral was to their left. Two horses, a soldier and a young boy were currently occupying it. After they came around the corner, she saw a large smoke house. The grounds were immense, much larger than she would have guessed. She noticed multiple small buildings, homes, she supposed. She noticed there were yurts as well scattered behind the barn. There was a large field to their right. Men were already getting the ground ready, even though it was still too cold. This early in spring you could still have a cold front blow in leaving ice and snow. Sometimes it lasted only days, last spring, it lasted weeks. The smokehouse was a longer walk than she would have guessed; it needed to be far enough away from the house, or in this case, the many houses and yurts not to mention the big house.

The General wanted to put her at ease, "What do you think? Its lovely here especially during spring, chilly, but nice." He smiled. "Do you like it here so far?"

She stopped walking and he with her, he turned to face her. "Yes, I do like it here. I feel safe. I am not hungry, nor cold. I will not give you trouble, if that is what you are worried about."

His head cocked slightly to the right and his brows creased. That was not the answer he had been expecting, he wasn't sure what he had expected, but her response had been discomforting somewhat. "I will not beat you, Elise. No one dare touch you again. And you will not be sent away."

Elise exhaled a small bit and with it the weight of uncertainty. She believed him and smiled. It was nice to be part of something again.

"I am glad you are here, now come. I want to show you my buck." He led her to the side of the smoke house where the bucks were hanging from their antlers. They were big bucks, beautiful, and majestic. "I killed this one myself." He pointed to the one in the middle. "He's going to make a fine fur this winter." She imagined that he would. He explained a little about what they were going to do, and how it worked. She listened and asked a few questions.

"Well, I'd better get started, I will walk you back to the kitchen."

They made small talk as they walked back to the main house. Elise was curious about the horses. She told the General she liked looking at them and would like to learn to ride. He promised to show her everything about the horses in the coming days, but for now there was just too much work to do. She was excited; she looked forward to the time that she would be able to spend with him.

He stopped just before the stairs to the kitchen. "Elise." She turned to look at him. "Thank you for preparing my return, I am filthy." He laughed, "it will be much appreciated after I spend some time at the smoke house."

She nodded. "Thank you for showing me your kill. You should be proud. He's a fine buck." The General nodded, to her, gave her a half smile, and waved goodbye.

The hours passed quickly as the meal was being prepared. Bridgette explained that the feast would last days with stragglers in between. The men that went with the hunting party would rest and feast tonight. The men that prepared the carcasses would likely feast tomorrow. Then there were men like Marcus and the General, who would do both. They would come and go.

Elise was down in the storage room grabbing wine and beer. She made a mental note to grab extra candles. It would be dark tonight with no moon. She kept herself busy, where she was needed, or she would run for this or that. Bridgette asked Elise to run to the smoke house and deliver a message to the General.

As she got closer to the smokehouse, she could hear several men laughing and talking. Some were speaking English, others French. It was not unheard of to hear French this far south. Since the last World War many men had died. The South American countries tried to attack the northern continent when it was vulnerable. Once, the US, Canada and Mexico combined to form the United Countries of North America, the borders were just like states. Many French Canadians moved farther south. Elise imagined for the warmth.

"Come on Luc, what the hell?"

Elise heard from a voice inside that she did not recognize. Then there was more laughter. Elise knocked on the door and the laughter stopped. The door was pushed open and the brute was staring down at her. He turned his head, spoke in French then, laughter erupted from inside. Elise was embarrassed feeling like she was the brunt of some joke.

The General came out, he had a sheepish look on his face, giving him an almost boyish quality. "I'm sorry to bother you, but Bridgette has asked me to seek you out."

"No problem, Elise. What is it?"

She explained the problem Bridgette had run into. "Bridgette wants you to know that after the feast and possibly a week more that we will need supplies. Somehow inventory got messed up and items are unaccounted for."

CLAN WOODSMEN: THE GENERAL'S REFUGE

"Thank you, Elise. Let Bridgette know that we have ample meat for a least two weeks, maybe longer. But the information is good, and we can discuss it in the morning."

"Yes, General. I will tell her."

Elise turned and walked away. She had taken about ten steps and turned to look at the place he had been standing. He stood there still watching her. She smiled at him semi embarrassed to have been caught thinking about him. He smiled in return, then went back inside. Once again laughter could be heard coming from inside the smoke house. Embarrassed, Elise ran back to the kitchen to inform Bridgette about the discussion.

The men had been teasing each other and discussing women. One had talked about his new woman that had arrived the same time as Elise. He had joked that she may not be as pretty as Elise, but she warmed his bed nicely.

Robert, the brute, had asked the General, "So, have you taken that little dove of yours or is she still up for grabs?"

Marcus pointed at the general and laughed, "WELL?"

The General just smiled and shrugged his shoulders. The men laughed and one of them yelled out, "Come on Luc, what the hell."

Then the knock came, and Robert answered it, hollering over his shoulder, "Speaking of, look what has flown in."

Luc had been embarrassed to see Elise standing there hoping and praying she didn't understand French. He'd have to ask her later but for now he had bigger problems. It was a good thing that a majority of the commanding soldiers in the group had gone hunting because they were all in the smoke house together and they had something to discuss.

It was time to go back into the city and scavenge, or it was time for a raid. The stocks needed to be replenished one way or another, action would be needed. The men's laughter and joking turned into a heated debate. The argument could be heard well outside the smokehouse.

The General may have been head of the clan, but he trusted his men, he respected them all, and all their opinions mattered. He never decided the fate of the clan. They all voted, but this evening, he did not like the outcome. He wasn't going to worry about it tonight. He would worry about it tomorrow.

CHAPTER 4

The men in the smokehouse were relieved when others showed up to take their place. The General found Elise in the storeroom grabbing candles, "Are you busy, Elise?"

"No General, I'm getting a few extra candles, that is all."

"Then I'm ready for my bath. Finish your task then, meet me in my room."

He turned and left without her acknowledging his request. He seemed unhappy about something, when only hours before he had been. She was sure of it. She figured he was tired. She was only partly right; he was tired but raiding always bothered him. He enjoyed his hunting and his time training with his men, but raiding was like Russian roulette, dangerous. The outcome was never the way you planned it. Hunting was easy. They typically used their crossbows, rarely guns. There were too many variables in the woods for guns. The sound alone almost always brought trouble.

In their raids, they had to use guns. He didn't like hurting people. He didn't allow his men to rape, but other than that, all bets were off. If they surrendered, they lived. If they fought, they were taken prisoner, or they fought to the death, and his men didn't lose. It was worse in the cities, more dangerous, more random variables. When raiding, at least you know your enemy. He never took it all, just some. He wouldn't do that to them. He knew what they had to do to survive, no different than him.

Elise poured the pitcher of water over his hair. She liked the closeness growing between them. Another thought crept into her mind as she scrubbed the General's scalp. Him. Her unknown lover. Did he think about her? Did she want him to? She had enjoyed his lovemaking. It was thrilling and erotic. The two men in her life were as different as night and day. They were both passionate and unique lovers in their own way. She wished they were the same man.

The space between her legs became moist as she thought about how erotic her first night there had been. He brought the passion she contained to the surface and made it boil.

His eyes were no longer closed, he was suddenly looking at her. Almost as if he could feel her body heat, smell her arousal, and read her thoughts. He spoke to her, his tone husky, it was a soft masculine timbre that made her melt. "Is that what you want Elise?"

She put the soap and cloth down that she has just picked up. "What do you mean?" she asked him as she took a few steps back.

He could see the smoldering heat in her eyes. "Don't play games with me, Elise."

She quickly told him, "I'm not, I don't know what you want from me."

"I want you to finish my bath and get out."

She picked up the cloth and soap once again. She rushed through her task, wanting to be alone to collect her thoughts. She began lathering him, unaware of what her touch was doing to him. She used his pitcher to rinse his shoulders. When she finished, he closed his eyes dismissing her without a word or even a gesture. She wasn't sure why he was so displeased with her. Elise was ignorant to the fact that he knew exactly where her mind had gone. She didn't know what he wanted from her. One toss in the sack doesn't make it love. He had told her to bun her hair. She would never delude herself to pretend it was nothing more than him proving a point and showing her that he would be obeyed, no matter what.

The feast began as people crowded into the great dining hall. There was an elderly couple and many children ranging in ages. There were also fine-looking women; they did not look like slaves, nor prisoners. Bridgette explained to her that if a man took a wife, she was free, like him. Only a few men had wives when they came here. The other women were prisoners, like them. Elise made her rounds pouring wine for everyone who wanted it. All were happy and in cheerful spirits. Elise found herself in a good mood. It was hard not to be.

Everyone was kind to her; no one treated her like she was beneath them. The men especially enjoyed themselves. Elise received a few whacks on her butt for her effort. Some of the men began to get rowdy. A pair that started a fight were kicked out into the yard. Some followed to watch. Everyone was laughing and having a good time. The food was good, and like the General had said, there was plenty. She found herself laughing and enjoying the antics of the soldiers. Some sang songs, some were in French. She enjoyed listening, wishing she could understand.

The night seemed to be getting longer, and Elise prayed for her bed. It had been a long day, and it was taking a toll on her body. She yawned a few times, watching people come and go. She was going to finish passing out the wine in her bottle and see if she could disappear without anyone noticing.

The General beckoned Elise to him, indicating his glass needed to be filled. She poured his glass, finally emptying her jug. She turned to leave but he stopped her, "Stay where you are." She did as she was told. The general stood up, and the crowd quieted, knowing that he was going to speak. "We have had a good start to our spring. This hunt will bring us food for weeks." The crowd cheered. "This," he held up his glass, "is for the Le Bucheron Clan." He downed his glass and so did his men. He said something in French causing the men to bang their glasses on the table. The General grabbed Elise, crushing her to him. He kissed her forcefully before the crowd. When he let her go, the crowd grew loud once again. They were teasing and joking.

Elise, thinking him drunk, was embarrassed and ran from the dining hall. Much laughter came from the crowd. The men knew exactly what that was about. The General sought Marcus out in the crowd, the younger man smiled at him and saluted him in a half drunk, half smart-ass I-told-you-so. It made him smile. He decided he wasn't going to let her just run away, so he set out to find her.

Bridgette had seen it all, but she did not feel sorry for Elise. The General was a handsome man, kind and generous. She would be thankful someday that he had chosen her, even if the way he claimed her had been a little unorthodox. At least there would be no confusion where his men were concerned.

Bridgette went to the bathing chamber hoping to find Elise and help relieve some of her embarrassment. She had guessed right. She knocked lightly, then entered. The sound of the feast could be heard, even on their side of the house. Bridgette came right to the point, "Do not be embarrassed; that was not for you."

"What do you mean, not for me? He's drunk, and I do not care to deal with that."

"Elise, I have yet to see him drunk, his men, yes, his cousin, definitely, but not him. You don't get it do you?"

Elise looked up at her, semi-impatient to be alone, "Please enlighten me then."

"That, my dear, was for them." She said her piece, then turned immediately and walked out.

Them? Who? The men? She was too tired to think, she wanted to relax and go to sleep. Elise sat in the rocking chair by the fire. She was unsure this is where he would want her to be, but here she was. Clean and calm, she sat warmed by the heat and read until she fell asleep.

She was startled awake when she heard his voice outside his bedroom door. His voice was brutal and angry, "I don't care what time it is Bridgette. When you find her let me know." He walked in angry; she could see it in his face, his body language, how he disrobed. He yanked off his shirt and flung it onto the floor.

"General," Elise whispered it and yet he jumped. He turned to face her.

"Have you been here all night?"

"Well, no I had a bath."

He smiled, yanked his door open, then disappeared.

She was unsure if she should stay or go. Finally, she decided to go to her room when he reappeared, closing the door behind himself.

"I wasn't sure if you needed anything else from me tonight. If it's okay, I would like to go to bed now."

He had calmed, his tone neutral, "Why did you disappear from the dining hall?"

"I thought you were drunk. I did not want to deal with that." She told him honestly.

"No Elise, that was for my men, to show them that you are mine and that no other man is to touch you."

Elise understood that he had claimed her, and no other man was to interfere. He wanted her, and he was going to take her now. He grabbed her roughly and took her to the bed. He disrobed her and laid her down across his mattress.

"Please don't," she whispered.

He realized that it was now or never. She must know that he is only one man. He can be two lovers, and tonight, he would be the lover she needs.

She didn't think that he would hurt her, but she was upset just the same. A tear ran down her cheek. He kissed her face tenderly where the tear had fallen. He whispered something in French and kissed her neck.

His voice turned to a seductive timbre as he breathed the words onto her skin, "Ma Chérie. I must have you. I have missed you these past days, and I have longed for your touch."

The realization of the two men came into one, as he revealed that he was in fact her lover, her only lover. She felt like she was hit with a ton of bricks. She felt betrayed, used, and foolish. Hadn't she wanted that all along? With the sudden rush of emotions, came the realization that everyone had been laughing at her for being a stupid fool. Ice cold water rushed through her veins. She sat up and slapped him, hard across the face.

"You bastard! You son of a bitch. Why didn't you just tell me?" She felt shameful as tears rolled down her face. "Now I know why everyone was laughing at me."

He was shocked at how she had received the news. "Wait, what? No, you're misunderstanding. It was never like that." He didn't know what had happened or how to fix it, but she was hurt. There was no denying that.

She jumped off the bed and ran for her robe to get the hell away from him. He jumped in front of the door. She snatched on her robe, "Get out of my way."

She went to slap him again. This time he caught her wrist in his hand, putting pressure on it, not enough to cause damage, but enough to let her know that it didn't matter, she wasn't going anywhere. He pulled her to him, he tried to kiss her, but she turned her head. "You're staying with me, and I'm going to make love to you."

She was angry. He could see the fiery passion in her soul. "You're going to have to rape me because I will never give myself to you again."

He wasn't going to force her; he wanted her willing or not at all. What had happened? He thought telling her would have been best. Now she thought the worst. He let her go. "Please let me explain. I want you to stay."

"Are you asking or forcing?" she asked him. She was shaken by her own reaction. She was angry, but not about the lie itself. She was actually relieved that it was him. She wanted that all along. The moment she first saw him, she knew she could love him. She didn't want to be some joke between him and his men. That was unfair, but then again, she was only his servant, his prisoner. After she calmed down a little, she realized he could have beaten her and still could. She had no right to refuse him.

"You're staying, and by God, you're going to let me explain myself."

She sat herself down in the rocking chair. The fire was dying, and she absentmindedly got up and put in another log.

"Please don't be angry. When you came that first night, I just wanted to see you, but I didn't want to frighten you. My intentions were not to take you." She looked at him and listened. She wanted to hear the truth, and hopefully, that was what she was hearing. "The men that went hunting came back bragging to everyone. They told everyone this wild tale about this magnifique creature they found in the woods. They said you didn't fight. You just came, like an elegant illusion in the woods. I couldn't wait to meet you."

"I knew you were all laughing at me in the smoke house."

"No, my darling, they were laughing at me because they knew I was going to be the one to claim you. Only Marcus and one other man knew that I even saw you that night. They know nothing about what happened between us. They wouldn't dare ask, nor dare say anything to anyone. I wanted to tell you sooner. I didn't like the lie between us, but I didn't know how to tell you. I should have told you the truth in the storage room, but I was jealous. I meant what I said, I did not like the smile you gave to Marcus. I love Marcus, he is more than my cousin, he is my brother, my best friend, but I wanted to beat him for that smile."

Elise smiled, imagining that.

He took comfort in her smile, her face relaxed. He was finally able to relax his shoulders. "Please stay with me. I'm exhausted and want to sleep. Just stay with me."

Being with him was where she wanted to be, she got up from the rocker and climbed into his bed. He did the same and she put her head on his chest.

"Good night Elise."

"Goodnight, General."

"Luc"

She raised her head to look at him, "What?"

He smiled, "It's Luc, please, just call me Luc."

She kept smiling, "Alright." She stuck her hand out to him, "Nice to meet you Luc." He shook her hand and she laughed. She laid her head back on his chest and kissed him lightly. "Goodnight."

"Goodnight Elise."

"Luc, what does Le Bucheron mean?"

"It means Woodsmen, now go to sleep, Elise before I change my mind."

Elise woke the next morning in bed alone. She yawned and stretched, content like a spoiled, lazy house cat. She was happy because last night she had slept hard in the arms of a strong sexy, virile man, that wanted her all to himself. This pleased her because she felt the same. She said a silent prayer hoping that this contentment would last, and she could once again be safe and happy.

She pulled on her fresh clothes, then added a log to the fire. She could feel the chill from the outside. A cold front must have moved in sometime during the night. The sky was dark, hinting at rain. She could hear the wind howling as she went to the bathing chamber. She washed the sleep from her eyes, then bunned her hair. She made the bed and tidied the room. She gathered the laundry, then made her way to her own room.

She took her bundle outside to start her first chore of the day. Laundry was easy if you kept up with it and didn't let it get out of control. Elise washed her own garments as well as the General's, Luc's. She said his name out loud then laughed because it felt funny on her lips.

It was indeed cold outside. She did not have a coat. Hers had been taken when she arrived and because of its state, she imagined it had been discarded or burned. She had no care for it. She found it one day when she and her brothers were scavenging.

The coat she originally had was dirty and torn. She found the new one inside a department store buried under piles of other items. She and her brothers were afraid as they went into the dark store. It had been raided many times; it was a scene that spoke of chaos. Their adrenaline had been rushing, places like this was where you were caught, because others had the same idea as you. She was excited when she found the coat. She wasn't sure if it was vanity or the adrenaline. It was plain, but it would keep her warm. It was dark orange, almost red, like a burnt peach.

She realized now thinking about it, that is probably why she was so easy to spot in the woods. She had not tried to camouflage herself. She had been hiding for months and had seen no one.

She finished the washing and rinsing and was about to hang the items when it started to pour. She grabbed her basket of clean items and decided to hang them in the bedroom by the fire. She hung what she could on the rocking chair, then went in search of something more useful. She didn't have much laundry, but enough, that the rocking chair would be overwhelmed.

She found what she was looking for in the bathing chambers. It was a wooden foldable organized hanger that was about the height of a table. She took the item back to the bedroom. She added more wood to the fire and decided that she would try to knit and sew again. She walked to the sewing room and found a small basket sitting in the corner. She grabbed multiple items to add to it, including some cerulean blue colored yarn, baby blue cotton, and the socks she started the other day. She had only just begun but was having trouble.

Elise figured she might have to seek out Bridgette, but first she was going to work on it. Like everything, the harder you work, the better you become. She tried to remember what Bridgette had shown her. She was doing well and only needed to fix a few things. Occasionally, she had to backtrack, but she was getting it. She was knitting cozy socks in a dull grey, almost charcoal color. Her feet were always cold, even now sitting by the fire. She wondered where Luc was, or what he was doing.

Her thoughts strayed. She wondered about her daughter and what she might look like today, had she not gotten sick. She remembered the night she had gone to the party. It was much like today, wet, cold, and dreary. She was a junior in college and had been studying hard for finals. Her friends conned her into going to a frat party. She had a one-night stand that created the love of her life. She got pregnant that night. She never told him. He was a loud, rich boy with daddy problems. She could do without his issues. She was pretty sure she had already gotten the best part of him.

She was able to finish her semester but knew that she couldn't go back in the fall with a baby to care for. She was young, but she wanted to be the best parent. Elise knew she was going to have to be mother and father to her child. She set aside her own goals and dreams of being in advertising. She always figured she would go back someday. She was a contradiction, even to herself, shy and quiet, yet adventurous. She preferred to listen rather than be heard. She loved to be around people but liked her space as well.

Her brothers were angry. One was deployed, the other was just getting back. They had seen too much fighting and death. They were angry at her for bringing someone else into the mess their society had become. That all changed the day her daughter was born. She was their world and they all adored her. Their parents had gotten sick and died within months of each other. Their mother had a heart condition. Their father died in battle. Her brothers were older, they had always taken care of her. After her parents were gone, they vowed they always would.

Elise wondered where her brothers were. She said a prayer, asking God to protect them wherever they may be, hoping that they found something like she had. She hoped that they were safe and warm and were not worried about her.

She needed a distraction, so she went to seek out Luc. She stopped in the kitchen to say hi to Bridgette. When she didn't see her there, she went to the storeroom. Elise was about to walk in when she heard multiple voices.

"What do you mean, Bridgette?" Luc's tone was harsh, and she was thankful that for once it was directed at someone else, just sorry that it was Bridgette.

She heard Marcus's voice next, quieter, less forceful, "Are you sure?"

"Yes," Bridgette replied, "someone is taking food; I am sure of it. I have been tracking our supplies. I write everything down."

Robert, the brute, replied next, "It would make sense why little things have gone missing, a crossbow and now a gun."

Luc spoke next, "We have a thief among us, but why? Are we not generous? Do we not share all, for the betterment of our clan?"

In the field, behind the barn, stood a newly erected yurt, and inside, a man was sitting on a cot with food hidden underneath him. The cross bow and gun were hidden under the floor. He smiled to himself. He had done it; he had perpetrated this clan. He hid in the woods for days, hoping to find their compound. He never would have believed that he would be picked up and found. He was fortunate. They had taken him prisoner, and he had allowed it. His clan was vicious; they had no mercy for the weak. He would find this clan's weakness. His clan would be proud of him. He would bring the General down and force the Woodsmen to serve him.

CHAPTER 5

Elise rushed away from the door, not wanting to be caught eavesdropping. She returned to the kitchen to see if she was needed.

Bridgette rushed in telling everyone the news. "The General is calling a meeting in the yard. Everyone is to attend."

The General was standing in the yard with Marcus and the Brute by his side. It took half an hour for everyone to gather. Men and women stopped tending chores and tasks, even men from the smokehouse. Everyone came the hear their General. The crowd was loud with speculation.

A man rushed to the General, the same man from the first night Elise had arrived. He informed him, "Every house and yurt have been checked. Everyone should be here."

"Thank you, Daniel." Luc replied to him. He turned to Marcus and Robert and told them something quietly for their ears only and they nodded in agreement.

The general raised his arms, so that all could see his hands. He slowly, but forcefully lowered his hands to the ground, signaling for quiet. He spoke loudly and his voice was strong, "I have gathered you all here because there is a THIEF among us."

The crowd made surprised and startled noises, ranging from anger to disbelief. They all started glancing around; the yard was loud with speculation. No one could believe it. It was not necessary to steal here. Simply ask. If they had it, they would provide it. No one was hungry, beaten, or abused. Everyone did their share. It was a family, a clan.

Again, he raised his arms; again, the crowd quieted. He looked around the crowd and saw people he trusted, yet there were others here that were new. He spoke loudly, slowly, and deliberately. "Make no mistake, whoever you are, you will be found and dealt with accordingly. We are fair here. We protect our own. Do not mistake this kindness for weakness, for I will kill you."

No one came forward; no one dared. His voice softened, "I understand being hungry, afraid, and unsure of your future, but here, you need not have those fears. Whoever you are, you need not come forward now. Come to me in private and explain to me. I am an understanding man with many emotions of my own, but thievery will not be tolerated. If you are unsure, come to Marcus or Robert."

Elise snickered mentally to herself, 'Oh yes, the brute is very sensitive.'

Someone from the crowd asked, "What has been taken?"

It was Marcus who spoke, "It is of no consequence, the thief knows and that's all that matters."

Another person chimed in, "Why would someone want to steal? We don't have to."

Robert replied, "Sometimes people make foolish choices. It could be lots of reasons, only the thief can explain. No more speculations. Go about your duties and hopefully this problem will resolve itself."

Elise was wondering who the thief was. She knew what had been taken, but the small group of men leading this discussion wanted to keep it private. Tiny drops of rain started to hit random marks, indicating that it was once again about to pour. The General thanked everyone for gathering so quickly and dismissed them so that may resume their duties.

The General walked over to Elise. He grabbed her hand pulling her along behind him. He pulled her through the big house and into the storeroom. He wrapped his athletic arms around her and kissed her. He smelled like the earth, rich and woodsy. His masculine aroma turned her on and brought moisture to her inner thighs. She wanted him. She wanted to taste him and feel his hands on her body. They kissed passionately; he pressed his forehead to hers. "I want to touch you all over. Can I have you tonight?"

She smiled at him and replied seductively, "Only if you blindfold me and kiss and touch me everywhere."

He became rock hard thinking about taking her right then. Her words brought a vision of their first night together and made him want to take what was his. He pushed himself away from her, before they let their lust take over and they forgot where they were, not that anyone would dare interrupt them.

"Is everything ok?" she asked him.

"No, but it will be. We can talk more tonight. I must go chat with the men at the smokehouse. I want to look at the fur and check on their progress. I won't be long; go to my room and wait for me. I will want to bathe before dinner. It will be a fun evening, hopefully, less rowdy."

She smiled," Less embarrassment?"

He smiled back, "Definitely."

When he turned to leave, she called him back, "Luc?"

"Yes?" He smiled a big bright, toothy smile at her. He looked charming and handsome. It was a genuine smile. His smile made him look years younger than his thirty- eight years. War had not aged him like it had most men. He liked her calling him by his name.

"Is there anything special you would like to wear?"

"Whatever you lay out for me will be fine, thank you." He turned and left.

She made her way to his room. Feeling sleepy, she sat on the bed, she just needed a short rest.

She felt groggy as a hand gently shook her leg trying to wake her. She jumped up realizing she had fallen asleep. She had not gotten anything prepared for him.

"Elise, it's ok. I came to tell you that I may be a while yet. I didn't want you waiting for me. Some issues came up and I was needed. I never made it to the smokehouse, but I'm heading there now. If you prepare my bath, it should be perfect timing."

She was relieved. He kissed her forehead and told her that he would return shortly.

The sun set. The sky was a pastel ombre of violets to oranges. The rain had come and gone and left a crisp cool evening. Elise was finished with her preparations. The fire was warm and inviting, as she rocked and thought about her day. Luc entered the room and noticed Elise right away. He smiled; she returned the sentiment.

"Close your eyes, I have a gift for you." She just looked at him and expanded her smile. "Please." He asked sweetly.

She did as he asked. Something warm and odd shaped was deposited into her lap. Something foreign that she could not recognize. She opened her eyes immediately. There was the smallest, most beautiful kitten she had ever seen. It was a Tortie, with bold contrast. Her whites were white, her greys were smokie. She had patches of tabby mixed in and two patches on her face.

Elise laughed, hugging the kitten to her chest. "Oh, Luc. She's beautiful."

"She's all yours, darling." He replied, happy that she seemed to love her gift.

She jumped up, cradling the kitten to her breast and hugged Luc with her other arm. "Thank you, I love her." He hugged her back, content.

"She is still small, so maybe we find her a box to sleep in, maybe even something to keep her cozy. Let's see what we can find."

After a limited search they found something perfect for Elise's new kitten. "What will you call her?" Luc asked as they got the kitten cozy, and secure.

"I'm not sure. I will have to think about it."

"Now that the kitten is settled, I need to bathe for dinner."

Elise picked up his clothing as he disrobed and climbed into his waiting tub. She was getting used to this ritual between them, and the more she bathed him the more sensual it became. He closed his eyes as she poured water on his hair; she scrubbed and rinsed his body, igniting the flame within herself. This time she would not make him wait.

CLAN WOODSMEN: THE GENERAL'S REFUGE

She took out her bun, letting her hair cascade down her back. He watched her, his eyes suddenly smoldering with heat. She untied her belt and took off her work dress. She was commando under the dress. He made a mental note to remember that in the future. She unsnapped her bra and let it fall to the floor. She let him stare at her. She did not smile, she only showed him her own need through her eyes, for they smoldered with passion to match his own.

Elise poured wine and help Bridgette with dinner. People came and went throughout the evening. She met new people and found that she could have many friends here. Many women talked to Elise. They asked about her, not in a gossipy intruding way, but in a way that said, you are one of us now, and we would like to know you. One was Jene, she made an impression on Elise, making her feel warm and invited. She was a lovely woman with dancing eyes and a fast smile. Her smile was stunning with two big dimples. She had two small sons with her. She held one because he was less than one year old. The other was eight or so, and quickly took off to find his comrades.

At one point during the meal, a subject had been broached that everyone, including Elise, wanted to know. A man stood and directed his attention to the heads of the clan. Luc, Marcus, and Robert gave him their full attention. "I understand that you wanted no gossip, nor speculation. Unfortunately, that's all I've heard since this afternoon. People are wondering if we are in danger here. We have never been raided ourselves." He sat down and everyone waited for the answer.

Out of respect, Marcus and Robert let Luc speak first. "We see no immediate danger." That was only a half-truth because he was worried about that exact thing. "Our high outer walls have kept our enemies at bay."

Robert stood next indicated that he wanted to be heard. "A few things have come up missing, this does not mean danger. When someone is starving or afraid, they know they must survive, yes?" The crowd acknowledge with a few nod's and few confirmed yes's. He continued. "We have a survival mechanism deep inside us, written in our DNA, and we are all different. I have seen people hoard out of necessity, knowing that they must prepare. We have all done this. We are all survivors, otherwise we would not be here."

He sat down, believing he had made his point and put everyone's minds at ease. The three men did not want their group to worry, they would deal with this. They understood that paranoia was better than complacency.

However, they would keep it to themselves. No one else stood up. Everyone seemed to take the knowledge in stride. Elise left the dining hall to check on her kitten. Luc wasn't the only one to notice this and wonder.

She picked up her new little darling and kissed her. She smelled her and loved the smell of a baby. Luc walked in moments behind her, catching her in the embrace. He smiled, he did not like where his mind had gone, even if it was only for a fraction of a second. He had learned the hard way in life to never underestimate a woman. She smiled at him. "I wanted to check on my baby."

"Yes, I can see that. Are you returning to the hall." He said this in a way that was not a question, but more of a command. She kissed her baby, then tucked her back into her blankets. Elise followed Luc back to the dining hall.

People had started to leave for the evening, only a handful of men stayed behind. Jene told Elise goodnight and that she would like to visit soon. Elise wanted that very much. The few remaining men started speaking to each other in French. Soon the conversation turned into a heated debate. Elise made a mental note to learn French. One of the men stood semi-angry and walked out. Marcus called to him, but he kept walking. He threw his hand sideways, indicating that he was done with the conversation.

Marcus just shook his head, "Stubborn man," he told his remaining comrades in English.

They all laughed for they knew Brent's temperament. He would cool down after a smoke and return. They all knew this. The men continued their talk, less heated, more relaxed. They had needed that laugh. Ten minutes later Brent returned. There was teasing as he did. He looked sheepish, knowing that his buddies knew him too well. The men decided that it was late, and they would continue the conversation in the morning.

Elise followed Luc to the bedroom. He had never actually said the words, but she felt that this was where she belonged. She checked on her kitten then sat in the rocking chair. She was tired but knew she would not be able to sleep right away. She was curious about the men's discussion, but she would be patient and let him tell her. She picked up her basket of sewing items that she had left within reach. She could hear Luc behind her moving things around. He picked up a chair from the table and brought it to the fireplace so that he could be with Elise.

She focused on her items, letting him think. After about twenty minutes of silence, he finally spoke to her. "Do you speak French, Ma Chérie?"

"No, but I will learn if you want to teach me."

He nodded, "Yes. I will." He took a moment before continuing." I have a lot on my mind tonight. I don't know that I will be able to sleep for a while yet." She understood how he felt. She let him continue without interrupting. "We are unsure what to think about the missing items. Nothing major was taken, but it still sends alarm bells off in our minds."

She responded to him. "Weapons in the wrong hands can be dangerous. I wouldn't call it nothing." He looked at her for a moment, and she continued. "Unfortunately, when I was searching for Bridgette, I heard your conversation in the storeroom. I hadn't meant to eavesdrop, but it happened just the same."

He took in this knowledge, realizing that he must be more discreet in the future. If she knew, who else knew. He told Bridgette not to say a word and Robert assured him that she could be trusted. He knew this already for he trusted her with the inventory. He was not angry with Elise. He respected her honesty, and thinking about it, she had spoken her mind in every situation. He trusted Elise; he didn't know her very well, but he felt in his soul that had found his match. She was equal to him, worthy of his affections, time, and someday even his love.

"I hope that you do not say a word or mention this to anyone, not even Bridgette. I do not want it overheard."

She smiled at him. "You need not ask. I will say nothing; my loyalty is to you."

This made his heart swell. He wanted to hear that; he needed it. "Unfortunately, we all have a different opinion about what is going on. I am on the fence. I will not let my guard down and yet I do not know what to think. Robert thinks that it is harmless hoarding. Marcus the opposite. He wants to hide the weapons. I do not. I do not want to show that we are afraid. Every man tonight has a different plot in his mind, it is too time consuming. We need to be planning our raid, not worrying about this."

"So, you will raid soon?" she asked him.

"Yes. I do not wish to discuss it, okay. I am not a fan of raiding."

"Then why do it, there are other ways," she told him passionately.

"I do not want to discuss this anymore tonight." She turned her attention back to her knitting, knowing by his tone that she had been dismissed. She heard him get up and leave the room, sorry that she did not leave the subject of raiding alone.

Luc laid in the bed watching Elise, she seemed to be having a nightmare. He started to shake her. She begun mumbling in her sleep. He shook her some more. "Elise, Elise wake up." He told her quietly, with much gentleness in his voice.

"Jack, Jack?" Somewhat taken aback, he left her in bed and took another walk.

Who was this Jack? Her husband? Her lover before she came here. He became jealous of this man. What had happened to him? Why did Elise dream of him and call out to him? He wandered without thinking and found himself at the smoke house. He stood and looked at the fur; he touched it and examined it. It was now an empty shell, void of its former glory, and yet still magnificent. The pelts were fine. Another idea came to him. He was surprised he had not thought of it sooner. He became excited to share his thoughts. He rushed back to main house and pounded on his cousin's door.

CHAPTER 6

Luc sat at the table staring out into the coming morning. It was going to be a good day. He wasn't tired despite his lack of sleep. He had a range of emotions running through his mind. He wanted to see Elise before starting his day. He looked at her often, growing more impatient as the sun rose while her kitten slept at her feet.

Elise rolled over, pulling the blanket over her head. She had slept fitfully through the night, waking multiple times. She had been alone each time and had felt the loneliness of her isolation. Hearing her stir, he went to the bed, sat down, and patted her butt. She laughed; she was relieved that she wasn't alone after all.

"Good morning, how did you sleep?"

Elise pulled the blankets off her herself, turned, and sat up in bed. She surprised him when she leaned over and gave him a quick hug on the neck. "I'm sorry about last night. I am sad that you stayed away," she replied back to him quickly.

"No, I came and went. I was here in bed with you some of the night. When I came back the first time, you were fast asleep. I couldn't sleep so I watched you for a while."

She was surprised to learn that he had been there some of the night. "Who is Jack, Elise?" He could see the surprise in her eyes as he asked the question. His question had come out more blunt than he meant it to be, but he wanted to know.

She laughed, "I guess I was talking in my sleep," she responded without answering his question. He stared at her and his jaw twitched. She could see the storm moving in. "Jack, is my brother."

The answer caught him off guard. He responded back, "Your brother?"

She took a deep breath, "Yes, my brothers and I were separated, maybe, a month ago. I'm not even sure. We had been hiding in a little house in the middle of nowhere. We were hungry so we decided to go to a store we knew well. Each time we went there it had been raided, but no one was ever there when we were. We were always quiet and quick." She paused. He nodded for her to continue, holding his questions.

"This last time was different we were caught unaware. My oldest brother, Kyle, took control; he drew them away from us. Jack and I slipped out, but there were more men on the outside. He told me to run, and we both ran and ran, then we got separated. I ran and ran more, my body just took over, I couldn't stop. My brothers warned me about what happened when a woman was caught. I ran until I puked. I was in the woods; I couldn't even remember how I got there."

"You must have been scared," he responded feeling great empathy for her.

"No, I was beyond scared; I was terrified. The raiders didn't notice as we slipped past. Even though we weren't followed, I ran and ran anyways. I hadn't been in those woods before, so I got lost quickly. The more I tried to back track the more lost I became, so I walked and hid. Just trying to survive. When your men found me, I hadn't eaten in days. I couldn't have fought them if I tried. I was not a tracker. My brothers were soldiers, that is the only reason I survived as long as I did. When I was alone, I tried to think about what they would have done and what they had taught me. My intentions were to get back to that store, but I got lost."

He pulled her into his arms, thankful that his men are the ones that found her. "Oh, Elise. I will protect you. I hope that you never have to feel like that again. I will do everything in my power to take care of you, always." She believed him. "I'm sorry about your brothers. Hopefully, they got away. Hopefully, some day you will see them again."

She smiled at him. "I pray for that exact thing every day."

The men gathered in the giant storage shed that housed the vehicles. Only the original ten from the regiment were ever allowed inside. They trusted each other without a doubt, fought side by side, and had protected each other. They checked the vehicles often. Problems during a raid could get them killed. It was dangerous enough if everything went along smoothly, and raids never went smoothly.

"Well, Luc, are you going to give the men your spiel?" Marcus finally asked after being in the shed for over an hour.

Luc looked sideways at his cousin. "Yeah, well I'm thinking."

Marcus laughed, "You're always thinking, for fuck's sake you're the great thinker, always have been, eh?" The men laughed. They knew Luc well enough to know that if he wasn't ready to discuss something, that was his go to excuse, 'I'm thinking.' Always.

Face down, under the hood in the heart of the Jeep, he finally spoke, "I want to discuss something with you all. Hear me out before you say yay, or nay, please. That is all I ask." He looked up and wiped the engine grease off his hands with a small cloth. The men understood his tone, his no nonsense, "I am the commanding officer, so listen up," tone.

"I have been thinking. I do not like raiding. It bothers me." The men listened. They did not have to be told as much. They knew him and knew that he was against it, however necessary it may be. "Last night, I could not sleep, so as I often do, I strolled around. I found myself at the smoke house. Thinking about how fortunate we were to have killed so much game on our last great hunt."

Robert unable to resist himself, asked him in French. "Even with that little sweet treat in your bed?"

The men snickered. Marcus smiled, Luc did not. "Yes Robert, even with Elise in my bed." He smiled after his comment. He couldn't help himself. "Like I was saying, I was thinking, what if we didn't raid this time." The men all looked at each other, still not saying a word, letting him finish. "What if we took some of the meat and fur and traded with the Monroe's this time."

The men all liked the idea, even though most of them enjoyed the raiding. They yearned for the smell of battle. The undeniable truth was that deep-down men were conquerors. Some men needed that drama, that thrill to be able to exist. Not all men, felt that way which is why they gave men the choice, soldier or farmer. Some men did not have the beast inside them. But these men were soldiers. The adrenaline was more part of their souls than their bodies. The need to dominate and excel at everything they did. They were natural athletes. Their bodies were made for war.

As much as they wanted to raid, they recognized a need for change. So, they would try this idea and give their leader something he asked for, since he rarely took or asked for anything himself. That is another reason no man here begrudged him Elise. Robert had seen it that day in the yard. That is why he felt shame by how he had reacted to her. He was usually a fun, teasing man, but her reaction to him brought out the beast inside of him, the conqueror, the man that would give no quarter to a woman, nor his enemy. He knew the second he saw the want and the need in his General's eyes, he knew he would back down and someday ask Elise for forgiveness.

The men talked for hours, deciding, planning. They would go tomorrow before the sun rose and hopefully be back before night fall. The Monroe's were close. They shared the same woods, somehow, they never ran into each other. Clan Le Bucheron had been fair with the Monroe's, or at least in their eyes, they had been.

Luc wanted to spend the rest of the day with Elise. He was conflicted about how tomorrow would end up. He wanted to make the best of life in the present. He found her in the bedroom, sitting with her kitten. She was making baby talk with her, cuddling her close. Elise had just sat down and was about to finish her sock, she almost completed one of the two.

She smiled when he entered; he was filthy. She jumped up to get him extra clothing to put on. She laid her kitten on the bed and started making small talk. She told him about her socks and about how she would make a nice blanket for her kitten. She looked forward to the extra distraction. He was glad that she seemed to be enjoying her time at his home, her home now.

He was using his pitcher to wash his face and hands. He had pulled off his garments and threw them in a pile. "Elise, would you like to go ride one of the horses?"

She looked up from her task. "Now?"

"Yes, now."

Her face lit up in the most exquisite smile he had seen from her.

"Oh, yes, please."

"Good, me to."

Suddenly unsure, she held up the item she had chosen for him to wear. He gave her a thumbs up, then realized that she may not have any pants to wear. After asking her and getting a negative response, he dressed, pulled on his riding boots and they went in search for Bridgette. Bridgette took them to a different storage room that contained many personal items. The General told Elise that some items had been scavenged, but that quite a lot had been there when they found the compound. Bridgette had organized it so that items could be easily found. They found Elise multiple pants, but no boots. Nothing fit, they were either too small or too big.

Elise felt silly in the old-style strapped sandals she had been given when she first arrived. She had never ridden a horse, but she was sure it was smarter to be in boots, anything but sandals. Luc assured her that she would be okay, and that he would not let her fall. They walked to the corral, she could see multiple men, a few horses and even a child. He greeted them all by name, giving compliments or engaging in small talk with everyone.

He thanked one of the men for getting the horses he had asked for and his own, into the corral. Luc opened the corral gate and ushered Elise inside. She was nervous never having been around horses before. There were four horses, all of them unique in their own way. The man named Billy, who had brought the horses for them, jumped off the fence to help. He grabbed a beautiful filly named Comet. She was a stunning chestnut with kind eyes. As he pulled her bridle over to Elise, he spoke softly to her, rubbing her neck.

"You can touch her, be soft, and kind, and she will be good to you."

Elise liked the horse right away. She rubbed her neck and touched her hair. She could smell the earthy aroma of the horse, the natural scent of dirt and debris that gave the horse her unique smell.

She called her name and the horse nudged into her. They had picked each other instantly, woman and horse. Luc came up behind Elise and rubbed the horse. Elise enjoyed his chest being pressed into her back; she loved the intimacy of the nonchalant position.

"Horse Riding and Horse Care 101. Never stand behind a horse." Luc said this in jest, and everyone laughed. He moved beside her and pulled Comet around, keeping Elise beside him. "She is a good horse, calm and mild tempered. She's not a runner; I'm not surprised you picked her. Now, do you see how I have her? You take her and lead her around."

Elise did this and noticed that where she went the horse followed without an issue. Elise smiled, relaxing. The horse was indeed calm, and this soothed her.

Luc came up beside them, rubbing the horse. "Now, I'm going to saddle her for you. I believe it will be too heavy for you to do. You will have to practice over time. Lead her over to the fence, I will show you how to do it all." He picked up the saddle and hefted it over the horse. As he showed her how to adjust and buckle it, he explained the importance of everything he was doing.

"Don't worry, I will show you every time and eventually you will be able to do it yourself. Now, put your foot here, grab the horn, and pull yourself up." He demonstrated it as he said it. "Watch again. Foot, horn, pull. Easy." He moved out of the way and positioned himself to be able to help Elise should she need it. She repeated what she had seen and pulled herself up.

She was frightened at first. She felt high, and unsure of herself. Sensing her mood, Luc told her to relax because the horse could feel her reactions. He rubbed the horse and pulled them around. Elise started to relax and feel better. She asked if she could do it herself. He handed her the reins. She felt thrilled; she was enjoying herself.

Luc got on his stallion and came up beside them. "What do you think? Are you ready to explore the compound a little?"

They rode out of the corral and down the field past the smoke house. On a horse, it didn't take long to cover much ground. They rode and talked, enjoying each other's company. There were fields as far as the eye could see. Spring here was indeed beautiful. The fields had a mix of yellow and purple flowers, with an occasional red. He turned his horse to the right and her filly automatically followed. They continued until she could see the outer walls. She could understand how they had yet to be raided. The wall was high, ten feet perhaps and solid rock. It was simple and yet an effective masonry masterpiece, for it was sturdy and its purpose currently being fulfilled.

As they rode, he told her about his plans for tomorrow and how the men had all agreed. He confided in her his fears about the future. He was unsure of how the Monroe's would react. He hoped they would not consider it weakness. Elise could do nothing but listen. She was no soldier and definitely not a man. Men and woman thought differently. They handled situations uniquely and saw the world through much different lenses.

When they finished their ride, he showed her how to care for the horse. They cleaned and brushed their horses and gave them treats. He put the horses in their stalls and fed them. Elise understood why he might not have time for this often, it was time consuming. She had enjoyed the time they had spent and would cherish it, anxiously waiting until they could do it again.

The sun was setting as they made their way to the big house. They both needed a bath. They smelled like sweat and horses. She readied a bath and they enjoyed it together, making love, tasting the passion each had to offer.

They ate in their room that night, wanting to be alone, just the two of them. They ate and talked. He watched her as she took care of her kitten. He read to her a book about famous Generals. She listened intently and started her second sock. She was intrigued by him and mesmerized by the sound of his voice. As he read, he explained things to her. They discussed things he had seen, dealt with or survived, when he himself was a soldier.

They talked almost all night, not realizing that time had slipped away. For them, it seemed to stand still while they enjoyed each other. She saw a new side of him. He was a well-educated, smart, strategic thinker.

Elise stood by the window watching as the group mounted. The sun had yet to show itself. She touched her lips where moments before Luc had kissed her forcefully and hugged her tight, promising he would be home soon. She stood there in the dark room watching the twelve men on horses riding out, the sun had yet to show itself. She said a silent prayer that everything would go well. She blew him a kiss that no one else would see.

The men had been riding all morning. When tribe Monroe came into focus, they could see them working in the fields. Although, they were farmers, some of them were also craftsmen. Luc's rocker was one of the items he had taken from them. It was beautiful and spoke of fine hand skills, effort, and talent. The General was curious and excited. He hoped the visit would go according to the plan he envisioned.

CHAPTER 7

The old man watched as a half dozen or so men on horses came into view. His men gathered around him. The man recognized the riders. They had raided before, yet something was different.

This time he was not afraid of the Clan Woodsmen. They were fighters and soldiers, and yet they did not inflict pain. They did not come to rape. They took what they needed but never more. They always left enough. He looked at his own tribe. They were farmers, not fighters. Even if they tried to fight, they were no match for these warriors.

The men were riding horses, not their typical vehicles. No weapons could be seen, yet he knew men like this would never be caught unarmed. As they came closer, he noticed that crossbows were strapped to their backs and knives strapped to their legs. He was curious, and his men were wary.

Luc told the other men to hang back a little. He wanted to be the one to approach and speak with Monroe. He wasn't surprised that Troy Monroe walked out to him. He was no fighter, but he was no coward either. He had a kindness in him. He was surprised that such a gentle man was able to survive in this time, but survivors came in all forms.

The old man, Monroe, came forward and stood in front of his group. The man they called General got off his horse. The other men stayed back, watching the crowd. The old man could see the alert focus that each one of them contained. Monroe knew he was an easy target. He had no main gate, no fence, and no wall to protect them.

"Monroe."

One word, that was his greeting, formal, straight forward, and to the point.

The old man nodded yet said nothing.

"We have come today to offer a proposal to Tribe Monroe. We have had a great hunt. We have meat and fur. We would like to trade in return for produce, as much as we can agree upon."

Monroe was surprised. These men had never asked before. They had only taken, and never offered anything in return. He was curious. "May I see the fur you would like to trade?"

Monroe's men only hunted when there was no food and small game at that, nothing large, or fantastic. They only had to hunt their first winter. After that, they had never run out of food, even when Clan Woodsmen had taken from them. They planted more than enough.

Luc nodded. He gestured for Monroe to follow and took him around to the wagon. There were multiple pelts to choose from.

Monroe touched them and felt the silkiness of them. "These are magnificent. This buck must have been a monster," Monroe stated with curious eyes; eyes that reminded Luc of a child, curious, and full of life.

"Yes, he was. You should see his points." Luc replied proudly.

The old man laughed, "Yes, I can imagine. Did you shoot this one yourself?"

Luc smiled and replied, "'Always do everything you ask of those you command.'"

The old man smiled. "Patton."

Luc smiled back at him, a genuine reaction that showed his true nature.

The General and Monroe talked loud enough so that everyone standing around knew what was going on. Monroe's men were confused, some thought it was a trick. Monroe was a trusting soul. He knew these men were straight forward, not devious. They made their intentions known. He trusted the reason they gave for being there. The General's men were relaxed, watching and analyzing. They did not have the look of war in their eyes.

Marcus and the others dismounted and followed the General into Monroe's main house. It was smaller than their compound, but they had less men to care for. Some men followed; others stayed outside while the Monroe's admired their horses. The group chatted and speculated why the clan was there.

Once inside, the men got down to business. The meat was laid on one table and the pelts on another. Men from Monroe touched and admired the buckskin. They debated and bartered. It took hours to agree. Monroe offered food and wine to the warriors. He liked the General. He thought he was a fair man. Luc and Monroe ate and talked like old friends. Both sides relaxed and got to know one another. The Woodsmen and the Monroe's interacted like neighbors, rather than opposing clans.

The Monroe's took all the meat and fur that had been offered. Luc felt the food that they were given in return was more than generous.

Luc mentioned to the old man, "Do you remember that rocker we took the first time we came here?" The old man nodded. "I love that rocker." The old man laughed. "What would you say if I wanted another?"

Monroe thought about it for a moment. "I would say, what do you want to trade me for it?" He asked the younger man mischievously.

Luc thought about it for a moment. He wasn't sure what else he could offer the old man. "You make me a rocker, and a garden bench, and I will bring you a colt."

The old man's eyes widened. A horse was worth much more than what he had to offer. Luc sensed his unease. "I wouldn't have offered if I didn't want the trade. It will be a good trade for me if you accept."

Monroe nodded; how could he refuse.

He couldn't help himself. "Are you married, General?"

"No, I am a widower." he replied bluntly.

"I'm sorry for your loss."

"Thank you, it happened a long time ago."

The old man nodded, he too had lost his wife and understood the want to leave the past in the past. He changed the subject quickly and asked him, "Would you like to do this again? I would take the meat, in exchange for farmed food."
Luc nodded in agreement. He would prefer this to the alternative of raiding.

The clan thanked their hosts and took their leave to make it home by dark. The men left feeling that the trade had been fair and worth the effort.

Monroe's group watched the warriors mount up and pull away towing their wagon. They left the same way they came. Only General waved his goodbye. Unknown to the men, a girl of eighteen, watched them leave through a small window with longing in her eyes.

Elise sat at the table by the window. The sun had gone down. It was darker than twilight, but just barely light enough. She was finishing her dinner as she watched the riders coming into view. She rushed out of the bedroom and down the hall. She wanted to be where he could see her. She wanted to throw her arms around him. She was relieved that he would be home tonight. The group looked travel weary and dusty, tired, but well.

He noticed her right away. He smiled and waved to her. Her hair was free, blowing in the wind. She looked stunning and exotic like some ancient queen. He was mesmerized by this Greek statuette standing there waiting for him. He wasn't the only man mesmerized. She was a ravishing creature.

She watched and took in the scene. Other people had come to greet the men and help. Everyone was curious.

Luc dismounted. He walked up to her and pulled her into his arms. His embrace was a crushing forceful hug that told her that she had been missed. He wrapped his hands in her hair. They kissed long and hard forgetting the world, not realizing that everyone was watching. He finally let go of her, he kissed her nose, and told her that he needed a bath and would be there soon. He said that they had much to talk about.

She walked away and smiled to herself. She had enjoyed his embrace, the smell of him, the feel of him. He smelled rustic and manly, like horse and pine. Sexy and intriguing, she wanted him, she wanted to feel his hands on her skin and his fingers running through her hair. His chiseled features made him sexy, but his alpha male instinct made him irresistible.

She ran to his room and got his things together. She pulled out his robe and prepared his bath. He joined her shortly, explaining that the others could take care of the rest. He wasted no time bathing; he had other things on his mind. Elise washed and rinsed his hair and scrubbed his body. She watched him get out and dry off. He wasn't shy and didn't mind her watching.

She went to the bed to grab his things for him, but he was behind her before she turned around. He pressed his body into hers and smelled her hair. He moved her hair aside and kissed her shoulder. She stood there enjoying what his touch was doing to her body and her mind. Elise rolled her head sideways so he could take her mouth and tongue. He kissed her hungrily as his hands found her breasts. He touched and teased her nipples, turning them taunt and alert. She was moist and ready for him. He turned her around and lifted her dress.

The dress itself wasn't sexy, but the fact that she was commando underneath made his cock rock hard. He pulled her legs up onto his hips and drove inside her. Luc laid her on the bed and made love to her with wild passion. She matched his movements over and over. He kissed her hard. He wrapped her hair in his hands and pulled causing wild emotions inside her. She enjoyed being used by him. He made love to her for hours. He would slow down and enjoy her. Then, he would turn wild again, pounding her and enjoying the different positions and speed, watching her face contorted in ecstasy. They kissed and touched all over. Finally, they both climaxed. Having been completely sated, they slept, naked, and content.

Trevor sat on his cot, thinking of his plan. He sat and thought about his life, who he had been, and who he had become. War and hunger changed a person. It had changed him into someone he did not recognize. The Woodsmen were strong, capable, even violent, and yet they had not lost their humanity.

He hadn't been mistreated; he wasn't beaten down or abused. He wasn't ridiculed. He had been given a choice, soldier or worker, hunt or have duties. In all his life, he had never been given choices, only pushed in the direction his father and now his brother had wanted.

His father had been a cruel man, even before this started. His father had beat him and his brother, making his brother just as cruel. He was not surprised the day his brother had challenged their father for leadership. It was a brutal fight, that had nearly killed them both. But his brother had been stronger, only just.

Upon joining the Woodsmen, Trevor chose to be a soldier, the clan accepted this easily. They were teaching him how to fight harder and better. Someday soon he would use this against them. The clan were teaching him their way of life. It was foreign to him. He felt like a fish struggling for water on the shore. He only knew the cruel, hateful side of life. These people had been good to him, but it didn't change anything. He wanted to be leader of this clan and he would take what he wanted.

CHAPTER 8

The days turned into weeks and the weeks into months. The sun was high in the sky now, and the days were getting hotter. They had already planted the few fields they were accustom to. Elise's new life had started to become routine. She enjoyed the closeness that developed between herself and Luc. She missed him when he was busy, and they sought out each other often. They made love as if each day would be their last.

Elise sat in the rocker by the window, knitting a blanket for her kitten, Rose. The kitten was growing, and the more she grew, the more mischievous she became. She glanced up often, to peak out into her world, watching this and that. The men were practicing hand to hand combat and were using their knowledge, not just strength, to overpower their opponent. Luc and Marcus mostly watched, enjoying the sport itself. Occasionally, they would stop the combatants, to demonstrate something together. They encouraged their men, giving them praise or constructive criticism.

Elise watched the men complete their session and break for lunch. She heard Marcus address the crowd before they were dismissed, "Please enjoy your break. Drink water and eat. After we return, we will be going into the field and practicing with our crossbows. You are dismissed. Meet back here two hours from now. That is all."

Elise left her sanctuary in search of her lover. She found him in the kitchen. He was laughing with Bridgette about something and was happy to see her.

"Elise, tonight my men and I must have a meeting. Please do not wait for me to eat. I have some time now and would like to ride with you."

The two lovers rode the grounds. Elise had been on Comet multiple times now and no longer feared her. She was accustomed to the saddle and the gait of the horse. She felt comfortable and at ease.

"We must go on a hunt tomorrow. More than likely we will not be back for many nights. We want enough for ourselves and enough to trade with the Monroe's." She understood. The food had lasted longer than anyone had first expected.

"Can I go with you?"

"Hell no! No way." His reply was more cruel than he intended.

She was hurt. He must not trust her to stay out of the way. He probably thought she was a stupid, weak woman that was helpless. Unfortunately, she was only partly right. He did not want her there to distract him; distractions were dangerous. Animals can be just as deadly as any human. A cornered animal fought, and always to the death.

He changed his tone. His voice softened, but still held the note of authority and made it clear that he owed her no explanation. "Listen, Ma Chérie, no woman has gone with us before. The men will not agree. I want you with me, but, for safety reasons, I want you here more."

His answer did not appease her tattered ego. She spurred her horse forward, into a light gallop. He hollered something in French. She was sure it wasn't good. He sat on his horse looking at her back as she rode away. He knew she was angry. Damn woman.

Elise rode back to the stable. She had Billy take off her saddle. She began to clean and brush her horse. Luc came up behind her and he whispered something in French. His tone seductive. Even though she was angry, she melted into him. He told her that he was sorry. She kissed him and decided she would let him win this battle. Asking to go on the hunt had been a long shot. It was not his rejection that hurt her, it was what he said and how he said it.

The men gathered in their shop. They looked the vehicles over, checking oil, tire pressure, all the things that were required to make sure driving went smoothly.

Marcus was the first to bring up the subject. "Tomorrow, I say we get up before dawn. I think we need to try a part of our woods we've never hunted before."

Robert spoke next, "I see no reason to change a good thing. Like they used to say, 'if ain't broke, don't fix it'."

Brent puffing on a smoke, looked up from his task. "Who the hell is 'they', Robert, your momma?"

Robert laughed, "I'll show you, your momma, bitch." The men all laughed.

Luc broached a new subject, unsure how the men would react. "I was thinking that after this hunt, I would like to check out a store that Elise told me about."

The men all started talking at once. Marcus knew he hated to scavenge. He knew there must be an ulterior motive behind his request. He said nothing; he just watched his cousins' body language and waited for Luc to tell them more.

Robert spoke, sarcasm dripping off his words, "Why the hell would you want to go do that. Your woman needs pads or something? Geez, lets die over that." A moment passed and no response.

Marcus finally broke the silence. "Well, Luc?"

The General replied, "I'm thinking."

Robert laughed. Marcus shook his head. Some of them sighed.

Brent shook his head, "You just can't drop a bomb like that and vanish emotionally."

Luc responded semi-aggressively, "I said I'm thinking, damn it."

The men decided it best just to go about their business and finish their tasks. They knew Luc would tell them when he was ready and not before.

The idea sounded stupid to him. He could have predicted how his men would react. No one went looking for someone, especially someone they didn't know, in a region they were unfamiliar with. It was suicide. He would never be able to convince them, and yet, he couldn't get it out of his mind. It wasn't fair to even ask them. He just couldn't push the thought aside. What if he could find Elise's brother? What if.

Without looking up, he spoke again, "Look, I would never demand nor expect any of you to do something you don't want to do."

Something about the General's words made them all stop. It may have been how he said it or his tone. Maybe it was a feeling of dread, but the words hung in the air like an imaginary vision of past, present, and future battles. It reminded them that he, himself often did things he neither liked, nor wanted to do.

He continued, "I'm going to paint a picture for you." He shared Elise's story of how she had come to be here with them. As they listened, they were all pleased that Clan Le Bucheron had indeed been the ones to find her. They loved their commanding officer and were grateful for the happiness the intriguing woman had brought with her.

He described how he felt when Elise first told him her story. He projected his thoughts, emotions, and wants. He ended his spiel with these haunting words, "If you were her brothers, would you not want to know? Would you not go to the ends of the earth to find the ones you loved?"

The men's debate started instantly. The men talked, argued, and commented all at once. It was unintelligible and without order. Nothing would be heard; no comment would be able to be countered.

"Stop!" One word was shouted, not by the General, nor Marcus. Robert wanted to be heard. His tone strong and angry. He would fight to be heard if it came down to it. The men stopped arguing and Robert asked, "Have we not all lost ones that we love? You, Luc, should know the hurt of loss, maybe more so than the rest of us. This woman is clouding your judgment."

The pain of the past flashed across Luc's face, only for a fraction of an instant, and yet his reaction had not gone unnoticed. Robert did not feel sorry for his comment because it may be the only remark keeping them between life and death.

Marcus replied next. "We do not do search and rescue. Her brothers will either survive or they won't. It is up to God, not us."

Luc ran his hands through his hair. Brent noticed this and knew his general was between a rock and a hard place. He knew what he wanted and had no idea how to accomplish it.

"I will go with you, even if it's just you and me. I will not turn my back on you." Brent said this with honesty and courage in eyes. He drew a long puff of smoke and wondered if he would die for his comment.

Luc believed him, knew what he said would be true, but he would never jeopardize his friend's life, even if it meant that he'd go alone. "I appreciate that Brent, but I will not jeopardize, your life, my life, any of our lives. You are all right, but I cannot stop thinking that maybe we can help them. We may not know them, but someday WE may call them brothers. I am sorry to have brought this up now because we should be planning our hunt. We were one regiment before we became one clan. I trust and admire each one of you. You are my brothers, my family." The General was sincere in how he felt, and they all knew it.

Marcus with a mischievous smile added, "Yeah, well you're a selfish prick. We all know this."

The men laughed, and Luc ran at Marcus. The two men grabbed each other in a wrestling bear hug. Luc put Marcus in a head lock and smacked his head. The men laughed and cheered. The men ended up on the ground, and Marcus grabbed Luc's hand, using it to smack him with it.

"Why ya hittin' yourself?" Marcus taunted multiple times. Marcus and Luc laughed; they had always fought ever since they were kids. Marcus had always called Luc, General. They were less than a year apart with Luc being the oldest. He always took charge, but Marcus didn't mind. He would follow Luc anywhere.

It was always funny to Marcus that Luc must have been destined for the title General, because during the war he had become just that. They had been rowdy and tough growing up. They played every contact sport they could. They grew up in a little town out in the woods of Quebec. Their mothers were American sisters and their fathers were French Canadians. Their fathers had been best friends, they met the sisters while vacationing in Florida. They knew it was destiny, love at first sight.

The men started calling out bets to see which cousin would win. It was all a joke, no one won. They usually called it a draw. The men had been fighting each other all their lives; they were virtually equal in every way.

The men spent the next few hours deciding that they would indeed check out a section of the woods that they had never ventured into. They knew that it would be more dangerous, so they would need to bring guns, not just their bows and knives. They previously planned to bring their new men but changed plans and decided against it. The original Woodsmen didn't want to add new reactions to already dangerous situations. The men knew each other inside and out; the new men had their own reactions to situations, reactions the Woodsmen did not know. Too many variables made the outcome harder and harder to determine.

Luc climbed into bed. His woman was asleep, her kitten at her feet. He cuddled up next to her, holding her tight. She smiled in her sleep, and this made him happy. He didn't want to leave her in the morning, but he had to do what he had to do. Was Robert right? Was she clouding his judgement? Was she making him soft? He would embrace the hunt. Maybe that was exactly what he needed to put things back into perspective. He never went against his men, but then again, he never had to. Luc slept little that night. The weight of his responsibilities heavy on his shoulders. He got up for a walk and found himself banging on his cousin's door.

"You may not sleep, but for shits' sake, the rest of us do," Marcus barked at him as he opened his door. Marcus knew who it was; it was always Luc, especially this time of night. Luc just stared at him. "Spit it out or f off."

Luc laughed, "Wow you're a grumpy bastard tonight."

"I'm sorry, come on." He opened his door wider so that his cousin could enter. They both laid on Marcus's bed. Luc propped up a pillow. He was surprised that Marcus wasn't accustomed to his late-night visits by now. He was his confidant; he came to him more often than not.

Marcus knew why he was there. He spoke first. "You're not going to let this go, are you?"

Luc put his face in his hand. "I don't know, I just don't know. Is Robert right, does my judgement seem clouded."

Marcus hated his answer but told his cousin anyway. "In this instance, I think yes. It's just too dangerous. We have no idea where to find either of them. This brother Jack may have been seen; they may be together. First of all, we don't know what either one looks like. And she told you, people had come upon them, one brother for sure had been seen. They could both be dead, who knows, Luc. Who knows? There are just too many variables."

Luc couldn't argue with his cousin. "You're right Marcus, I must let it go." He stood up. "I'll see you in a few hours. Get some sleep."

"Yeah, I think you should take your own advice." He told his cousin, knowing that Luc would probably wander longer before going to bed. Luc walked out, closing his cousin's door.

Elise was standing near the window looking out into the darkness as Luc walked into the bedroom. She rushed over to him, embracing him. She told him, "I was unsure of the time. When I woke up, I was afraid that you had already left for the hunt."

He smiled at her," Why Ma Chérie?"

She ran her hand down his chest, "Because I wanted you to make love to me one more time."

He pulled off her robe, letting it fall to the floor. He neither touched her, nor spoke, he just looked at her as he disrobed. She made no attempt to cover herself. Her nakedness only spurred her arousal. A thought came to him. He wanted to play the Casanova she had once responded to and seemed to enjoy.

"Go to the bed, Elise. Close your eyes and wait for me." His tone was neither seductive nor sexual, it was pure authority.

She was taken back a little, the General was present, when she was sure that only moments ago it had been her lover. Elise did as she was told. She could hear him searching for something.

One drawer, then a second. He chuckled as he closed the second drawer, and she wondered if he had found what he had been looking for. She was curious, and yet, she did not peek.

She could feel his weight on the bed, and the smell of him sent chills through her. His aroma was sex. He smelled masculine, earthy, and powerful. No wonder he was the Alpha. His aura was pure authority. He whispered to her, "Keep your eyes closed just a moment longer." He kissed her cheek, and she could feel the softness of something silky touching her eyes. Elise imagined it was the way a cloud would if feel if you could reach up and snatch it from the sky. She could feel his hands and material cover her hair. She subconsciously reached up and gently guided her fingers where her eyes should be. The blindfold was soft and silky. A rush of moisture filled her inside and suddenly she was turned on.

Elise and the General were still up when it was time for him to go, neither had slept. They were too awake to sleep after they had made love, so instead they had romantic pillow talk. They talked about the future, never about the past. He told her how eager he was to return to Tribe Monroe. He liked the old man. His conversation was stimulating. Luc had been impressed that Monroe had recognized a quote from Patton. He could tell that Monroe would be a powerful ally, maybe not in strength, but in knowledge and skill. He wanted a great hunt. The Monroe's variety of canned and pickled items were amazing, and he wanted his meat and fur to be worthy of the exchange. The sun was coming up when, they said their goodbyes.

She watched the men gathering their supplies and horses. She knew Luc would be tired but wasn't the least bit sorry. She had enjoyed all that had transpired between them. The intimacy in body and mind thrilled her. She was no fool; she had fallen in love with him. He made no declaration himself, and she hoped that if he didn't feel the same, he would someday. She knew he cared in his own way. He didn't treat her like an object, he treated her like a partner, a friend, and most of all a lover. She watched and waited until the men left.

Filled with anxious energy, Elise knew that she could not go back to bed, so instead she started on her daily routine. She was going to do anything and everything to occupy her time. She made a mental note to seek out her friend Jene. Jene was married to Brent, and she knew that she would also need a distraction from worry. Even though she had two small children, to occupy most of her time, Elise felt that anything might help.

Bridgette and Elise spent the day doing inventory. They made a list of things to do, make, clean or fix. With General and Marcus gone they had more time to do the things that were extra chores on top of the daily ones. They spent some of the day in the clothing storeroom and part of it in the food storeroom. The food storeroom was easy, something either got replenished or it didn't. In this day and age, things were available, or they weren't, simple. Everyone made do without.

The two friends had fun in the clothing storeroom. They found multiple items that alone were worthless to them but combined might make them something worthy of their time. They would repurpose the cloth to make something useful. It was hot out now and Elise wanted something cooler, shorts or short pants, to help with the heat. She found some clothes made of khaki material that she and Bridgette might be able to transform into something good. Bridgette found a few pieces of material for herself. The ladies took their items to the sewing room and made the most of their day.

They cut, sewed, and measured as they chatted about the hunt, wondering how and what the men were doing. They opened a window and could feel a light breeze. It was enough to keep them cool. The women took a small break and went down to the kitchen. They noticed that the food storeroom's door was open, yet they were sure they had closed it. They disregarded the issue guessing one of them must have forgotten, so they closed the door and moved on.

They took a small plate of food with them as they continued their tasks. Elise was happy to have finally learned how to sew. She had never been any good at it. Bridgette's time and attention to detailed had help Elise master something she never thought possible. They stayed in the sewing room until dark. Their day slipped by as they got lost in their own fun.

"Do you love the General, Elise?"

Elise was neither embarrassed nor insulted by her friend's blunt comment.

"Yes, Bridgette, I believe I do. Why? Is it that obvious?" she laughed.

Bridgette thought about it, "No, I just see the way you look at each other, I see how he treats you. Do you think he loves you back?"

Elise sighed, "I don't know my friend, I cannot pretend to understand what is in a man's mind or his heart. I have learned that you need to keep one eye open where men are concerned, they will always surprise you. And when you think they will react one way, it is the exact opposite you will get every time."

At the same time, somewhere deep in the woods, a group of men sat around a fire. The men passed around jerky and talked. Luc was the only one among them to be dragging; he was dead tired though he didn't let it show. On the outside he was the rock, but on the inside, he was an ocean of emotional turmoil. He was not distracted from his duties, he was a soldier, and he would defend and fight to the death. The men took a vote on who would be on watch the first night. Luc did not volunteer knowing that he would fail, and he was too proud to fail.

Elise and Bridgette told each other goodnight sometime around midnight. Elise was exhausted. The events of the day had finally caught up to her. She practically dragged herself to the hall that contained her section of the house. She passed a soldier that was to stand watch that night. She did not recognize him. She was still learning the inhabitants of the Clan Woodsmen. She told him goodnight and he smiled and nodded his sentiment.

The room was dark; the only light came from the small candle she had carried from the sewing room. Elise felt the breeze from the window she left open. Right away, she noticed the disheveled and ransacked room. This was not how she had left it. She turned to go and fetch someone, Bridgette, the guard, anyone. As she turned, she felt a knife pressed into her back. She had missed the man hiding in the shadows. She screamed as she was shoved to the ground. She could hear the man run away and grunt as he jumped from the window.

The door flew open, the guard and Bridgette had both come, hearing Elise's scream.

Seeing Elise on the floor, the guard went to her and held out his hand, "What happened?" he asked Elise.

She was shaken and had to sit on the bed.

Bridgette looked around the room, "What happened here Elise?"

Finally finding her voice, she told them, "There was a man. He, he shoved me down." Elise examined her arms, seeing that a bruise was forming where she hit the ground.

The guard walked around the room looking at the mess. He went to the window, but saw no one, so he closed and latched it. He told the women, "I will be in the hall outside your door. I will send for another man to take my place in the great hall. Keep your window closed tonight, and we will investigate tomorrow. You didn't see his face? You didn't notice anything about him?"

Elise shook her head in a negative response. Elise thanked the man as he dismissed himself.

Trevor sat in his yurt, alert and out of breath. His heart raced with adrenaline. With the General gone, he didn't anticipate anyone would have walked in on him. He hadn't really thought it through at all. He just saw the window open and climbed in. That was his problem, he was always impulsive. He wasn't looking for anything in particular, just looking. He planned to take whatever he wanted, but that bitch came in and surprised him. He sat there ready to do battle. He felt courageous, but in reality, he was stuck like a caged rat. It took him a long time to calm down. When no one came he finally relaxed. This clan was more stupid than he had guessed.

Alone with Bridgette, Elise cried. She confided in her friend, "I was scared, I saw the mess, and then," remembering something, continued, "There was a knife pressed to my back, I'm sure of it. Then I screamed and he pushed me. It happened so fast. I was terrified. I'm glad you came when you did, but he ran as soon as he pushed me."

Bridgette just shook her head, she didn't know what was going on,

"I'm going to sleep in here with you tonight. I will make something on the floor. I don't want you to be alone."

Elise thanked her. The two women settled in; they were tired, yet neither could sleep. Just before dawn, Elise finally gave in to her exhaustion and fell asleep.

CHAPTER 9

Bridgette sneaked away quietly and let Elise sleep. She had things to do before they started the chore of making candles. Eventually, they would pick up where they left off in the sewing room.

Elise woke when the door creaked shut. She sat up in bed and looked around the room. She wondered what the man had been looking for. She wouldn't know if anything had been taken. She yawned, climbed out of bed and went to the bathing chamber she shared with Bridgette. She washed her face and braided her hair instead of a bun. She imagined that a braid and a bun were the same in her General's eyes. Her hair was back and out of the way; that was all that mattered. She picked up the mess as best she could. She had to guess where it all belonged.

Books were on the floor and clothing was thrown here and there. Objects had been dropped. It was like a child had come through and without thought or care, tossed the place. The person obviously wasn't worried if they were caught. A smarter thief would have searched and taken what they wanted inconspicuously.

Elise picked up the clothing and either rehung them or stuffed them into drawers. She pickup up the pieces of a broken hurricane lantern and grabbed an old towel to clean up the oil. She shook her head, what a mess. As she picked up the books, a picture fell out.

She looked down at the picture. It was upside down and the names, Brittney and Blake were written on the back. She bent over to pick it up. She flipped over the photo and her eyes went to the woman. She looked like she was in her thirties. She was beautiful, with smokey gray eyes and dirty blond hair. Her lips were full and her nose was petite. She had kindness in her face and she seemed happy. Elise turned her attention to the other person in the portrait. A boy, five or so, with black hair and smoky charcoal eyes.

There was no question that these two were related. The boy had the same smoky eyes of his mother, yet they were darker, more alert. Elise wondered who they were. Had they been the owners of the compound before the Woodsmen had come here? She made a mental note to ask Luc. She tucked the photo back into the binding and with much care she closed the book.

The day came and went and so did the next. Elise and Bridgette spent most of their time together making candles and sewing. On the fourth day that the men were gone, they agreed to divide and conquer the chores. Elise started laundry, while Bridgette made soap. Elise enjoyed candle making but making soap she could do without. Bridgette didn't mind since she loathed doing laundry. They were a perfect match.

The hunters had been unsuccessful so far and moved quietly from camp to camp each night. They saw animals, but no animals they would eat. They saw a cougar with her young. She was stunning, and graceful. She sensed their presence, yet she could not see them. They watched her awhile, enjoying the way she interacted with her young. The men were surprised to see this one so far northeast. Cougars tended to stay in Texas and Florida or farther west like Wyoming and Utah. The men were warriors first, then hunters. They knew how to blend in and disguise themselves. They had camo and ghillie suits and could virtually disappear. An animal or person would know they were there only if they wanted them to.

They saw small prey like rabbits and squirrels but nothing big enough to tempt movement or chance being seen. Finally, on that fourth day, a small deer wandered into their kill circle. She was young and jumpy. She grazed and the men waited until two more deer showed up. The mother watched her young and ate beside them. A noise startled them, and they took off into the woods. The men followed quietly, but quickly. They knew they would miss their chance if they didn't. The deer jumped and ran until there was a clearing. The men hung back just inside the woods.

They couldn't believe what they found. The clearing was stunning, a field as far as the eyes could see. There weren't just the three deer they had followed. There was a herd of deer. They couldn't believe their blessing. The men all said a silent prayer of thanks. Luc gestured for his men to fall back. He wanted to talk with them. They moved far enough back so that even a whisper wouldn't spook the animals.

"We can't go in there, guns blazing like cavemen." Luc told his group.

"Yeah, no shit. They will all be spooked." Marcus added.

Luc continued where he had left off, "What if we took multiple animal's home."

"Yeah, I thought that was the point." Brent replied without thinking.

Robert shook his head, "We have to get as many as possible."

The men talked and debated, they realized that if this were going to work, they would have to be on point. They decided to split into three groups. Three men would move to left and three farther to the right. Four of them would stay put.

"Okay men, on my signal, have your animal picked out and shoot. If possible, get as many as you can."

The General gave his signal; the ready hunters fired. For a fraction of a second, the whole field stopped, frozen in animation at the sound of the crossbows. The animals fled. The men watched as animals jumped into the woods, scattering in all directions. The field emptied in an instant. They were surprised with what was left. There were five animals, two bucks and three smaller deer. The men felt like conquering Vikings; proud, and yet humble, knowing that they could not have done this alone. The hunt had been a blessing.

Elise and Bridgette sat in their sewing room organizing the material for their new clothing when Jene walked in with her baby.

"I am getting lonely without my Brent," she confided in the women. They understood how she felt; they missed someone as well. "What about you Bridgette? You miss your Robert."

Elise's eyes widened. In all her life she never would have guessed that Bridgette was with Robert.

Bridgette smiled mischievously. "Sometimes, like when I go to bed." Bridgette looked at Elise, "You didn't know?"

Elise smiled, "No, I didn't. You never told me. I guess I'm just not that observant."

Bridgette responded to her, "He does not make his affections obvious. Men know not to bother me, but that's all. I don't know how he feels towards me. Somedays, I think he must like me a little, others I'm not so sure." She finished the last with a sigh. Elise knew how she felt.

Jene stayed for a while and talked. Jene liked some of the blue material that she noticed on one of the tables. Elise decided she would surprise her friend with a baby blanket. Jene excused herself with the justification that she needed to feed, bath, and ready her boys for bed.

The time slipped by until Elise and Bridgette finally excused themselves from sewing.

"Bridgette, I'm going to go to the library for a while, so if you want some relaxing bath time, it's all yours."

Bridgette thanked her friend because that is exactly what she needed.

Elise scanned through the shelves, looking at this and that, trying to decide what she wanted to read. The evening was slipping away, and she had to light the hurricane lanterns that hung around the room. She tried keeping herself busy, but during any quiet time her thoughts focused on Luc.

She looked for a book on Patton. He seems to be well educated on General Patton. She would like to be able to converse with him and understand his feelings and any ideas that he had. She had never killed anyone, she had never been in battle, but she knew the feeling when adrenaline kicked in because of the unknown.

She was not a soldier, nor a warrior but if anything, she was a good listener. She didn't find anything on Patton in the library. Maybe Luc had something in his room. He had many books, and even though she picked them up earlier, she hadn't paid attention to the titles.

She looked through more books in the library, finally selecting a book about women from the wild west era. Some of the woman had been courageous, others outrageous. They ranged in color and size, but one thing they all had in common, was that they were all skirts well ahead of their time. They were women that men couldn't tame and didn't have a name for. She was excited to read the book. She hoped it would give her courage.

There were things she wanted to do but wondered if she would be allowed. She wanted to learn how to hunt. She was already denied that opportunity with a definite "hell no". She wanted to learn how to fight like a man. She wanted to be able to defend herself. Elise did not want to be weak or cowardly. If Luc refused to teach her, then she would watch, she would learn regardless. She had enjoyed watching the men as they battled each other in practice. Elise knew the real deal would be much different. She figured fighting to the death would be much faster, more chaos.

There are two kinds of people in this world, fight or flight. Time and time again, her response to danger was flight. She didn't want that. She felt like a coward. She needed to train her brain to stop and analyze. She heard that warriors and athletes could slow down their surroundings or situation; their minds allowed this, so they were able to concentrate, observe and react to the situation at hand. She wasn't sure about other flight people, but her mind always sped up, like it was running to get out of a situation. She often panicked, she was a runner, she knew she had flight instincts. She wanted to be able to stand her ground. Live or die, she wanted to be able to prove that she had what it took to be a survivor.

She looked through a few more books realizing that there were many here that she would like to read. There was a cosmic amount of knowledge in such a confined space. She was finally ready to call it a night but had yet to eat or bathe. She turned out all the lanterns, grabbed her book, and candle and headed to her bathing chamber.

Elise laid her head back against the tub. She put a hot cloth across her eyes and relaxed. She thought about Luc and wondered about the picture in his book. She wondered about her brothers, hoping that they were ok.

The vision of where and when she had last seen them flashed through her mind. She remembered the remnants of chaos that were everywhere. Abandoned vehicles, trash, random piles of discarded items. She shook the image from her mind. Elise was happy that this quiet sanctuary had become her home. It was almost surreal, like a celestial palace in the middle of ruins, an oasis in the heart of the desert.

Her thoughts turned to her daughter. She knew better than to dwell on things from the past, the things you couldn't change. She missed her family, and as of right now, she was alone and void of them all. She felt melancholy. She knew that it didn't matter how she felt because, unfortunately things could always go from bad to worse in the blink of an eye. She didn't want to be "Debbie downer", as her brothers would call it.

She pulled the cloth off her eyes and lathered it up with soap. She started washing her arm and remembered the bruise. It was a deep purple showing that it was healing. She wondered about the intruder, wondering why he was there. She was a lot of things, but she wasn't stupid enough to leave the window open again. She learned that lesson. She wondered if the thief and intruder were the same person. It was the only thing that made any sense. She was deep in thought when the door opened, making her jump.

Bridgette peaked her head through the door, "They're back Elise, the men are home."

With those few simple words from Bridgette, Elise pushed everything from her mind, except one; she wanted to see her lover, her friend, her General.

CHAPTER 10

Elise rushed to finish her bath. She dressed quickly, grabbed a lantern, then ran out of the house and into the yard. The night air was refreshing. The breeze lifted pieces of her hair sending them in multiple directions.

The moon was high, casting a light glow across the compound grounds. Some men were taking care of the horses, others sorted and moved the camping equipment. The men that went hunting were already at the smokehouse. Marcus and Robert had hung the buck by his antlers and were starting to clean the second animal when Elise arrived. Marcus looked up as she walked towards them.

"He is not here." Blunt and to the point. Dismissed without another word.

Robert with his back turned, turned slightly towards her, "He's out at the far field." He pointed in a direction, she nodded her thanks and walked to find him.

Elise found him in the clearing with some of the other men. They would need to make more rack space to hang the animals. She could see him talking to his men but could not hear him. He noticed her, smiled, and waved. He talked for a few minutes longer, then he pulled his horse around so that he could get to her. As he galloped to her, she watched in amazement at how stunning he looked on his horse. They looked magnificent, equally graceful and powerful like they had been made for each other.

When he reached her, she stood there, looking up at him. He lowered his arm for her to take it. She climbed into the saddle with him. They kissed, and he realized that he had missed her more than he thought. The kiss was tender and affectionate, not seductive, nor hungry. She laid her head on his shoulder, and they sat there taking in the smell and touch of each other.

"I like the braid, Ma Chérie." He told Elise, while rubbing it between his fingers. He liked the silky touch of her hair. He enjoyed tangling his fingers through it while he made love to her.

"I missed you, General." Elise told him quietly. He held her tighter for an instant, in a quick half-hug, then started moving his horse forward.

He stopped at the smoke house and sent Elise on her way with the promise that he would be with her soon.

The hunters agreed that the Monroe's would get a buck. All of him, his pelt, his meat, and his antlers. This pleased Luc the most because he knew that the Monroe's had been generous in their giving of their own precious food supply. The canned fruit and vegetables had lasted them a while. He told the men that he wanted to waste no time in seeing the Monroe's. "Let's see this taken care of quickly. I am anxious to be there and back."

He made sure that all the men had been relieved from the smokehouse, to relax and clean up, before he made his way to the big house. He wanted to nap before that evening's celebration.

Clean and fresh, Luc climbed into his covers to nap. Elise joined him and the two fell asleep. Elise and Luc joined the festivities late. They enjoyed their nap. They cuddled together and slept long and hard. They walked into the dining hall hand in hand.

The men were discussing the hunt and what they had seen. People were surprised to hear about the cougars. It was unheard of for cougars to be in their part of the country.

Elise made her way around the tables and people; she was pouring wine or helping Bridgette in some way. The men talked amongst themselves. The woman chatted with one another. There was much to celebrate. She noticed that Jene and her family were absent. Elise understood the want to keep her loved one to herself.

The soldier that came to Elise's rescue the night of the intruder walked into the hall. He spoke quietly to Luc and Marcus. Elise watched as the storm rolled into Luc's eyes.

"Elise," he shouted at her.

The crowd quieted and everyone watched. She had been startled even though she had been watching him.

"Come here." His tone was angry, he hadn't spoken to her like that since she first came to the clan.

"Yes, General," was all she could say.

"Why did you not tell me about the incident that happened while I was away."

The crowd watched. They could say nothing and knew that he was angry.

"I'm sorry; I didn't think of it." Being called out in front of everyone embarrassed Elise, so she turned and left the hall.

The crowd talked once again, but quieter. The soldier continued to explain to Luc and Marcus about what had happened, giving them all the details and concluding that no trace had been found of the intruder. Luc was concerned, not because anything might have been taken, but because someone could have hurt Elise. He was angry at her for not telling him. It wasn't logical. He knew that, but he was angry anyways.

The crowd finally died down late into the night. Elise and Bridgette had long since gone to bed, when the remaining few men said their goodnights. The General walked to his hall with a heavy heart. He could see in her expression that he had hurt her. When he got to his room she was not there. He made his way back down the hall he had just come from. He opened the door to the room she had only slept in a few times when she first arrived. Seeing her asleep, he left her there. Luc took a walk to the smoke house to clear his thoughts. He had too much going on in his mind, he needed to simplify things. A walk always cleared his head and gave him the answers he was searching for.

Elise woke the next morning. Luc had neither come to retrieve her, nor stay with her. She knew by the late hour that they must have left for tribe Monroe. She made her way to the bathing chamber. She started her daily ritual which including washing her face and doing something with her hair. She was feeling sorry for herself. He had hurt her feelings, and she wanted some alone time. She didn't intend to fall asleep. Luc did not come for her, which made it worse. He had been hunting for days and did not even miss her last night. She hadn't lied to him. She was too happy to see him to worry about something that had happened days ago. It was literally the farthest thing from her mind. She had best stop worrying about it and move on. She needed to do laundry and finish the sewing that she had started. When Luc returned, she would talk with him and make it right.

The men had gotten a late start and wondered if they were going to make it home that night. Luc took less men this time. The road to Monroe's was deserted. They had yet to cross paths with anyone or anything. Fortunately for them, they lived out in the country, even when travel was easier, they were farther out. The ruralness helped the few tribes who lived in the area. There were only two he knew of, themselves, and Tribe Monroe.

There were six men, including Luc. They brought both the buck and the colt. The colt was under two. He was a fine-looking palomino stallion. He felt confident that he would make a good trade with the Monroe's for the things he had requested. The men were quiet on their journey, each seeming to have something on their minds.

Luc wondered why Elise chose to sleep elsewhere. He remembered how lovely she had looked both times he had checked on her. It took everything he had not to snatch her out of bed last night. Then again, when he checked on her before he left for the Monroe's, he stood there for minutes just looking at her. She was lovely, he blew her a kiss and closed her door quietly instead of doing what he really wanted. He wanted to make love to her. He wanted to touch her all over. He wanted to see the passion in her eyes.

He understood she was hurt or possibly even angry with him for yelling at her in front of everyone, but not enough to leave him without even trying to discuss it first. They hadn't said the words, but he thought she knew how he felt, that he wanted her with him. He could force her, but that was not how he wanted her. He wanted her willing or not at all. He wanted her to be her own person, not a person who only served him and did his bidding. He wanted a partner, not a slave. He wanted her to be his, forever.

He didn't think that he could live without her. Luc understood that he hadn't known her very long, and he didn't know her well at all, but what he did know was that she belonged in his world. He needed her.

The Woodsman had almost reached their destination. They could see Tribe Monroe's hamlet in the near distance, when Luc noticed Troy Monroe come out of his barn and wave to him in greeting. The old man recognized them immediately, without fear or trepidation. Monroe wore a smile on his face. He was genuinely happy to see his neighboring tribe.

The men pulled their horses up to Monroe. A few of his men had come to join Monroe and offer their greetings as well. It was obvious that these men had missed the old days when people were more social. The men halted their horses a few feet from the Monroe's. No one felt the need to hang back or speak privately. Both clans had already developed a bond between themselves and knew that they had allies in each other.

Luc smiled, "Monroe."

"General."

Men were always good with fewer words, relying on body language, tone and facial ques. These men were happy to see each other. Other men swapped handshakes and hellos.

Luc and Marcus got down off their horses. They were ready to get down to business with Monroe.

"Come take a look at your new palomino." Marcus said proudly. The colt was from Marcus' stallion's blood line. He felt they resembled each other. He knew he would make Monroe a fine stud when he was old enough.

The old man touched the colt's neck, looking him over.

"What do you think?" Luc asked him.

"He is exceptional. I am proud to take him." He looked at Marcus, "I will take good care of him. He will be a brat."

Marcus laughed. He believed the old man. He was a man that when he gave his word, he meant it.

CLAN WOODSMEN: THE GENERAL'S REFUGE

Monroe gestured for the cousins to follow him inside his barn. "First the trade, then I have a gift for you."

Monroe walked over to something covered in cloth, he yanked it free. Luc was blown away by the stunning rocking chair the old man had made. It was different than the last. This one looked like it was made of mahogany. It was rich and vibrant in color, like red wine. The back had more detailed work with flowers and vines. It was like the old man knew that it was for a woman.

Luc went over to it rubbing his hand along the arm. He pushed it to rock. "It's lovely, and I know she will like it," he told him cryptically.

The old man smiled. He had taken great care because he knew the trade was far more worthy than his simple pieces of cedar. Next, the old man walked over to another cloth and pulled. Underneath was a garden bench very much like the rocker. It was intricate and well made. He knew Elise would like both pieces. The rocker was for Elise, but the bench was going to be for all the ladies. Marcus had suggested to him that the women needed something for themselves, a garden, or a space that was just for them. His mother and aunt had gardens when they were alive. He knew they needed distractions just like the men.

Luc was surprised that Marcus had thought about it. He remembered the fresh flowers in his mother's kitchen and how she would be in her greenhouse early on Sunday mornings. He was surprised that he hadn't thought of it. As much as he and Marcus were alike, they were just as different. That was another reason why they were such a good team. Luc and Marcus complimented and thanked the old man for his pieces. They appreciated them both and knew that he had taken great time and effort to make such precious pieces of furniture.

Monroe took something off a work shelf and handed it to Luc, "This is for Clan Woodsmen. It is a gift."

Luc took the object out of the canvas cloth. He was astounded. He did not expect the 11x17 canvas. The portrait was amazing in detail, the colors were vibrant, and eye catching.

The picture was of an old man standing near a group of riders. The picture was muted and blurred, all except three people. The likeness and attention to detail was astonishing. Everything from the crossbows to the wagon were visible. Luc, Marcus, and the old man stood front and center. It was a re-creation of the first time they had come to trade. Luc and Marcus were complimentary. They admired the attention to detail.

"No boys, I did not paint this." He paused a moment. "It was my daughter. She has a photographic memory and paints every detail, exact. She painted this for you."

The men were surprised. "Why?" they both asked.

The old man smiled and shrugged his shoulder. "Who knows why woman are the way they are and why they do what they do." He said this in jest, but the statement was true to all of them. "Come boys, it is time to see the meat."

They were surprised since Luc and Marcus were usually the ones that got down to business. The old man walked out of the barn leaving them behind.

Marcus nudged Luc in the ribs, "Did that old man just call us boys?"

"Twice," Luc held up two fingers as he spoke. Both men laughed, then followed him out into the sunlight.

The Monroe's took the six riders inside for food and wine. The buck was inspected, and the food exchanged. Once again, both parties felt like it was a worthy trade. The men sat and talked and enjoyed their meal. Luc had been listening, but he couldn't get Elise's almond shaped green eyes out of his head.

"So, what is bothering you my friend?" Troy Monroe asked Luc.

"What makes you think that something is bothering me?"

"I know a man with troubles on his mind," he replied to Luc.

"Woman problems." Marcus butted in with a half-smile.

Luc just raised his eyebrow at his cousin. The old man asked for a woman to come to him. He spoke to her softly, then she disappeared. The woman returned fifteen minutes later and only nodded at Monroe. Whatever was going on they were both on the same page.

Marcus angled his head so that only Luc could hear him. "What do you think that is all about?" Luc just made a face a gave a half shrug; he wasn't worried. Marcus continued, "What do you think about inviting the Monroe's to have a meal and a round of games; a little friendly competition so to speak?"

Luc smiled at his cousin. He didn't have to answer, Marcus knew that he liked the idea. The two men returned their attention to Troy Monroe. Marcus told the crowd about his idea, and immediately, the entire group of men got into a deep debate about it. They laughed and talked about the games they would try. The men all agreed on a crossbow match. They couldn't agree on football or baseball. The warriors all wanted some form of contact sports, the farmers the opposite. They decided to flip a coin for it. Monroe called the coin in the air. The farmers were relieved when it landed in favor of tribe Monroe. This got a huge raucous laugh from the clan woodsmen.

The men were planning a day for the barbeque, when several of the clan Woodsmen stopped to stare. They were caught unaware by the beauty that had entered the dining hall. She was tall and slender, with stunning turquoise eyes and long wavy, blonde hair.

Her features were delicate and instantly attracting. Luc had been looking at Marcus and the old man, when he saw something in his cousin's eyes that he hadn't seen in quite some time. When he looked up, he noticed the reason for the sudden change in atmosphere.

The old man smiled and beckoned her to him. She hugged him as he sat with his comrades. "This, gentlemen, is my daughter Sierra."

She looked around the room and gave a quick nod and wave. He stood up and so did all the men, showing their respect not just to the leader of the tribe, but also his daughter.

The old man pointed to Luc, "This is the man, they call General." He told her. She nodded and they both extended their hands in formal greeting. He turned to Marcus, "This, my dear, is his cousin and right-hand man, Marcus." They extended their hands to each other as well.

Once again, Luc saw something in his cousin's eyes. He knew him well enough that no one else had noticed it, no one, but him. There was a slight change in his expression and eyes that told Luc what he guessed was true.

Marcus spoke as he held Sierra's gaze. "You're a talented artist. Your father is proud, and we are pleased to accept your painting."

"Thank you, Marcus. I only paint what I see, my idea of the world, nothing more." Marcus smiled to her and nodded his head.

He then turned his attention to Luc, who spoke next. "Yes, we are pleased to have your painting, we are pleased to meet you. However, the day grows long, and we wish to be home tonight."

The old man nodded his understanding. The men all walked into the yard to get their horses ready. The old man watched as man after man filed out of the main door, only the cousins remained. Luc turned and walked out. Marcus took one last look around Tribe Monroe's dining hall before he followed his General out.

The men laughed and talked a few more minutes, lingering like family members or old friends delaying the moment they have to say goodbye. Finally, they said their goodbyes. Luc and Marcus were the last to jump into their saddles.

Luc spoke first, "Goodbye Monroe. We will see you and your people fourteen days from now."

"Yes, my friend. You're sure you can handle us all?"

"Do not question it, Monroe. Until then," he waved goodbye then turned his horse in the direction of home.

Marcus was last to leave, he told Monroe, "Until next time Monroe, goodbye."

Monroe hollered out to them all, "Safe travels my friends."

Monroe turned to go into his barn when something caught his eye. Once again from the window, Sierra watched the Woodsmen ride out of her life. She felt hope this time, knowing she would see him in just a few short weeks.

She had loved him since the first time they had come to raid Tribe Monroe. She was only fourteen, but she knew she would love him forever. She was kept hidden because her father was terrified that these warriors would hurt her or kill them all. They were strong and demanding, but they hurt no one. They proved over the years that they were not cruel. Sierra had known the moment she had first seen him, that she wanted to marry the warrior. She knew that two weeks would seem like a lifetime. She needed a distraction. She changed her clothing, pulled out a canvas, and painted.

CHAPTER 11

Elise finished her chores early. She wanted to be alone and skipped sewing with Bridgette. Elise wasn't done feeling sorry for herself yet. She was missing her general. No distraction would work. Her book only made it worse. She sat by the window in the dark, with her cat, Rose, in her lap. A storm had moved in. The wind was blowing fiercely as rain fell hard against the windows. She absently ran her fingers through her hair. She left it down and hoped that Luc would be distracted by it. She wanted him to make love to her. Luc may not want her here when he arrived, but she wasn't going to take any chances. She wanted to see him and find out what he was angry about. It seemed like forever, yet the men still had not arrived.

She laid on the bed that she shared with him. If he didn't want her there, he would have to move her himself. She enjoyed the smell of the pillows and aroma of her General pouring out from every section of the bed. Instead of trying to stay awake for him, she would just fall asleep, naked in his bed. She removed her robe, laid it across the rocker and climbed into bed. She tossed and turned for what seemed like hours, and still he did not arrive.

It had taken the men longer to get home than expected. When the storm arrived, it made traveling worse. They slowed to a snail's pace. All he wanted was to get home to Elise. When they arrived it was quiet, everyone had long since gone to bed. The guards on watch were the only people that knew they were home. They pulled the wagon into the barn and would deal with the food in the morning. The six men took care of their own horses instead of waking up Billy, the stable hand. The men were tired, it had been a long day.

After their horses were taken care of, the cousins walked to the big house together. They didn't want to track mud and water through the house, so they stripped down to their undershorts. The men said their goodnights, then went to their sides of the house.

Luc noticed Elise right away. He closed the door quietly. She didn't move or make a sound. He watched her for a moment, then took off his last remaining garment, and crawled into bed.

Elise felt the bed move and she turned, in that direction. She felt the coolness of his skin. She reached out and ran her hand along his back. She continued to his neck and felt his wet hair. He turned to face her. Elise propped her herself up with her head on her hand. They just looked at each other for a moment. Finally, Elise broke the silence.

"I'm sorry I didn't tell you about the issue with the room getting ransacked. It was my fault I left the window open."

"That's not why I was angry, Elise."

"Why were you angry then?"

"It doesn't matter anymore."

Elise was getting angry at him. "Well, it matters to me. I have the right to know why I was yelled at." She sat up in bed holding the blanket to her chest.

He didn't like her tone, nor her comment. He replied even more heatedly. "You have the right? What right do you have, Elise? If I say it no longer matters, then by God, let it be."

He could see the fireworks in her eyes as soon as he finished his comment. She jumped out of bed, naked and angry. All he could see was her nakedness. Nothing else mattered, he wanted her.

"I actually wanted to make things right. Now, I just want to be alone."

Luc jumped out of bed and grabbed Elise by the shoulders. "What do you want from me? What do you want me to say?" He was hurting her arms, and she tried to pull away from him. "What do you want, Elise?" He asked her again angry and harsh.

"The truth."

"You want the truth? The truth is that I wasn't angry at you, I was worried about you." He paused then continued, "I can't live without you. I need you. Is that what you want to hear?"

She calmly replied to him, "Only if it's the truth, Luc."

He crushed her body against his and kissed her forcefully. "I don't lie, I won't start doing it with you." He said this in a husky, seductive timbre. She kissed him and pressed her body into his. He picked her up and laid her on the bed. They made love for hours. Their passion was wild and forceful. When their bodies were finally appeased, Luc cuddled Elise into his body. They listened to the rain as they fell asleep.

Elise woke the next morning, she could still hear the rain outside. She had always liked rainy days. She moved around in bed and felt her partner. Luc was still beside her; he must have been tired and decided to sleep in. Luc woke up the moment Elise started moving. He had awakened earlier but decided that he was going to devote his day to her; just the two of them.

He pulled her to him, and pressed his face into her chest, she laughed. His hair tickled and sent chills along her body. She loved the smell of him. She loved to lay next to him. Elise thought about what Luc had told her last night. He needed her.

"I'm glad that your men found me. I have come to be happy here. It has been a blessing."

"I am glad too. But I'm especially glad that I have you in my bed." He told her seductively.

She smiled at him; her eyes narrowed just slightly.
He recognized that as her "I'm in the mood" look. He liked the way her eyes told their own story. She could seduce him with just a look. He whispered something to her in French. Luc kissed Elise all over her body. They explored each other for hours, better understanding each other with every new sensation. They were passionate together, as if they had been made for each other. He was erotic in the things he did to her.

They made love again and again that day; they chose only to venture out for food. The rain had not let up, so they read to each other. Luc read to Elise about famous General's again. She read to him about the women from the wild west. They enjoyed each other, and once again fell asleep wrapped up in each other.

Luc woke the next morning and placed soft kisses on Elise's shoulder. She smiled at him and hugged him close to her. They laid in bed talking and enjoying the lazy morning. Their pillow talk was soft and sweet.

Luc asked Elise, "What do you think about starting our day off with a ride?" Luc was already sitting up, propped up with a pillow.

She answered him as she was pushing herself into a sitting position. "Oh, yes. Luc, I would love to ride all day, every day if I could. I find it very therapeutic. Like nothing else in the world matters."

She said this in such way that he believed she would do just that if she were allowed. Luc could tell that something in her mind had triggered. She had a funny expression on her face that told its own story.

She was hesitant, but wanted to know the answer, so she asked anyway. "Luc, who are Blake and Brittany?"

Luc was stunned for a moment, as if he had been electrocuted. She continued quickly after seeing his expression.

"When the intruder came in, he knocked a bunch of your books onto the floor, and when I cleaned up, a picture fell out of one of them. I wasn't sure if you knew who they were or not."

He nodded his head realizing that she was just being curious. "Well, Elise. They were my family. Brittney was my wife, and Blake was my son. They both died."

"I'm sorry, Luc. I didn't mean to bring up something so painful. I didn't realize. Please forgive me for being nosy."

"No, Elise there is nothing to be sorry about. It was a long time ago. I would have been curious myself." He smiled at her. He didn't want to sour their day with talk of the past. He loved them, always would, but he needed to focus on now. Besides, talking about it only hurt.

"I know the hurt of losing a child." He turned to her. Elise had a tear running down her cheek. "I know that you must think about them every day. I think about my daughter, more often than not."

Luc hugged Elise to himself. They sat there holding each other. They both had loss, and yet still had compassion and strength for one another. They had needed to find each other. Neither one talked any more about it. They knew when the time was right, they would finish their conversation.

Luc and Elise finally made their way out of the house and into the yard. After walking in silence, Luc spoke to her, "I have something for you. Come with me to the barn."

Elise was intrigued, wondering what kind of surprise he had for her, especially since they hadn't left the inside of the house in days. The bench and rocker had been unloaded and left inside the barn, next to the wagon. Luc held Elise's hand as he dragged her inside.

"I traded Monroe for this, I thought you would like it, since you seem to enjoy mine."

Elise was surprised by the rocker. It was beautiful and ornate; feminine and sturdy. She immediately sat down on it and loved the way the back was made. It was not straight, but slightly curved. The rocker was comfortable. She knew she would enjoy it for years to come. She stood up and looked it over again. The rocker was a burgundy, almost like wine. It had delicate flowers and stunning vines all over it.

"Luc, this is fantastic. Did Monroe make this himself?"

"Yes, Elise, he did. He's a clever and observant character; he understood right away that it would be for a woman."

She smiled up at him and hugged him. "Thank you, this is the best gift I've had in a really long time. I will definitely use it, and often."

"I know, darling." He told her as he returned her smile.

"Now look at this," he said to her as he pulled her over to the bench. "This bench will be for all of the women here. You can make a space for yourselves, a garden or something similar."

She nodded. It would be wonderful if they had a garden. She knew many of the women would indeed enjoy that. The bench was just as lovely as the rocker, they were similar, and yet unique in their own way.

"I think we will leave the bench here for now, but we can take the rocker inside."

Elise watched as he hefted it over his shoulder and started carrying it out of the barn. Elise followed behind Luc. They went through the dining hall and into their hall of rooms. She jumped in front of him and opened the bedroom door.

"So, Ma Chérie, where would you like it?"

"In front of the window for now, please."

He took it over and placed it in front of the window. "Perfect," Elise told him.

He smiled at her, "Now how about that ride."

She responded happily, "I've never been more ready."

Luc walked over to her. He kissed her hard and forcefully. He let her go and gave her butt a whack, "Let's get out here before we don't."

She smiled and laughed. They both knew if they didn't get out of the bedroom, their passion for one another would take over. She had already fallen in love with him. She knew it the moment they met. Elise felt that Luc cared. He didn't say the words, but he didn't have to. He may not love her, but he showed his feelings in the way he dealt with her. In these hard times, he had been thoughtful enough to have the rocker made for her. She knew that he had other things that required his time, and yet here he was, spending time with her. Luc may not love her, but he cared. She could live with this, forever, she hoped.

They walked around the compound, past people working in the garden, men battling, and people doing their odd chores. Elise was hesitant to broach the subject, considering how he had felt with the hunting issue.

"I would like to help in the garden, I have always enjoyed planting, watering, pulling weeds, just being around nature in general. I don't mind the hard work; I find it therapeutic. Sometimes if I need an answer to something, I focus on my work, and God will just slip it into my mind. Suddenly, I have my answers. It works for me more often than not."

He smiled. "I know how you feel. My walks do that for me. When I can't sleep or an issue is heavy on my mind, I just walk. Sometimes it's like a bomb going off. Poof, eureka." He laughed, put his hand to his head and made the motion.

She understood, "Exactly, mind blow." They both laughed.

"You know, Elise, I do not mind, nor will I care if you should choose to help in the garden. I'm sure your help will be much appreciated. Its time consuming, and the extra help is always welcome."

"Thank you, I won't let it interfere with my other chores."

"Do not thank me, you will be tired, sore, and smelly one day, and you will be cussing me." They both laughed. He continued, "Besides, I have no doubt you will make sure your other duties are taken care of first. I myself enjoy gardening from time to time." They were enjoying this time together, with every moment they better understood each other.

Their horses were saddled, and they were ready for their ride. As they led their horses away from the stable, Marcus walked up to them.

"Going for a ride, I take it?"

"What gave it away Marcus?" Luc asked him sarcastically, with a crooked smile. Elise only smiled; she enjoyed the verbal jousting that took place between the cousins.

"I didn't get my invitation. It must have gotten lost in the mail." Marcus winked at Elise when he said this.

"Well, Cuz, it's probably because you weren't invited," Luc told him bluntly. Marcus could see his cousin's irritation, and he chuckled. "Did you need something, Marcus?"

"I'm hurt Luc, do I need something to seek you out?" Luc just stared at his cousin. Marcus chuckled again.

"Actually, come and find me when you have some spare time, and please for God sakes not at two in the morning." Luc nodded, and the men dismissed each other. Marcus watched Luc and Elise ride away. He wondered if his cousin had gotten around to telling Elise that he was in love with her.

They rode around for a while enjoying the weather. The sun was high in the sky and it gave off incredible warmth. The rain had come and gone and left puddles of water in random places. Luc took Elise around to the different water catchments that were sporadically located around the compound. He got off his horse, inspected and re-covered each one. After a few hours, they offered their horses water and walked, giving their horses a rest.

Elise had been thinking. Her mind wondered to the past, "I wish we didn't live in this time. I want takeout. Pizza and a beer. A hockey game. Anything other than what we deal with every day. Not that I don't enjoy this with you, right now. I'm just tired of the constant planning and preparations for survival."

"A hockey game? Who's your team?"

Elise looked at Luc sideways, men always heard what they wanted. "That's what you got out of my spiel."

They laughed. "I'm a Red Wings fan."

"Oh, Elise no, my darling, no."

She continued, as if she hadn't been interrupted. "I'm a Red Wing, on the cusp of a Black Hawk. And you I'm guessing are a Montreal fan?"

"Le Blu, Blanc et Rouge…. Les Habitant!" They both laughed. He hugged her to him. "I'm with you on that one, I miss hockey, but I miss other things. Like pizza, beer, and takeout." He said with a wink. He shrugged his shoulders, "I miss it all, the convenience of life. This is what happens when we get too selfish, you, me, all of us. We are left with the fall out. Literally." She nodded.

Elise smiled, then continued on the same thought path, but slightly different subject, "I would love to walk on the beach with you, smell the breeze. Feel the sun roasting my shoulders. You and me, on a vacation. That would be romantic. Have you ever been to beaches in Hawaii? It's like your walking on the fucking sun."

Luc laughed. "I have not been to Hawaii, but I've been down to the beaches in Florida, and I tell you, there's nothing like the water. Teal and clear. The sand looks like sugar."

Elise replied to him, "I have not been to Florida, but I've heard the beaches are fantastic. The sand in Hawaii can be different colors. There's a beach on Maui that has black sand, and there's other beaches where the sand is pink. It's cool how the same island has so many different shades of sand. I love the Hawaiian beaches, there's wildlife around every corner. Sharks, eels, and many different fish. The turtles swim around people, like they're just another fish in the sea. They don't care, they have the Hawaiian mentality for sure. Life's a beach my friend."

He smiled. He could picture her swimming around, having a good time. He could picture them together. "I'd like to walk with you on the beach someday."

They both took a deep a breath. They knew someday was a long shot.

CHAPTER 12

Luc and Elise enjoyed their afternoon together. They finished their walk, then took their horses back to the barn. Elise cared for her horse while Luc left his with Billy, making the excuse that he needed to find Marcus. He figured that whatever Marcus needed to speak to him about was not pressing, but important enough that he didn't want to discuss it in front of Elise. He told Elise that he would catch back up with her in the barn in a few minutes.

Elise enjoyed caring for her horse. She cleaned and brushed her. With her task completed and her horse groomed, Luc still had not returned. Elise asked Billy if he needed any help. He gave her a negative respond. She asked Billy to tell Luc that she returned to the big house. Billy nodded and said goodbye with a wave.

Elise walked back hoping to see Luc on the way. She did not, so she went straight to the bathing chamber she shared with Bridgette, taking advantage of her alone time. She washed her hair and enjoyed the smell of the soap. She closed her eyes and was so deep in thought that she did not hear the door open and close. Suddenly, the feeling of being watched crept over her. She opened her eyes and jumped, then relaxed, seeing Luc. He was leaning back against the wall. He had one foot propped against it and his arms were crossed. He looked handsome standing there, so relaxed with a crooked smile across his face.

"Why are you in here?" He asked her, the crooked smile not leaving his face.

"Why not?" she asked him.

His tone changed slightly, "Why not, because we have our own bathing chamber in the bedroom."

She just looked at him for a moment. "Well, you never told me that I could use it, so I never have."

"I didn't know you needed an invitation, woman."

Her eyes got big. The storm rolled into both of their eyes. "Woman?" she replied heatedly.

"You share my bed, woman, my bath isn't good enough." His tone, attitude and remark caught her off guard. She took a sharp intake of breath.

She replied to him heatedly. "You never said that I was allowed anything. Remember I'm just your servant." She stood up, naked and wet. She was angry.

"You're not my servant, Elise."

"What am I then, your guest?"

His voice got louder, "You want to leave? Then by God woman, go. No one is keeping you here."

She turned her back on him. He walked out, slamming the door behind himself. She sat back into the tub, immediately sorry. What had just happened? Hell no, she didn't want to leave.

She touched her stomach, she wasn't sure, but she had missed her period that month. She hoped it was stress, but the thought of having a part of Luc sent thrills running through her. She would wait. She wasn't going to tell him if it turned out to be stress. She'd had this problem before, and she hadn't had sex then. Stress can definitely alter your tides.

Luc stormed out of the house and went for a walk. He was unhappy about the discussion he had with Marcus. Instead of internalizing it, he took it out on Elise. He didn't want her to go, he didn't want her anywhere but with him.

Marcus told him that the men wanted a meeting, and it would happen after the sun went down. They didn't want anyone to know about the meeting. It was about a scavenge that needed to be done. This put him in a sour frame of mind.

Elise finished her bath. She sat in her rocker that looked out into the yard. She dried her hair the best she could, then braided it. She watched the Woodsmen moving about, coming and going. She watched Luc talk to some of his men. It was hot out; she opened the window for a slight breeze. She closed her eyes and drifted off to sleep.

Luc came into his bedroom quietly, he had seen Elise in the rocker, sleeping. He didn't want to wake her. He watched her for a few moments before he sat down. He felt the small breeze that drifted into the room. He could smell his woman's hair. The smell was light and fresh. He closed his eyes, thinking about the pleasant day they had shared before he had turned it sour.

He wanted to be clear when she woke up. She wasn't going anywhere, whether she wanted to or not. He may have said something stupid in anger, but she was going to understand where he stood on the issue. He had already told her that he needed her. They fought and still she had come to his room. Maybe he didn't have to tell her after all? People fight. They don't just leave each other; they fight for each other. In any relationship, whatever it may be, people need to learn to fight, and then be able to mend those fights and move on together. No one agrees all the time. That is what makes each relationship so unique. Each person brings something new to the table.

Luc thought about what he would say to Elise, and then he also drifted off to sleep. Unlike her dream which was peaceful, tender, and calming, his was harsh and anxious.

Elise woke to Luc giving her a gentle shove. The sun had gone down, and it was twilight outside. She yawned, "Wow, I must have needed that nap, when did you come in? Just?"

"No, Elise, I've been here with you for a while. I took a nap as well. I am about to go meet with the men. We are going to discuss some things." She nodded at him. He continued, "Eat, don't wait for me. I may be awhile."

She replied to his comment, "I may pass on dinner tonight, I'm not feeling well. I may read for a bit, then go to bed. I guess the ride wore me out. I'm sorry about earlier."

"I'm sorry too, it's over and I don't want to dwell on it."

She got up from her rocker and lit a hurricane lantern. "I don't want to leave here, or you." She told him quietly.

Luc got up and pulled her into his arms. He told her in a deep sexy voice, "It doesn't matter, I wasn't going to let you leave, even if you wanted to. You are mine, and I am not letting you go."

She kissed him passionately and held him close to her. That was all she needed to hear.

"You know, Elise. You are not my servant, nor were you ever. You have always been free to come or go."

"What do you mean?"

"We, meaning the Woodsmen, may be arrogant but we feel this is a good place. We let people believe what they want, until they discover this is the best place for them. Once a person realizes that we are not 'the enemy', and we believe that they are not 'the enemy', they are free to come and go as they please. Does this make any sense?"

Elise said nothing, her eyes narrowed, he could see the wheels turning in her head.

"You are different, Ma Chérie, you are mine. But I am yours as well."

Luc walked to the shop where the vehicles were kept. They might as well check everything out while they were in there. He was the last to arrive.

"You used to bust our balls, when we were late, especially the last guy to arrive." Robert said this sincerely, but with a smile.

Marcus couldn't let it go either, "Come on General, what's changed? You prefer your room, to the company of your men." He said this with a smile and a laugh. They all laughed.

Luc shrugged his shoulders, and smiled, "What can I say boys, the skirt is better looking than you bunch of outcasts."

Marcus punched Luc's arm; Luc just let it go. "Have you told her yet?" Marcus asked him.

Luc looked sideways at his cousin, "Told her what?"

Marcus paused then replied, "That you're in love with her."

Luc shook his head. "Get real, let's get this discussion started." Luc's expression and tone had changed, the men all understood their General. He was in no mood to play.

They started on one of the Jeeps. "Gas is about half a tank." Robert told them.

Marcus answered his problem. "That means we have maybe one more mission in this vehicle, unless we can find fuel. I say we go farther this time. Into a bigger city. There are probably abandoned homes, and vehicles everywhere. We can siphon gas."

Luc spoke next, "I don't like it, smaller towns are dangerous enough. Now you want to go into a big city. You have lost your shit Marcus."

"I'm not talking a major city; just bigger than the two smaller ones we have already been to. There's enough of us, we can do this."

Brent spoke next, "Maybe we try and find the place Elise was talking about. Maybe it's a place just big enough. What do we really need?"

"Did she ever mention the town's name?" another asked.

Luc looked around at his men, "No, okay guys, list what we need. Just shout it out. I know we need lumber."

Marcus was the first, "Fuel in general, propane, kerosene, gasoline, diesel."

"We could use bedding, any kind of bedding," one of the men responded.

Robert added, "Bridgette wants us to look for bathroom items as well, soap, shampoo. Anything really."

"I need diapers, if I can get them, hell my wife gave me her own list." This had come from Brent.

The men laughed and someone threw a rag at him.

Robert responded to Brent's comment, "Damn it, I knew you needed lady pads, you freakin' panz."

Luc laughed, "I'm sure everyone has a small list, but for now I want to discuss the main list. Food is and will always be a priority." Everyone nodded, that was a given. Luc continued, "The lumber around us has pretty much been taken, so regardless of how I feel, we are going to have to move to another place we have not been. Has anyone looked or been looking at a map? Any ideas? Let's have them."

Robert pulled out a map and laid it on a table. The men gathered around. Many of them pointed at different places and made comments.

Marcus pointed to a spot, "This is us. We need to make sure that wherever we go, it's worth the gas, and that the gas we already have can get us home."

Luc lovingly gave his cousin a pat on the back. "Does anyone know where Elise was found?"

One of the men that was hunting the day Elise was found, stepped forward, and pointed to the map, "This general area."

Luc thanked him. They all looked and made guesses. Unfortunately, no one had any real idea where she may have come from. She told Luc that she wasn't sure the direction, she had been wandering for weeks. That didn't help, she could have come from so many different directions. He needed to move on from that thought.

The men moved onto the next vehicle. It was an older modified military truck. There was plenty of room, thank God, it was a diesel. It was a sturdy, five-ton camo beast, with six wheels and a flat bed. They had raided a deserted National Guard lot and got lucky. It ran with no problems and had plenty of juice.

The men continued their conversation. Luc, asked the men, "How's the ammo looking? I need more bolts, I have lost a few in our hunts."

Luc nodded. "So, this beast has more than three quarters of a tank. This is probably the best option, with one of the Jeeps. How many of us need to go? I will go on this one for sure." He paused and looked around. Marcus and Brent held up their hands. Luc continued, "I'm thinking nine men this time. Two men stay with the vehicles, while three snipers are in a triangular style perimeter. That way someone always has eyes on your back. I'm thinking two pairs to scavenge." He moved his hand palm down in a wavering motion, indicating that he was undecided in his own mind.

Marcus nodded, "Yeah, I think that will work. We need to see which Jeep has the most gas, and possibly syphon gas from the other to match the beast."

Robert added, "Maybe we hook up one of the trailers to the beast. That way we have the room, should the need arise."

Marcus responded, "Yeah I like it, I think you are right." Luc and the other men nodded, all in agreement. "I want to strap any and all of our jerry cans to the trailer."

Some of the men got started, they gathered all the jerry cans. If any gas remained, they combined it, then took the empties. After all the cans, barrels, anything that could hold fuel, was loaded, Brent walked over and strapped everything down securely using ratchet straps.

The other men moved on to the other Jeep. This one was a newer Wrangler; it was a four door with more room. They would take it this time, it had more cargo space, more people space, and the off-road capability was just as fantastic.

The men talked and debated for hours; they finished late into the night. They planned to leave early, just after dawn the following morning. The men all knew how to prepare themselves. They had their military style tactical chest protection. They would take multiple guns, knives, and their crossbows. They preferred the crossbows and knives for defense, because of the noise factor. Guns could draw more attention than what they bargained for. They were all tough fighters; they had each other's backs and knew how to survive, but no one went undefeated forever.

After the meeting, Luc walked back to his room with a sense of anticipation. He wasn't really worried this time; he was more curious. This would change the morning they intended to leave. He didn't know about the other men, but his adrenaline would kick in the moment he started to dress. His heart would beat faster with every weapon he hid or strapped on himself.

Elise was asleep in bed, she looked peaceful. He pulled off his clothing and climbed into bed with her.

Elise woke the next morning alone. She knew Luc must have started early. She figured he had too many things on his mind and hadn't slept well. She was feeling rotten. Her tummy was upset, she wondered if she had eaten something bad.

Since the last few days had been spent with Luc, her chores had piled up. She had laundry and a room to clean. She knew she would seek out Bridgette at some point. If there was any time left over, she would help in the garden. She climbed out of bed and hoped that her nausea would improve with her schedule.

Elise used the bathing chamber attached to the bedroom. This would be the first time. She should have used it earlier. She realized the fight they had was her fault. Looking back, it was stupid, and had been unneeded.

She cleaned the bedroom and started her laundry. She could hear the men in combat but could not see them. She washed her laundry and thought about the barbeque that would take place soon. Elise knew that she wasn't the only one that looked forward to it. It would be something common in an uncommon world. It would be like the world she grew up in. Maybe, things like the barbeque were needed to get life back to normal.

Elise was so deep in thought that she did not hear Luc come up behind her. She was wringing out her laundry and about to hang it when he finally spoke, "Elise."

She jumped, then laughed. "Luc, you startled me."

He smiled. "Yes, I see that. Sorry."

"No, it's okay, don't worry." She could see that he was dirty and sweaty. He looked like he had been working hard. Probably in hand to hand combat.

"I just wanted to say hi to you, I was working with the other men on some things and needed a break."

She nodded her head, "Well, hi then."

He replied the same sentiment with a crooked smile. "Hi." He walked up to her and kissed her cheek. His expression changed and he became serious.

"Please, don't stop. We can chat while you finish, I didn't want to distract you." She continued what she was doing. "Tomorrow, we are going on a scavenge."

Elise paused and looked up at him, she held a wet item half in and half out her basket.

He continued, "We are going to find anything we can."

She listened and digested the information he was giving her.

"Is there anything you need? I can't promise anything, but I will certainly try."

"I'm not sure, can I think about for a bit?"

"Sure, let me know this evening, before we go to bed."

Luc stood and talked with Elise for about twenty minutes. He told her about the place they picked out. They had not been there before. He confided his worries about the location being bare, with nothing to collect. His men didn't know the area so the danger would increase. Luc did not want to scare her. He wanted her to be aware, not ignorant. "I need to get back to what I was doing. I just wanted to give you a heads up." He brushed a stray hair from her face lovingly. He placed his hand on her arm and gave her a light squeeze. They smiled at each other and gave a quick kiss in parting.

Elise finished hanging her wet laundry and set out to find Bridgette. She found her in the food storeroom. "Bridgette, why do the men need to go on a scavenge? I thought the food would be okay for a while."

"It is, however, we need other things, like fuel. I've asked for soaps, shampoos, cleaning supplies in general. We are also running out of the materials we need to make our own, so whatever they can find will be helpful."

Elise asked Bridgette, "Do you have a personal list?"

"Not really, the men don't really say anything, but they grab personal items for us if they find them. Is that what you need? We still have a few."

"No, I'm good there for now, I just didn't know. Luc asked me, but I can't think of anything I need."

The two ladies chatted for a while. Elise finally dismissed herself to see if her laundry was dry. She finished her chores, while the day was still young, and the sun was high in the sky. Elise guessed it was sometime around noon. She needed some food and a rest before she helped in the garden. She felt overheated and splashed her face with water. She brought some crackers, jerky and a small portion of dried fruit with her. She set her plate by the window, opened it, and hoped for a breeze. She sat in her rocker and tried to eat.

Her stomach had other ideas and rebelled against her. Elise felt worse than she had before. She pushed the plate away and closed her eyes. She figured the heat had taken her energy. She must have been more tired than she originally thought and fell asleep quickly.

She napped for about forty-five minutes. When she woke, she was refreshed and felt better. She popped a few dried pieces of fruit into her mouth and went to help in the garden.

Luc and his men spent some of their morning doing their usual daily activities. At noon, the nine men that would leave the next morning changed their daily tasks and began to prepare. The vehicles were virtually ready, but they decided to do another round of checks and double checks. They checked the oil levels, gas level, and tire pressures. They made sure the trailer was hitched properly, and everything securely tightened. They took the map and discussed their route. They assigned each man his position.

The men left their meeting just before dusk. Luc walked with Marcus back to the house. They both noticed Elise in the garden. She was down on her knees pulling weeds.

Marcus smiled, "I'm going to clean up, and I will see you for dinner."

Luc gave his cousin a pat on the back and replied, "Sounds good."

They parted ways. Luc made his way over to Elise. He walked up to her as she smiled up at him. "How's it going? Have you been out here awhile?"

She stood up, dusted off her hands and answered him. "Yeah, I'd say a few hours. I've been pulling weeds and familiarizing myself with the items in here. We don't plant a variety, but at least we plant a lot of what we do plant, if that makes sense."

He nodded his head, "Sure. Are you enjoying yourself?"

"I am actually." She paused, then continued, "I do have one request." She showed him her already blistered hands, "gloves."

"Yes, I see that. I should have some already. I will go see what I can find for you. Are you about done? I'm ready to eat and bathe if you want to join me."

"Yes, I'm about done. I can finish whatever tomorrow." Elise gave the head gardener his tools; she thanked him for letting her help, then walked to the main house with Luc.

The couple bathed together and enjoyed each other's company. Elise helped Bridgette with dinner and served only Luc, Marcus and

Robert. The rest of the men wanted their own private time that night.

Bridgette told Elise that it was traditional for the men to have a private night before a scavenge. Dinner went quickly and everyone said an early goodnight. Luc and Elise went straight to bed. They chatted for a short period of time, then kissed each other goodnight.

"I hope you and your men are safe tomorrow. Hurry back to me."

Luc kissed Elise, one last time, and whispered in her ear, "I will Ma Chérie."

They fell asleep wrapped up in each other's arms. Elise said a silent prayer before drifting off to sleep.

CHAPTER 13

Elise woke to the sound of velcro being adjusted. She sat up in bed and watched Luc don his tactical attire. The room was dim indicating that it was early morning. In a corner, a hurricane lantern softly lit the space. Luc already had on BDU style tactical pants. They were multi-functional, breathable, and easy to move in. He had a t-shirt underneath the vest he just finished putting on. The vest hung on his shoulders and had pockets and velcro attachments around his waist. She yawned and caught his attention.

He turned in her direction and smiled at her, "I'm sorry I woke you."

She smiled back, "I'm not."

He turned his attention back to his dressing. She looked down at his feet and noticed his boots. He was virtually in black from top to bottom. He looked sexy, and dangerous.

Elise knew from her own brothers being in the military, that the government only gave you so much. If you wanted multiple items or different colors, you were on your own. Tactical gear could be pricey, but the government gave you different allowances, so it evened up. She imagined he got most of his items during the war. Items such as these had been looted or purchased prior to the problems in society. Her brothers had multiple sets themselves.

She watched him stuff gloves into one of his pockets. He started attaching multiple cases on his vest. "What do you have in those?" Elise asked him curiously.

He pointed to one he had already attached, "This is a multi-tool." He attached another one, "This is a mace type spray."

She nodded, "What about weapons?"

"Well, we keep the guns locked up, so we get those just before we get into the vehicles, but I have four knives on me, in random locations. I have one here." He pointed to his hip. It was a visible weapon inside a sheath.

"I have one in my boot. I also keep one inside my vest, and I strap one on my opposite leg. I carry two guns, and my crossbow. One gun will be holstered here," he pointed to his leg opposite the knife, "the other will be a rifle."

"Wow, that's intense."

"If you think it's intense now, wait until we leave the gate. My adrenaline has already begun in anticipation." She could imagine. He continued, "The rest of the cases that I attach to my vest will be ammo. I also carry a little food, you never know." He told her this and shook his head. He tried to shake memories that could not be forgotten. Luc took a deep breath, he opened his drawer and pulled out two hats. One was a black baseball cap that he immediately put on, the other was a black sniper's soft brimmed boonie. Luc walked over to the bed, bent over and kissed Elise. She threw her arms around him, and they gave each other a squeeze.

"Luc, please be safe."

"I will Ma Chérie."

He turned and walked out of the bedroom. He was at the door when Elise stopped him. She couldn't help herself, she felt rushed and panicked. She had to tell him, "I love you."

He turned around and moved quickly to the bed. He snatched Elise up, and held her tight. She responded with the same emotion. He kissed her hungrily, as he moved her hair away from her face. He kissed her multiple times, on her cheek, her chin, then finally her nose. He set her away from himself. He cupped her chin with his hand. "You are precious to me. I will miss you, and I love you." With that parting statement he walked out the door.

Luc walked into the dining room. Marcus and Robert were there waiting for him. Marcus pulled a bottle of brandy from behind his back. Robert smiled at Luc, then laid three shot glasses on the table in front of himself. Marcus poured each of them a shot.

"Well, gentleman what are we toasting to?" Luc asked.

The men each grabbed their shot glass.

Marcus, smiled, raised his and spoke. "Here's to us, our men and our freedom, may we live and love, or die fighting."

Robert and Luc raised their glasses and both answered, "Salut!"

The men drained their glasses and put them on the table.

The three men walked out of the house and made their way to the shed. Luc, Robert and Marcus were the first to arrive. Luc and Marcus threw open the large double doors. Robert got in the four-door Jeep, started the engine then drove it out of the shed. The others had started to arrive. Brent was the first. He jumped into the beast, started the engine and drove it out of the shed, parking it next to the Jeep. The nine men gathered their weapons and checked their ammo supply. Each man was prepared. They all had multiple weapons ready for an attack at a moment's notice. They turned on and checked their personal radios for clear communication.

Each of the men were dressed similar to Luc, other than color. The men were in an urban camo pattern with greys, greens, blacks, and minimal whites. Only Luc and Marcus were in black from head to toe. The men had joked that cousins looked like avengers of death. Anyone seeing them would die on the spot. The men had joked and teased each other while preparing for their unknown day. They needed levity in a sea of adrenaline, and an ocean of uncertainty.

Luc walked around and made sure his men had what they needed. After twenty minutes, the nine warriors were ready to roll. They packed extra supplies like flashlights, sleeping bags, and food. They tried to be prepared for multiple scenarios. Brent drove the beast with Robert and another man inside the cab, while two men sat on the flat bed with their backs against it. Luc drove the Jeep with Marcus riding shot gun, and two men in the back. Robert was the map guide. He had always been the best; he could read maps with ease.

Two men were waiting at the main gate to let them out and shut it behind them. Luc rode out first, with the beast following. The two men in the back of the beast waved goodbye, as the gate was closed. The gate guards returned the sentiment and waved goodbye to the men leaving. The men left behind said a silent prayer. Each a little different, but asking for the same thing, a safe journey and return for the nine men leaving the compound.

Elise was too awake to go back to sleep. She watched from the window as Luc drove away in the Gobi colored Jeep. She said a quick prayer, knowing it was one of many that she would say until the men return home safely. She dressed and began her chores.

She wanted to talk to Bridgette about making something nice to wear to the barbeque. When she finally cleaned her room, dressed herself and left her side the house, the sun started to come up. She walked quietly to the kitchen. Bridgette was already there putting together a small breakfast. They ate oatmeal and dried fruit. Elise tried eating but her stomach rebelled against her.

Bridgette's eyes narrowed, "Elise, are you pregnant?"

"I'm not sure."

"When was the last time you had your monthly?"

"Oh. Goodness. A month, two maybe. My periods are all over the place. I've been feeling crappy, and tired, but that doesn't really mean anything."

Bridgette winked at her, "You're not going to believe what I've got. The men raided someplace a couple years ago and brought back all kinds of women crap. I don't think they even knew what they were grabbing." She waved her hand back and forth. "Anyways, we have a pregnancy test, if you want to take it."

"Yeah, I guess I do. Let's eat then we can go."

Brigette and Elise continued to chat and finished their meal. The ladies cleaned up and went to the bathing chamber that they originally shared. Bridgette pulled a box out of a drawer and handed it to Elise. Elise thanked her and excused herself. She made her way to her bedroom.

Nervously, she unwrapped the box and read the directions. Anxiously, she walked around the room and waited for the results. As she walked by the window, she stopped and thought about Luc. She stood, looked out into the yard, and wished she could see him. Regardless if she was pregnant or not, she told Luc that she loved him and meant it.

She walked over to the stick, picked it up, and read the positive result. She stood there stunned. She was pregnant. She returned to the window, sat on her rocker, and just rocked. She was so deep in thought she did not hear Bridgette knock.

"Elise."

Elise jumped from the sound of Bridgette's voice, "Yes?"

"Are you good?"

Elise got up from the rocker and went to the door. "Yeah, of course. Do you need help with anything today?"

Bridgette responded with a negative shake of her head.

"Well. I have a few ideas for the barbeque. How do you feel about sewing today?"

"That sounds great, I'm in," Bridgette responded to her with a smile.

The two ladies made their way to the storeroom for a quick peak at anything they might want to modify. After selecting a few items, the ladies went into the sewing room. Elise immediately opened the window. The breeze felt nice on her face, feeling more like a caress.

Her thoughts returned to Luc. She imagined the last time they made love. She could tell by the breeze that it would be a hot day. At least this part of the house was in the shade, which helped. Elise had chosen a light pastel shirt, teal, almost the color of sea foam and a white long skirt. Bridgette found a yellow dress. The women compared notes on what they thought about their own pieces; they even gave each other some extra ideas. The morning turned into afternoon. The ladies chose to take a break. Elise was suddenly feeling fatigued. They agreed to find each other later after lunch and continue.

Elise opened the window and sat in her rocker. It was quiet in the yard that day. The men that usually practiced hand to hand combat or weapons training were either gone or opted for a rest day. She closed her eyes and drifted off to sleep.

The men passed no one on the small country road. They eventually turned onto a new county road (CR). The second and the third CR had been as uneventful as the first. Robert indicated that soon they would stop moving from CR's to a county highway. That could mean more people, traffic, or problems. The men passed by a small deserted area they'd raided previously. Finally, they reached the county highway. They had not seen this stretch of road before. They turned onto the county highway and proceeded cautiously. They saw nothing unusual. No one had followed them. All nine men were on high alert, rarely speaking, but always watching, and scanning. This road was a mix of abandoned farms and woods. No vehicles littered the streets this far in the country.

The more miles, the less country, the closer they came to the town. Little neighborhoods started popping up sporadically. More garbage and abandoned vehicles could be seen; most of them looked abused, not worth stopping to look at. Still, they saw no signs of life, but imagined that in one of these little house's, someone would be hidden. They stayed alert and moved quickly.

They came to a city center of sorts. It had multiple stores, ranging from hardware, to clothing. Most of the stores looked trashed. Windows were broken and things randomly thrown about. No rhyme or reason to the chaos. The parking lot was immense, the size indicated that the small town expected much growth before the war had changed it.

Luc stopped the Jeep in the middle of the parking lot. He parked the vehicle so that it faced out and the back was easily accessible. The beast pulled up close to the Jeep, but far enough away so that if either vehicle had to bail out, they could do so quickly.

The men stepped out of the vehicles and stretched. No one spoke, they didn't have to. Each knew their job, and quickly got to it. One man laid down on the ground, rifle ready, his back to the vehicles. The second man assumed the same position but in front of the vehicles, tucked between the two. The third man laid down on the ground, facing the opposite direction. The men had eyes on the world and each other.

All three men wore their sniper's hats to keep out the glare of the sun. The men knew it was up to them to stay vigilant. It meant all of their lives.

Brent got out of the beast, stretched his legs, then hopped back in. With his rifle ready, he sat like a bank robber in a getaway car, ready to move at a moment's notice. The fourth man that rode with Luc, stretched and took Luc's place as driver of the Jeep. He would be ready to move just like Brent.

Marcus, Luc, and two other men got ready to go into the first building. They checked their radios, cocked their weapons, and took them off safety. Moving in pairs, they started their way inside. It was a sporting goods store. This was good news; they should be able to find supplies like ammo, bedding and batteries. Possibly even fuel.

Elise woke from her nap. She felt better, but still tired. She knew from her first pregnancy that the first trimester took a lot out of the body. She remembered that her breasts hurt terribly the first time, but this time not at all. When Bridgette told her about the test, she had done it half in jest, and half to relieve her mind. She hadn't expected to be pregnant. Elise was unsure how she felt. Excited, terrified. This was not a world that anyone should bring a baby into, but she couldn't think of anything that would bring her more joy. She was happy, and worried. She was unsure how Luc would take the news. She would worry about that when he got home. First thing, she would seek out Bridgette.

Elise found her in the bathing chamber, doing minor chores. She was glad that Elise had sought her out. The duo made their way back to the sewing room. Elise put her hand on her tummy and smiled.

Bridgette smiled at her. "So, are you going to have a baby?" Elise nodded. Bridgette hugged her friend. "How many months do you think you are?"

"I'm not sure exactly, maybe two. Maybe not quite."

Bridgette laughed, "So, maybe a January, February baby?"

"Yes, that's about right I guess."

"How do you feel?"

"I'm scared, happy, I've got a million emotions going through my mind. Bridgette, please do not say anything until I tell Luc."

Bridgette relieved her mind, "I will tell no one. This is your news to announce not mine. My lips are sealed my friend, don't worry." Bridgette winked at Elise.

They began their projects. Elise grabbed some white ribbon and teal lace from the table. She sat in the rocker and enjoyed the breeze. She suddenly had the thought that she would need to make baby clothing. She had a lot of time for that, and it gave her something to look forward to. Bridgette had been working on her item. She held it up to show her work. Elise gave her the thumbs up acknowledging that she liked what she was looking at. The pair had been working for a few hours when Elise and Bridgette got hungry. They made their way to the kitchen for a light snack.

The men went inside and were amazed at how enormous and dark the space was. Luc and Marcus both pulled out flashlights. They went right, while the other men went left. They both had drawstring bags to pack whatever supplies they found. They came to an aisle with camping items. There were bags throw into a large pile, most were unwrapped. They grabbed several and kept going, the idea was to get in and out quickly. They moved from aisle to aisle. The aisles were mostly deserted. The shelves were bare, except for the occasion pile that someone had discarded. They went into another camping aisle and found two bottles of propane. Marcus grabbed them and threw them into his bag. They continued until they met the other group.

They nodded to each other, then returned the way they came, stopping again and again, hoping to find anything they had overlooked. They spotted some flashlights and grabbed them. They hoped that batteries were already inside, but they had no time to look now. They would check later. The two groups met in the front and came out of the store at the same time. They walked out into something they did not expect.

CHAPTER 14

Luc, Marcus and his two men went just beyond the inner door, where they stood for a moment taking in the scene.

"Whoa, shit." Marcus cried out.

Luc put his hand up to stop the other two men, then he put his finger to his mouth. The three men that had been on perimeter watch now stood with rifles aimed, all in a single direction. Brent and the second driver had their windows down, guns aimed. Three pick-up trucks were headed in their direction, at full speed, with pure aggression. Luc pulled his pistol from his leg as the four men ducked back inside, out of sight.

Quickly Marcus told the two men, "Find a back way out. Get onto a roof. Anything you can to gain a height advantage."

With guns ready, Marcus and Luc retreated to opposite sides of the store's main entrance, repositioned themselves and watched.

One of the enemy trucks pulled up, cutting off the only escape route the Jeep had. Three men were in the back, guns aimed at the Woodsmen.

Robert spoke, "We don't want any trouble."

One of the men replied, "To damn bad. You're in our market, Friend."

Robert returned his comment, "I'm not your friend. Back down and get the fuck out of here."

The man pulled his gun and shot Robert. Gun fire immediately irrupted from all directions. Luc's men ducked down trying to find a safe spot to return fire. Marcus and Luc fired multiple shots. The driver of the enemy truck was shot. One of his men pushed him out and took off, just as the other two trucks showed up. Luc and his men were outnumbered, two to one. Suddenly, sniper shots came from the roof. Once again shooting took place, from all directions.

One of Luc's men got to Robert. He was wounded but would be okay, he'd survive. Gun fire continued. Luc took as many shots as he could from his limited vantage point. The two men that entered the store with the General, now came around the side of the building, taking out the tires of an enemy truck. The other two trucks took off, leaving their comrades.

The five men that were left stranded in the broken vehicle, threw down their weapons in surrender. Two of the men were shot, one badly, the other only a flesh wound. Seven of the Woodsmen swarmed the five opposing men. The men hollered commands as Luc and Marcus joined them outside.

"Get outta the truck. Get down on your face, hands behind your head."

Luc's men had the four enemies under control. They zip tied their hands and feet. The fifth man was too badly injured to be a threat, he had bled too much.

Luc walked over to the two men that were in his original building-entry group, "How did you get off that roof so fast?"

They looked at each other, then at Luc. Only one of them spoke, "We were never on the roof."

Luc looked at his men, "Oh shit." He immediately looked around the roof line and yelled to his men. "Sniper! Sniper on the roof."

The men bugged out in all directions. They ducked and moved behind the vehicles. It was then that the Woodsmen realized their collective mistake. The enemy they thought had bled too much, was now standing above two of Luc's men, with a weapon drawn. Their backs were to him. Out of the silence a single shot rent the air. The man toppled back into the truck bed. Luc looked over at his men and realized whomever it was had saved them.

Luc told his men, "Friendly fire. Friendly fire. Stand down." Luc yelled out, "Who are you? Show yourself."

The man shouted back, "Why? I don't know you, so, I don't trust you."

Luc replied to him, "Then why help us? An enemy of my enemy is my friend. You helped my men; therefore, you are already my friend."

There was no reply, no response. The men did not move from their positions. Luc tried again, "Please come down. Show yourself."

The man on the roof debated with himself, then made his way to the men waiting below. Luc's men were looking in multiple directions, constantly watching. The man came around the corner, his rifle hung on his shoulder, a pistol in his hand. Luc watched the man; he was a soldier. He could tell by his stance, how he held his gun, and the graceful way he moved.

Luc spoke first, "Who are you?"

The man responded, "It doesn't matter."

Luc walked up to him and held out his hand. "I am Luc, and I am grateful for your help." The man looked at his hand; something about Luc made him feel that he could trust him. He lowered his gun and shook his hand.

"Jack."

Jack noticed a quick reaction of surprise. Luc smiled at Jack in a genuine way that put him at ease.

"Why did you help us Jack?"

"Those sons of bitches killed my brother."

Luc nodded his head in understanding. "How long have you been hiding up there?"

"I have a tent hidden, I've been here awhile, waiting for them to come back. I was starting to worry they had moved on."

Marcus walked up to them.

"Marcus, this is Jack."

Marcus quickly turned his head to look at Luc. Seeing Luc's smile, he turned to Jack. He extended his hand and Jack took it, wondering what this pair found so amusing.

"We better finish and load up before they come back."

Brent walked up to Luc and spoke with him. "General, we need to get home so Robert can get looked at. His bleeding is not slowing down. What are we going to do with these four?"

Luc took in the information, then spoke to his men as a group. "We are calling it a day. Robert needs some attention. Blind fold those four bastards and toss them in the truck bed."

He turned to Jack, "Come with us for a few days, rest and eat. We can bring you back here, but for now, get in."

"I can't come with you; I want to be here when they get back."

Luc did not like his refusal, "Why? So that you can be outnumbered? You will die. Besides, live to fight another day, have you never heard this? You will be warm, fed, and be able to bathe. You will not hate it. I promise. Let's go. Ride with me."

Jacks eyes narrowed slightly, "Are you really a General?"

Luc gave him a crooked smile, "Are you really a sniper?"

Luc turned his back to Jack taking for granted that he was following.

Jack did not refuse him again. He understood the wisdom. He could use the break.

The men loaded up and rolled out. They saw no one. Robert was in serious pain from his gunshot wound and passed out. It was up to the others to remember the way home. Marcus, Luc, Jack, and another soldier rode in the Jeep. Robert was with Brent; the rest of the men rode in the back of the beast. The men either watched the prisoners or watched their surroundings. No one seemed to follow them. They made a few deliberate wrong turns and took extra time double checking that they were not leading trouble home.

There was silence. No one spoke. Marcus watched and scanned as he drove. Luc looked out the window. He hoped Robert would be okay. He watched the trees go by, and the shadows the sun cast. The men were on high alert. The scavenge had been dangerous, they left with almost nothing. Yet, it accomplished something he wanted, without having to do anything. Fate had stepped in and taken care of it for him.

The soldiers at the gate watched the two vehicles approach from a distance. Men were ready to throw the double doors open. The beast drove through the gate and headed in the direction of the shed. Marcus pulled the jeep up to the house. The four men got out as their fellow clansman gathered around. Luc made a quick comment about Robert and two soldiers rushed to the shed to help him.

Elise and Bridgette heard the commotion and hurried outside. One of the men spoke to Bridgette and she rushed back inside. Elise went to Luc and threw her arms around him. She kissed him fast multiple times. "Oh, God, Luc I was so worried. I know you weren't gone long but I missed you."

"Elise?" She stood frozen looking at Luc.

"Elise?" The voice came again stronger, more certain. She realized she had not imagined it.

Elise spun around, "Jack? Oh Jack." She rushed to him and threw her arms around him. Jack squeezed her back. The two held on for what seemed like a lifetime. Luc smiled. All the people in the yard seemed frozen in time as they watched the two embraced.

Jack set Elise from himself. He walked over to Luc and punched him in the face. "You son of a bitch. You knew. Why didn't you tell me?"

Elise watched in surprise, unsure of what might happen next.

Luc spit blood from his mouth. He looked Jack in the eyes and replied, "Because I like to get punched in the mouth. You're welcome." With that comment he turned and walked toward the shed.

Marcus, laughed, some of the others turned their heads and coughed. No one was worried or afraid for their General. They all knew it had officially become "family business."

Luc walked to the shed with a smile on his face. He liked Jack; he's got balls the size of a show bull.

Marcus pulled up alongside him, "Come on, hop on I'll give you a ride."

Elise and Jack watched Luc jump on to the predator bars and ride the rest of the way to the shed.

Elise turned to Jack, "What the hell was that and where have you been?"

Jack responded, "Don't worry about it, it's a man thing honey. You wouldn't understand but I promise you, he does. How did you get here?"

He looked at her smiling at him. He had missed her. He thought she was dead. When he couldn't find her, he almost gave up, but something told him not to.

Elise looked around, "Jack where is Kyle?"

Jack looked at the ground. "The day we were separated he was killed."

Elise hugged Jack. She was sad, but she wasn't going to dwell on it now. She had Jack, and that was something to be grateful for. They needed levity in this darkness. She punched his arm. "Jack, you stink."

They both laughed. "All right, Maverick," Jack replied, laughing at their inside joke.

Elise took him inside and showed him to a bathing chamber. She gave him everything he needed and told him that she would find him something to wear. She left him and headed to the stockroom. She found multiple items for him to wear and took them to a room on her side of the house she knew was unoccupied. She knocked on the door to the bathroom her brother was in. He answered wearing a towel.

"Leave your stuff, and I will clean up. Follow me, there is fresh clothing and a bed for you."

He nodded and followed. She showed him to the room. He was surprised by the size of the place. It was a nice change to have a roof overhead versus sleeping on a roof.

She pointed to the bed, "There are some clothes for you. I will show you the storeroom where we keep the clothes later, that way you can pick out some things for yourself. Why don't you nap, I'll come get you for dinner, okay?"

He hugged her and said that he was happy and grateful.

She winked at him. "I'm sure that's exactly how Luc thinks you feel." She laughed and closed the door before he could reply.

Elise went back to the bathing chamber. She cleaned it up, got rid of the water and put her brother's clothes into a hamper. She made a mental note to wash them in the morning. With her brother taken care of, Elise went to the kitchen where she saw Bridgette crying over boiling water. "What's wrong Bridge?"

"Robert has been shot, the men asked me to boil water, get some cloth and cut it into strips."

Instantly, Elise was crushed with guilt in her excitement to have her brother back; she had no idea that a man was bleeding to death. She snapped alert and immediately started helping Bridgette.

"Take this water to the shed, I'll start boiling another pot. Give me a minute and I'll bring the water and more strips of cloth."

Bridgette nodded and left the kitchen.

Elise knocked on the door to the shed with her foot. She had a bag full of cloth and a pot of boiled water in her hands. Brent answered it, beckoning her inside. There was a small room in the shed that had been designated as an infirmary. She almost heaved at the sight of Robert in his condition. She quickly put the pot of water into Brent's hands and rushed out the door. She barely made it out of the shed when she started vomiting. She never had the stomach for these things and apparently now that she was pregnant, she was completely intolerant.

With one arm braced on the shed, she held her braided hair back with her hand. She was startled when a hand was placed on her back.

"I know it's a lot to take in, are you okay?"

Elise turned her face to look at Luc, "I'm sorry. How embarrassing."

"Don't worry Ma Chérie. I'll be at the house shortly. Go rest and wait for me." He kissed her head then disappeared back into the shed.

Elise knew that with Bridgette attending Robert, the other ladies would need help with dinner, if anyone would want it; they may be too preoccupied to eat. She went to the kitchen and chatted with the other women. They elected to leave trays of food out with multiple choices, simple foods that could be eaten when a person was ready. They put out plates, utensils and wine. Tonight, would be a buffet style meal.

When the ladies were finished, they went their separate ways. Elise saw her brother injured once. He had wanted whiskey to numb the pain. She went to the storeroom and found a bottle.

They probably already had some, but she made her way down to the shed anyway.

Elise knocked on the shed door for the second time that day. Marcus answered it but he didn't invite her in. She understood why and felt ashamed. She held out the bottle to him, and he smiled, took the bottle and closed the door. Elise walked back to her side of the house. As she passed her brother's door, she stopped and listened. She could tell by the way he was breathing that he was sleeping. She chose not to bother him and made her way to her bedroom.

She opened the window to let in the breeze. As she stood at the window, she noticed that one of the men was watching her. It sent chills down her spine. He quickly turned and walked away. She felt alarmed but not threatened. Dismissing it from her mind she sat down in the rocker and waited for Luc.

After a while, she heard shouts coming from the yard and noticed that someone was running from the shed. Elise could see and hear the man stop and ask people in the yard if they knew where 'the man Jack' might be. She stood up to look out the window. Luc's man was running to the house. It looked like whatever was going on was urgent.

CHAPTER 15

Elise rushed out of her bedroom and down the hall. Jack had been awakened and wasn't far behind her, his weapon in his hand. Together they rushed out of the house and met Luc's man.

"Luc sent me for you, Jack. They are about to interrogate the prisoners and he wants you there, he is done messing with these bastards." The man was breathless, "The prisoners have to be constantly watched. They've caused nothing but trouble since they were thrown into lockdown. They tried to fight their way out and injured one of the guards."

Jack holstered his gun and followed the man to the shed. As Elise watched the men walk away, she wondered what was going on. She didn't realize that there were prisoners on the compound. She turned and walked back into the house. Then something occurred to as her mind wandered and raced. Why did they want Jack involved? What the hell had happened today? Why was Luc staying in the shed? She was too curious and too jittery to do anything else, so she let her legs take her to the shed.

Bridgette was giving Robert a sponge bath while he slept. They knocked him out with whiskey, dug out the bullet, cauterized the wound, and bandaged him up. Bridgette had yet to leave his side. She undressed him with the help of the other men. He was unconscious and was starting to burn up. She cleaned up the room, and the blood. She didn't know what else to do but try and help him cool down. She was tired and hungry but couldn't bring herself to leave him.

The four prisoners were left on the floor in the room zip tied hand and foot. The men had taken the blindfolds off, replacing them as a gag, so they could not communicate with each other.

Two soldiers stood on guard outside the door. One man stood with his back against the wall facing away from the door, the second man sat in a chair adjacent to the door. The two men did not communicate, there had been too much chaos and they were digesting their day. They looked at the floor and each other, mulling over the happenings, arguments, and discussions that had been and were continuing to go on in the shed.

Luc argued with Jack about the prisoners, "Damn it, Jack, that is not how we handle problems here."

"Put a bullet in their heads and bury them, or we are going to be digging more bullets out of many more people. I've seen these bastards, they are ruthless. *They DO NOT care.*"

Marcus stepped in. "Jack, calm down, we want you here, but we are not killers. That's what makes us different from them."

Jack ran his hands over his face and through his hair. He was angry, but he knew they were right. He walked away from the cousins and used the space to adjust his attitude.

Marcus shook his head at Luc and went over to Jack. "We understand your frustration, but whatever you have going on with Luc right now, you need to put in your pocket and get over it. Alright? We agree on things here. No one does anything vigilante style, no one."

Jack nodded his head. The duo talked briefly, and Jack seemed to relax. Whatever Marcus told him improved his mood quickly.

Elise didn't knock this time. She boldly just walked into the shed. She didn't realize what a mistake it might be or the chaos it might cause. She knew that the shed was off limits to her; basically, everyone but the original group of soldiers that were under Luc's command when the war started. She wasn't sure why Jack had been invited inside, but she wanted to find out.

No one noticed her, she wasn't creeping, but she was intentionally being quiet. She briefly peered into a room that's door was partially open. She could see Bridgette washing someone's feet with a cloth. She assumed they were Robert's.

Elise turned her attention back to the shed. It was an immense building with multiple rooms and what appeared to be a second level loft. She could see multiple vehicles; four in total, two more then she had already seen. One was a pickup, the other, a two-door Jeep. There was workspace and work benches. She could see many tools, and what she believed were safes, probably for weapons of some form or another.

There were probably ten men scattered about. She noticed Jack, Marcus and Luc all discussing something. Brent and another man joined them, dragging a man she did not recognize.

Luc pulled the man's head back to look into his eyes. "We can do this the easy way or the hard way. Your choice." He pulled the cloth from his mouth. The man gave Luc a disgusted look, bent his head and spit on Luc's boot.

Jack walked over and punched the man. The two men still held on to him, then dragged him out into the open space that had a single chair in the middle of it. Brent and the other man sat the prisoner down then zip tied him to it.

Luc walked over to him and punched him. "I can't say the same for all four of you, but if my friend dies, I will kill you. He's bleeding to death in the other room because of your bullet."

Elise was unsure what was going on, but felt she needed to get out before she saw anymore. She turned and left the shed, feeling confident that no one saw her.

Luc and Jack had both been aware that Elise was there, and they both knew the moment she chose to leave.

Jack and Marcus took over the interrogation. Luc dismissed himself knowing that Elise had come to seek him out three times. He knew she must need him. He walked to the house knowing they were going to have a lot to talk about. She might even be angry with him for the way they were treating this man. Perhaps, if she knew what they knew, she might feel differently about these prisoners. He wasn't happy that she was in the shed, or what she may have seen.

As Luc walked into his bedroom, he noticed right away that she had gotten his bath ready and pulled items out for him to wear. He was alone in the room and decided to bathe. He finished his bath, was dressed, and still, she had not returned. Tired of waiting, he went in search of her.

He wandered into the different rooms, looking everywhere he thought she might be. He finally found her; she had her back to the door. He could feel the breeze from the window.

She was leaning over one of the tables of cloth. Elise was admiring some blue plaid cotton; it was soft and would be nice for baby clothing. When Luc spoke, she jumped, she had been completely preoccupied. He thought she was pondering what she had seen in the shed. "I've been looking for you."

"I'm sorry, I was feeling jittery and thought this would ease my mind a little, a small distraction. I can see that you have bathed. Are you hungry? I can fix you a plate."

"Not, yet, I want to talk with you." He sat in one of the chairs; she came and sat in the other.

They looked at each other for a moment, then finally she asked him, "Did you want to talk about something?"

"We have some prisoners in the shed, four of them. I want you to stay away from it. They are dangerous."

She nodded her head. "Jack is not one of your men, and yet he is invited to be there."

"Elise do not come near the shed again. Do you really think I would not notice you there? Your curiosity is not going to be appeased. These men are dangerous. And no Jack is not one of my men, but he will be. I trust him already. He helped my men; he helped save us. He is an asset. He is a soldier. He is there because I choose him to be, do you understand?" His voice and tone had changed, Luc was gone, and the General was present.

Elise was angry, she stood up, "I see, he's there because he's a man." She turned her back on him and walked out.

He followed her, yelling, "Elise, get back here. Those bastards killed your brother, there's more going on here than him being a man." He was angry and blunt. He turned and walked away from her.

Her tears started immediately, and she screamed at him, "Then I hope you kill them all."

Luc turned to look at her, "You're as bloodthirsty as your brother." Then turned and walked down the hall.

Elise walked back to her room and cried herself to sleep. She had wanted to tell Luc about the baby, instead she had been selfish and uncaring about how he might have felt. She had no idea how their day had gone. She didn't know how Robert was doing, and still she felt sorry for herself. Jack and Bridgette had both been allowed to be where she herself was forbidden. She felt like a pariah, not allowed where others were.

Luc walked back to the shed. He stopped in to check on Robert. He chatted with Bridgette for a while, finally dismissing her to go eat and clean up. He told her to take a break.

Before she left, she turned at the door, and spoke to Luc, "Is Elise doing ok? I know she was feeling bad earlier."

"I'm sure she's fine, Bridgette, just being difficult today for some reason."

Bridgette smiled at him. It wasn't a happy smile; it was full of sadness and displeasure. She responded to him cryptically, "She needs your tenderness. She's fragile right now. Be gentle with her, body and mind." With that statement she turned and walked out of the shed.

Luc snorted, in his mind he thought yeah, she acted quite delicate while she was screaming at me. Luc watched Robert sleep for a bit, then went to see what was going on with the interrogations.

Jack and Marcus were laughing about something when Luc walked over to them. Jack's expression changed; Marcus smiled even brighter when he noticed his cousin. They filled him in about what the four men had told them. The first prisoner proved to be the only difficult one; the other three were more than willing to answer any questions, without revealing too much. The prisoners were all returned just as they left the room, all but the first. They had beaten him badly, but he had revealed nothing other than his contempt.

Since the prisoners didn't know where they were, they gave Luc's men an idea of where their stronghold was from the parking lot. They all revealed other basic information about their clan. They described their leader as a ruthless man who would stop at nothing to kill them all. One had even revealed that he had killed his own father in order to be leader. The only one that seemed truly loyal to his clan was the first prisoner, the man that had shot Robert.

Luc told Marcus and Jack to take a break. He assigned a new set of men to watch the prisoners and even sent someone to watch over Robert. He instructed the man watching Robert to send for him if he woke up. As Luc walked out of the shed, he almost bumped into Trevor.

"What are you doing here? This area is forbidden to you."

Trevor nodded. "Yes, general. I was just curious about all the talk that has been going on today."

Luc nodded, "Go about your duties. Stay clear of this space."

Trevor nodded and tried to appear as if he were returning to work.

Luc walked back to the house wondering what he was doing. He had a sneaking suspicion that Trevor was more than just curious. He walked into the house making a mental note that he needed to stop and chat with Bridgette.

Luc walked into the dining hall and noticed that food was placed out. He fixed himself a plate, sat and watched several men scattered about the room eating. Marcus and Jack soon followed behind him. They made plates, then sat next to him. Bridgette came in with more food to add to the trays. She left the dining hall, then returned with wine.

"Bridgette." She turned to Luc, then came to stand beside him. "Why are you not resting?"

"I bathed, then felt too awake to nap. I figured my help was needed here."

"Go find Elise. She can finish."

"I'm sorry, General, Elise is napping." Luc made a funny look at Bridgette, and she continued. "She isn't feeling well, so I let her nap."

Luc stood up, "Go and wake her."

Bridgette was unsure how he was going to react but stood her ground. "No, I will not. She isn't feeling well. If you want to wake her, you will have to do it yourself." With that statement, she turned and walked away. She hid in the kitchen for a while unsure of how Luc would react when he saw her again.

Marcus laughed into his hand. Jack just looked at him wondering why he was treating his sister this way. Luc turned to leave, and Jack stood up. "Leave her. She isn't feeling well, let her sleep."

"Stay out of this jack. Do not meddle where it is not your concern."

Luc walked out of the house and down the path that led to the smoke house. He walked past it until he reached the compound wall then turned and walked back. Luc walked to the back of the house, through the kitchen. He noticed Bridgette sitting on a stool eating. He could see fear in her eyes when she saw him, and she stood up immediately.

"I had meant to tell you earlier that Robert was doing fine. He was sleeping when I left. I told the man watching that if he woke or anything changed to come get us. When it's time to relieve him, I will come and get you. Please do not go to the shed without one us. I'm sure that you know that there are four prisoners inside."

She nodded her head, and he walked out of the kitchen. She laughed realizing that she had been afraid for nothing. She knew he was kind and not cruel. She felt stupid for thinking otherwise and grateful that had dismissed her mutiny from his mind.

Luc walked back into the dining room to see Elise sitting with Marcus and Jack. Elise was eating as the two men sat drinking and chatting. Luc walked past the trio and out the door. He knew enough about himself to know that in his current mood, he would only sit there and pick a fight with anyone and everyone.

CHAPTER 16

The people sitting at the table watched Luc walk past them and out the door. Jack was glad he had kept going. Elise wondered why, but Marcus knew without a doubt the reason Luc was angry and avoiding them. He wanted to reunite the siblings, but one thing he hadn't thought through was how Elise's brother would react to their relationship. He most certainly had not thought that Jack would undermine him where Elise was concerned.

Luc walked around the compound for the second time that day. He wondered what was going on with Bridgette. She had never disobeyed him before. All day she had been protecting Elise, but from what? And now Jack? He needed to set things straight with Jack. No one was taking her away and no one was going to interfere with them, including Jack. Luc walked back into the house to find the trio still sitting in the same spot laughing and enjoying each other's company.

He sat down, calm and in control on the outside, but a boiling pot ready to explode on the inside. His walk had done little for him, other than to get him riled up. His walks usually calmed him, unfortunately today's walk had only made things worse. The group stopped talking the moment Luc sat down. Marcus brought up the barbeque, hoping to get him interested in something other than what was bothering him. The group made small talk, then Marcus excused himself from the group stating that he wanted to check on Robert. Jack stood and went with him.

Elise looked at Luc. "Could you have made that any more awkward? What's your problem?"

"My problem? Let's see your brother arrives, and suddenly this whole place has gone mad. Doing shit that is highly suspect; I would call it mutinous behavior."

He got up and walked out. Luc walked to the shed and peaked in on Robert. He chatted with his man watching him and told him he'd have some food brought to him. Luc walked up the stairs to the loft and found the two men he had been looking for.

Jack jumped right in, not holding any punches. "What's going on between you and my sister?"

Luc thought about a smart-ass answer, then decided that it was best to be honest, "Elise has been here for a few months now. She is mine. It is mutual and I love her Jack. I'm going to marry her."

Jack took a deep breath. "Alright, I won't interfere, but I won't stand by if there is something I don't like."

Luc smiled genuinely, "I would expect nothing less from you."

Luc extended his hand once again to Jack. Jack took it, both knowing it was a truce. Luc excused himself from the two men.

He made his way back to the house to get food for Robert's watchman. He grabbed him several items and water. He took them back and stayed with his man for a bit. They chatted about the items that they found on the scavenge that day. He went to take a look for himself. It seemed like a wasted day to some. One of his men had been injured and there was only a small pile next to the workbench of things they found. There wasn't much to account for: a few sleeping bags, empty flashlights, a few knives, a couple pairs of boots, and a few random pieces of clothing. No batteries, no food, no gas. Today was good for one reason only; they found Jack.

He walked back up the stairs to chat with Jack and Marcus. He told them about the lack of what they had been able to find. Luc didn't want to assume that Jack wanted to be part of them, so he asked him point blank, "Do you want to stay here and become part of our clan, our tribe, our family?"

"Of course, if you are going to marry my sister, that means we already are."

Luc nodded. "We are going to have to make another trip somewhere else. We didn't find much, and we needed a lot. I know it will be risky, especially with Robert hurt, but I think we should go tomorrow."

Marcus spoke next, "That will not leave enough men behind and what about the prisoners?"

Luc replied, "Maybe just the three of us make a run. Then we can dump the prisoners off somewhere."

Marcus shook his head, "We need to discuss this with everyone. We need to call a meeting."

Elise was helping Bridgette clean the dining hall. The remaining stragglers had already eaten and were just sitting around chatting. The women overheard many things, but mostly fragments of information. Luc, Marcus, and Jack all walked into the dining hall. Elise had her back turned to them. She was preoccupied with her task and had not noticed them come in. Jack walked up behind her and snatched at her broom.

Elise laughed, "Come on Jack, I'm tired."

He handed her back her broom, then pinched her cheek. He was smiling, all three men seemed to be in a better mood which was refreshing. She was too tired for their male egos.

Luc walked up to her and pulled her into his arms. She let him and felt better by his hug. He kissed her head, then spoke softly to her. His voice was sweet in its seductive timber. He whispered something in French causing chill bumps on her arms. She looked up at him with seductive eyes making him smile. "We need to have a meeting. Don't wait up for me. I'm not sure how long it will take."

He looked around the room noticing Bridgette. "Bridgette." She walked over to them, and he finished, "Rest and sometime early morning one of us will come get you, so that you may be with Robert. Someone else can do your things tomorrow. They can be divided among the other woman and Elise can help you. I'm sure extra work won't bother her."

She looked at Elise, but Elise gave her a slight almost non-existent nod in the negative. Bridgette understood this to mean that she needed to keep her mouth shut because Luc was still ignorant to the fact that his woman was carrying his child.

Elise smiled at Bridgette, "Of course Bridge, I'll do whatever needs be done, don't worry."

Bridgette nodded then went back to her duties.

Luc finally addressed his men that were present, "Gentleman please finish your conversations and meet in the shed in thirty minutes." He didn't have to further explain; they all knew this was an emergency meeting. Luc nodded to his cousin and Jack, then said something to Elise, and they walked out of the dining hall together.

Luc closed the door behind them, "I'm sorry I yelled at you."

He pulled Elise to himself; he kissed her desperately; he needed her; he wanted her. What she gave him was never enough. He craved more; he knew he would never be satisfied without her. He pushed her against the wall and hiked up her skirt. He whispered unintelligible soft nothings into her ear as he kissed a trail down her shoulder. She melted into him and opened her legs. He touched her, teased, and manipulated her flesh. His fingers sought out her moist cavern as he bit and nibbled at her neck. She arched her back in ecstasy, enjoying the way he used her for his own desire. He pulled her onto him. She cried out in pleasure as he entered her. He kissed her moans into his mouth drowning them with his lust. He wrapped his hand in her hair, smelling her, pulling, and getting his desired moan from her.

She cried out to him, "Luc, oh, Luc."

He pulled her arms above her head. He rode her hard against the wall. He bit her arm, showing her that she was his. Her body became wet with the thrill he gave her. She moaned for him, loving the feel and pressure of his teeth on her skin. Her moans only drove him further into their maddened passion for each other. They made wild, hungry love. They both used each other, filling a need that could only be sated temporarily. They climaxed together, enjoying the smell and taste of each other. When the couple finally relaxed and their breathing calmed, they helped each other undress. They bathed together, enjoying the intimacy they shared. When they were finished, Elise climbed into bed with a book. Luc kissed her and told her that he would be back.

"Luc, we need to talk."

"I know, Ma Chérie, when I get back." He blew her a kissed then walked out the door.

Elise wanted to stay up and tell Luc about the baby. She was unsure how long he would be; the past had proven that it could be hours. She was unable to read. She opened the book and realized that she was just too tired to focus. Elise ran her hands over Rose who laid down next to her. A strong breeze came in through the open window. It was a sign that a storm was coming. She closed her eyes and fell fast asleep.

Luc and his men sat around a table in the loft. They usual jacked around downstairs with the vehicles or with their tools. They chose the upstairs option instead to get as far away from the prisoners as possible. Some of the men did not want to turn around and go the next day, others didn't care either way. There was a lot of talking and debating.

Luc finally asked his men, "Okay guys, formal vote. Who wants to go tomorrow?" Four of the eleven men present raised their hands. "Who wants to wait a day, then go?" Seven men raised their hands. "Okay, so we wait a day. We need to meet up in the morning and decide the rest. I'm going to bed. I'm exhausted; this day has been a shit show. I'm sure you are all tired. Get some sleep. We can figure the rest out tomorrow. Good night."

The men all got up and went their separate ways. Luc, Marcus, and Jack made their way to the house. Luc left a man with Robert and a guard at the prisoners' door. The prisoners were restrained, and the door was securely locked. The guard was just one extra precaution. He instructed his men to secure the main door from the inside. He felt confident in their safety. He told his two partners goodnight, then went to his room.

Seeing Elise asleep, Luc quietly climbed into bed, not wanting to disturb her. He laid awake for some time thinking about the men in the shed, all of them.

Elise woke alone. She knew she hadn't slept by herself. She had woken at some point during the night and Luc was there. She woke up sweaty and went to the pitcher to splash water on a cloth, so she could cool herself. She was feeling hungry, so she took a walk to the storeroom. She grabbed a handful of dried fruits which helped calm her stomach.

She laid in bed a few moments thinking about her late-night walk around the house. Elise stretched and yawned, then finally climbed out of bed and got herself ready for the day.

She started her typical morning routine in her room. She cleaned, made the bed, then gathered her laundry. She remembered to get Jack's items, then made her way to the yard.

Elise washed and rinsed her laundry and was just starting to hang it when Luc came around the side of the house. He walked over to Elise and gave her a kiss.

"Good morning."

She smiled at him, then returned his sentiment. "Good morning, you were up early."

"Yes, I had some things to deal with. How did you sleep."

"Fine, I guess."

He nodded at her, "What did you need to talk to me about?"

"Well, Luc, let's take a short walk." She left her wet clothing sitting in the basket, took Luc by the hand, and started walking. They walked for a few minutes out into the field. She turned and looked at him. "I'm pregnant."

He looked at her and laughed, "No. Really?"

She was hurt. "I'm not kidding. I'm going to have a baby."

She turned around and walked away from him. The tears had already started before she reached her wet laundry. She wasn't sure what she had expected, but that hadn't been the response she thought she was going to get.

Luc just stood there watching the woman he loved, who was now carrying his child, walk away. He really had thought she was joking. He was angry at himself for being so insensitive. She was hurt; he could see it in her eyes and hear it in her voice. Suddenly, it all made sense and explained a lot. Looking back, he should have known sooner. Elise was tired and sick lately; it explained why Bridgette had been coddling her.

Luc walked to the shed. He was looking for Marcus. He found him and Jack sitting in Roberts room laughing with him about his injury. Robert was feeling better. He was even more gruff than usual. He nodded to Luc when he walked in.

"I see your still with us," Luc said to him.

"Your gonna have to do more than that to put me down," he smiled at Luc.

"How are you feeling?"

"You know Luc, pain is God's way of letting you know you ain't dead yet. Apparently, I ain't dead." The men in the room snickered at Roberts response.

"I'm glad. I need to talk to Marcus for a bit, then I'll be back to check on you, okay?"

Robert nodded. Marcus got up and the two men took a walk.

Luc smiled at Marcus; his smile was boyish and all charm, "I need you to take a ride with me."

Marcus punched his arm, "Let's roll."

No one inside the walls expected the Jeep carrying its two passengers to be leaving. They stopped at the gate; it was opened without question, then re-shut. The men at the wall were concerned, however they did not question their leaders' request. The two men inside the Jeep turned in the direction of the Monroe's and out of sight.

Elise finished hanging her laundry and went to help in the garden. Her laundry may take a while to dry since there was no breeze. The sun was hot, and her clothing stuck to her. She had been given the task of pulling weeds and got right to it. She was enjoying herself; the task itself was therapeutic for her. She thought about Luc's reaction to the news about the baby. She felt that she may have overreacted a bit, but at the time, his reaction stung. She decided that she would not hold a grudge about it. It was probably the farthest thing from his mind.

She worked in the garden for several hours. She thanked the main gardener for letting her help and dismissed herself to take a break.

She walked into the kitchen and gave Bridgette a smile. Bridgette was sitting on a stool eating her lunch as well. Elise cleaned her hands, splashed water on herself, then made a plate, and joined Bridgette.

"How's Robert today?"

"He's much better. I was with him earlier for a while and I will go back again later. He was more surly than usual, but I guess getting shot would piss anyone off, right?"

Both ladies laughed, then finished their meals. Elise checked on her laundry, pulled it down off the line, then folded it. She took Jacks clothing to his room, then put away the rest. It was barely after lunch and the sun was high in the sky, but Elise was tired and needed a small rest. She sat in her rocker and dosed off.

The men on watch at the gate saw the two-door Jeep come into view. The orders were hollered down, and the gate was opened, then closed. Luc was driving. He waved to his men and continued driving. Marcus and Luc pulled the Jeep back into the shed. Luc had accomplished only part of what he had set out to do. He told Marcus that he would find him later, and he walked to the house in search of Elise.

He found her sleeping in her rocker. He sat down next to her and watched her sleep. He thought she looked lovely, so calm, and peaceful. He touched her hand softly to try and wake her. She woke slowly, recognizing him and smiled.

Luc apologized, "I'm sorry about earlier, I honestly thought you were teasing."

"It's okay. It's possible that I may have overreacted a bit."

"I've been happier since you came here than I've been in a really long time. You should know by now that I don't just want you, or need you, but I love you with all my heart. I'm excited about our baby."

Elise smiled, that was all she needed to hear.

"There's something else though," Luc stood up out of the rocker. He got down on his knee in front of Elise and proposed. "I know that I didn't do things the right way when we met, but I've loved you since that moment." He paused, "Elise, I love you; you are going to have my baby. Will you be mine forever?" He held out his hand, "I know that we can't be married by a pastor or a preacher, but we can say vows in front of our clan. It will be the same to God. It's about the commitment."

"Yes, I will marry you. I love you."

They both stood up and embraced each other.

He kissed her face, "I love you, Elise." He looked down at her and wiped the happy tears from her face. "You're mine forever, Ma Chérie."

CHAPTER 17

The night came. Luc asked his people to gather in the dining hall. The happy couple announced their proposal of marriage to the clan. There was much well-wishing and cheers. Luc told the group they would have the informal ceremony the second night of the Monroe gathering. The group did not linger long as the soldiers knew they were once again going out into the unknown at dawn. They were nervous and needed to be mentally prepared. They feared it was too soon. They would have less men, yet possibly face the same amount of danger.

Only Marcus knew of the baby and the rings that Luc asked Monroe to make. They had gone to Monroe on a mission. Luc wanted to see if Monroe had a man of God that could perform the ceremony for him. Monroe told him that he did not but spoke to him about the importance of saying their vows to each other in the presence of his people and God. He figured that would be good enough for God. Luc felt the same, but with Monroe's reassurance, he finalized the idea in his mind.

Luc walked Elise to bed. He was tired but too full of adrenaline to go to sleep. He kissed her goodnight, then took a walk. Elise was worried for him. She did not want him to go on the scavenge but knew what kind of man he was. He would go simply because he would rather put his life in danger than that of his men. Elise was tired but could not fall asleep, so she read in bed until she finally dozed off.

Elise woke the next morning feeling full of dread. She did not see Luc before he left. She wanted to hug and kiss him goodbye but missed her chance. She laid in bed looking at the darkness outside. A storm was moving in; it was as if the weather was mimicking how she felt. She went about her day doing anything and everything to occupy her time.

The sun had come and gone, and the men had not returned. Elise hardly slept that night. Her mind was full of dread; she was wide awake in her anxiety. She kept moving between the bed and her rocker. She listened as the wind blew rain across her window. She tried reading to occupy her time. She paced about the room, going from bed to rocker, to window. She would stand and look out into the storm. The rain was coming down in sheets, like a monsoon. The sky cried the tears that she could not.

Her fiancé and brother were out there in the unknown. She was fearful for them. She cared about all four of the men that left that day, but especially for Luc and Jack. They took three of the four prisoners with them. She didn't understand what was going on or what they were thinking. Maybe when they returned, she would better understand. They took the beast hoping to find the things that they needed as well. She sat in her rocker reading. Her hurricane lantern was running low on oil, so she put her book aside and went to the storeroom. She was grateful for the distraction. Her anxiety had her suffocating in her seclusion.

In the storeroom Elise found what she had been after. She quickly filled her lantern, then replaced the bottle where she found it. Elise went back to her room and read. The short walk did not ease her mind. She was virtually alone in the house and could feel the unwanted privacy. The only person she happened to see was a guard in the hall. He had been listening to the sounds of the house. He greeted Elise when she entered the hallway between her hall of rooms and the storeroom. He nodded his hello, but otherwise said nothing. It wasn't a rude sort of ignoring, but more of a purposeful attention to everything else.

Elise finally slept, but she woke often feeling anxious and fearful. Her mind was not put at rest, for the next day came and went, and then the next. Still the men had not returned.

When Elise woke on the following morning, the sun was coming up and the promise of a beautiful day could be heard in the sound of birds singing. The sky was bright blue with pinks and purples as the sun showed itself. There were sporadic white puffy clouds that transitioned between greys and blues.

She climbed out of bed feeling better for the first time in days. She dressed and went to the kitchen. As she turned the corner from the hall, she noticed four men sitting at a table. She rushed in; Luc stood seeing her coming. They threw their arms around each other.

Luc kissed Elise quickly, then released his embrace. "We just arrived maybe thirty minutes ago. We needed coffee."

She looked at the other three men in the group and smiled. She reached out a hand and placed it on her brothers back, and he placed his hand on hers. He replied to Luc's comment, "Yes, much needed coffee."

"How did it go? And why in the hell have you been gone so long?"

Jack and Marcus laughed. "Three days isn't so long, Elise," Marcus replied.

The four men laughed. Unfortunately for them, she had been serious. Her smile darkened. "I was worried sick, sick to death."

Luc grabbed her again in an embrace. "I know, but to answer your question, it was productive and safe. So, it was worth our time."

"Why did you let those men go? Don't you think they will come after us?"

"We took them far away," Luc replied to her.

"They would be stupid to try and attack us again. They were fearful of their own clan. They were more than happy to be left where we left them," Jack told her.

"Why did we keep one of them?" she asked the men.

"We don't know what do with him yet. He is dangerous. We do not want to just set him free," Luc told her.

Jack decided to take it a little farther, "We are hoping he gives us a reason to have to kill him."

Elise looked at her brother with wide eyes, then at Luc. "I hope he does." The four men agreed with her even though no one voiced it aloud.

Elise sat with the men while they had their coffee. They filled her in on where they went and what they found. The conversation switched to the barbeque that would be coming in a few days, and how they would need to prepare. It had been over a week since they planned the barbeque with Monroe. In a few short days would be the actual barbeque. Two weeks seemed like a lifetime before the wars, food shortages, and diseases. Now it came like wildfire. The bare necessities in life were a struggle, and survival was number one on the priority list.

The men finished their coffee and dismissed themselves. They had a list of things to do and they needed to get busy. The nice thing about this gathering between the Woodsmen and Monroe's was that it was not a necessity in the form of food or shelter, but rather a necessity for the soul.

Elise had her own things that she needed to complete. She started her chores and after completing them, she went in search of Bridgette. The two women chatted about life, Robert, then finally they talked about their goals for the Monroe barbeque. Elise and Bridgette wanted to make sure that extra candles, nice smelling soaps, and nice cloth were available. The two women got busy ensuring that the Monroe's visit would be pleasant. They wanted them to feel like old friends or family coming home.

Monroe looked at his daughter. She was lovely, an image of her mother. He missed his wife. Life had changed for everyone, himself included, but until her death everything had been bearable. He was no fool. He could see the want, the passion, even the desire in his daughter's eyes whenever the Woodsmen came to visit. He himself thought the cousins were a rugged, handsome, and strong pair. He could understand his daughters' desire. When he broached the subject with her, he expected honesty. They knew no other way.

The father-daughter pair knew each other so well that words rarely needed to be spoken. Understanding between them was as simple as breathing, natural and without thought. He felt that his daughter was delicate, yet strong-minded and strong-willed. She needed a strong man to be able to deal with her. He felt that her choice was a good one.

"The image is a perfect likeness," Monroe said as he entered her room.

Sierra looked up from her painting and smiled at her father.

"You captured his hawk like intense eyes perfectly."

She nodded. Those eyes had been burned into her memory for years. She dreamed about them. They were the only eyes she could ever see.

"What do you think about a marriage between yourself and Marcus?" Sierra smiled at her father. He felt at that moment he would have been blinded by her radiance; it seemed a million times brighter than any star in heaven.

Luc smiled at Elise as he closed their bedroom door. The day had been long and busy, yet it had not drained them of their need for each other. Their passion fueled them as they stood naked like sensual Greek statues of fated lovers. Their magnificent bodies glowed with anticipation, adding to the lustful ambiance of the room. Luc caressed her neck with his hands. His hands were strong, could be violent even, yet touched her with tenderness and warmth. Elise ran her hand down his chest. Luc pulled her body into his and kissed her hard, wet, and fiercely. They needed each other as if it were the first time.

They had a passion for each other that ached as if they hadn't made love in decades. They were hungry for each other, a hunger that no one else could satisfy, no one else would ever satisfy. He kissed her face and she moved her face closer to his body. She took in his scent barely brushing her nose and lips across his neck. She savored the smell of him. The masculine and earthy taste of him made her immediately wet.

Luc ran his hands along her body, touching her breast, then her hips, stopping in the sweet, moist mound of her feminine geography. Luc kissed her as she moaned. She couldn't help herself; the feeling was more sensational than her body could handle.

Luc led Elise to their bed. He stood over her looking at her nakedness. He loved the way she looked back at him, unafraid and at ease with her own sexuality.

She smiled up at him. "I need you deep inside of me."

He returned her smile and climbed between her legs. He whispered something soft and sexy in her ear. He pulled her hair into his fingers and entered her. They touched and teased enjoying each other as they made love for hours. The exotic age-old movements made them climax together in total ecstasy.

Elise and Luc both laid in bed reading, enjoying each other's company, loving the feel of someone they loved close by. They were both relaxed and genuinely content; happy, if you could feel that emotion, in this time of realistic expectations instead of romantic disillusionment.

CHAPTER 18

Monroe stood with his people on the outside of Clan Woodsman's compound. His people were excited about this invitation. They had often wondered about this strong and humanitarian group of savages.

His daughter's anticipation was enormous; she knew what her father was going to propose to the leaders of this clan. She was excited and thrilled. She was home.

Monroe felt tiny and insignificant standing next to the great wall of what he suspected was a mighty compound. Fear was not in his mind; he had come to like the cousins and their people. He knew this barbeque would change all their lives. He just didn't know how much.

The perimeter guards could see the group coming and sent a man to fetch the cousins. Luc and Marcus brought Jack. The men stood waiting to extend their sanctuary to their neighbors, a group that may be smaller, yet no more insecure than themselves. Luc looked around his space as the gate was opening. He wondered what the Monroe's first impressions might be. The grass was green and tall in sections of the fields. There were random colors and displays of wildflowers. His clan's walls were immense, impressive, and possibly even intimidating. They offered protection from the injustice of what their world had become.

The men embraced Monroe and his men, then introduced Jack. Monroe looked pleased. As the two groups walked to the main house, they broke into smaller clusters of people talking, laughing, and teasing. Monroe pointed as a group of boys ran off chasing each other. "I have not seen a child in years."

Luc smiled and nodded. "We have many families here." The small group of men walked to the main house.

Elise and Bridgette were watching the group from a window. The ladies walked out to greet their neighbors they had never met, yet felt they knew well. Elise knew that Luc not only respected the older Monroe but cherished his new-found friendship.

Elise took in the scene around her. In that moment, it looked like nothing in their world had changed. Friends were laughing and talking again. The modern-day self-quarantines had been a result of disease, war, and the final issue of survival of the strongest. The scene before her looked like the world before it had changed. This barbeque was needed and would be cherished.

Elise spotted the man she believed was Monroe. He was a handsome man, even in his older years. His eyes were kind and full of wisdom. He was dressed simply. His overall demeanor spoke of a man who had lived and loved, a man that had not allowed the harshness of his environment to shape or destroy his love of man and life.

Elise looked at her people; everyone was happy and smiling. Her eyes rested on Marcus and saw the longing in his smile and the beauty he was looking at. She was stunning with wild, blond hair and sparkling eyes. Someone in the group made a joke and she laughed. Elise smiled seeing the smile on the beauty. Elise walked off the porch and up to the group making their way from the field.

Luc hugged Elise to himself and introduced her. "Monroe, this is my lovely Elise." Elise smiled.

Monroe took her hand in his and kissed it smiling warmly into her eyes. "Elise, my dear, it is lovely to meet you. I want to introduce to you my own lovely daughter." "Sierra my sweet, come here please." Monroe introduced the ladies and Elise hugged her. Sierra smiled at her, knowing that they had found a friend in each other.

The men continued to talk while Elise dragged Sierra away to meet Bridgette. The trio talked and laughed. They compared ideas about how the men would, could, and usually reacted when some form of competition is placed before them. Elise watched her brother, fiancé, and Marcus talking with Monroe. They seemed more than at ease with one another.

He told the cousins that he needed a private word. They used the excuse of touring the compound to give them distance from prying ears. Jack took the hint and started a conversation with one of Monroe's men. Elise watched as Luc and Marcus walked toward the field with Monroe. The men made it past the barn and stood looking out at the fields that surrounded them.

Monroe placed a hand on Marcus's shoulder and spoke to the cousins. "My daughter is at an age that she would like to marry. I am feeling more tired and older it seems with each passing day. I would like to see my daughter happy, settled, and well cared for before I go. So, without beating around the bush, Marcus, I would like you to marry my daughter. Perhaps, you can take a small amount of time to get to know each other to make sure it will be a pleasant arrangement. I would like this match, and I'm certain that she wants this as well. What are your thoughts?"

Marcus thought about his answer carefully, deciding that, as always, honesty was best. "I would like nothing more. I fell in love with her the moment I laid eyes on her."

Monroe smiled. "Good, then it's a match." Both men turned to Luc. He smiled and shrugged his shoulders. Marcus smiled back knowing without words what his cousin was saying. The trio walked back to join the rest of the group and Marcus quickly excused himself to search for Sierra.

Elise watched Sierra and Marcus walk away. Marcus approached the women to ask if Sierra would like to take a short stroll around the compound with him. She nodded her consent and gave him a brilliant smile that would have made the most precious gem envious.

"Thank you for taking this walk with me," Marcus swiped up a handful of flowers, and continued, handing them to her, "your father has just spoken to me about a marriage between the two of us. I would like to know your thoughts and discuss this with you." He waited a moment then continued again, "I'm sorry if you feel that I'm too forward, but if we are to be married, it's best you meet the real me now, and not some version of me."

Sierra nodded her head. "Yes, Marcus, I agree. I'm a shy sort, so you must forgive me. I'm not as blunt as you. However, I will be honest with you, and I will be as straightforward as I can."

He smiled at her, "That's all I ask, and in return, I will do the same. Do you want this marriage or is it something your father wants?"

She looked at him, then looked away. She took a deep breath and stared out into the fields. "I have loved you for as long as I can remember. I've wanted to be your wife since the first time you raided my group. My father wants this match because, he knows I desire it."

Marcus took her hand in his and kissed it. He said something soft and sweet in French. He kissed her lips softly, not asking, nor taking more than what he deserved. It was a sweet first kiss for the innocent Sierra. The kiss told her and him both all they needed to know. They would both agree to the marriage. This was more than fate; it was meant to be.

The two groups sat in the large dining hall drinking and talking. Elise and Bridgette walked amongst the men refilling their drinks and engaging in small talk. Food had been placed out, and everyone was eating, drinking and enjoying themselves. They talked about the baseball game that was going to take place later that day. Elise dismissed herself and made her way to her room feeling exhausted. She hated leaving the fun but needed the rest. It seemed that one moment, she had energy to spare and the next, she felt like she could barely walk. Bridgette assured her that she would wake her before the game. Elise laid on her bed and fell asleep, her cat curled at her feet.

Luc saw Elise slip out of the dining hall sure of where she was going. It seemed that she was getting tired easier as her pregnancy progressed. He knew she would need the rest for the night would be long. Luc pulled out the two rings he had Monroe make. The rings were made of beautiful polished wood. They were unique, Luc thought with a smile, much like his love with Elise.

He loved his family and still mourned their loss, but he was getting a second chance at life and love, two things people needed, and few ever truly got to taste and enjoy.

He was happy about the baby. The child would be loved, cherished, and nurtured by both mother and father, not to mention their entire clan.

Luc's thoughts turned to Marcus. Marcus seemed exhilarated since the talk with Monroe. He didn't think his cousin was lonely before, but he was certainly no fool. He did seem in love. He had seen the instant attraction between Monroe's daughter and Marcus but had not guessed it would have progressed so quickly into a union between the two. Yet watching them now, laughing and talking, sitting side by side, he should have foreseen the match.

With nearly everyone gathered into the dining hall Luc decided it would be a great time for announcements, so he went to wake Elise. He slipped out making his way to his room. He found her sleeping soundly tucked under a blanket. He sat beside her and touched her lightly trying to wake her. She woke with a start. Seeing Luc, she threw her arms around him and hugged him close. She told him about her dream, a dream that had been terrifying and realistic. Luc kissed her and spoke softly to her, reminding her that it was not real. He asked her to join them in the hall when she was ready. He wanted her there while he was going to announce a few things to the two clans before they proceed with their game.

Elise watched Luc walk out of the room and close the door quietly behind himself. Her dream had scared her. She hated anxiety dreams, the kind where you run and never escape. She shook the negative feeling from her head and splashed water on her face. She combed her hair and straightened her clothing. The feeling of dread left her little by little the closer she came to the dining hall. By the time she reached the dining hall, it was all but forgotten.

Luc watched Elise as she approached him. He indicated for her to sit in the empty chair beside him. She did as he asked. He grabbed her hand and brought it to his lips, "Are you feeling better, my love?"

She smiled at him, "Yes, I believe so."

He smiled back at her, "Good."

Luc stood up and the group quieted knowing that he was about to speak. "My people are pleased to have tribe Monroe amongst us, as friends, as neighbors, and as allies." The group cheered. "Most of you know that tomorrow evening, I am marrying my lovely Elise." Again, the group cheered. "But what you may not know is that soon after there will be another marriage ceremony. Monroe has trusted Clan Woodsmen with his lovely Sierra, so please congratulate, Marcus and Sierra."

The dining hall had become loud with the sounds of well wishing, congratulations, and much teasing on Marcus' behalf. After the crowd quieted down, Luc dismissed his group so that they could get ready for their game.

Monroe sat next to Elise as the baseball game began. The men had made rough benches from left over lumber. They were crude and rustic, yet perfect in their functionality. The two tribes argued and joked about which side Sierra would play for. Monroe's group argued that she was currently still a Monroe, while the Woodsmen argued that she was technically a Woodsmen. The two men who had been selected to be pitchers tossed a coin with tribe Monroe being the winners. When Marcus made it to first base, Sierra blew him a kiss from the home plate. Marcus became the brunt of the joke in the outfield.

The game was fun to watch and Elise enjoyed herself. The teams were pretty evenly matched, but because of the competitive nature of the Woodsmen, they were never behind. Monroe made small talk with Elise. She could understand why Luc trusted him and liked him as a friend. He was warm by nature, relaxed, and easy to talk to. He seemed to listen to everything, not letting anything slip by.

The game was a professional game of amateurs. She imagined that they had all played ball at some point in their past. Whether it was as a youth, young man, or otherwise.

Elise remembered a time when, as a young girl, she had watched her brothers play. Her oldest brother Kyle had been the best of the two going on to all-stars with his buddies. She remembered the smile on his face when he received his first trophy. She thought he looked like a king winning his crown.

Their parents had been so proud. She could see them now, her mother on one side of her brother, her father on the other, congratulating him and telling him how they felt. She preferred to remember her brother that way, not wanting to imagine the last time she saw him. He had not died on the battlefield as a soldier. In her eyes, he had died a hero just the same. He had saved her life and Jack's; he sacrificed himself for the ones he loved. That is a hero in anyone's eyes. She thought about her baby and decided she would name him Kyle. If it weren't for her brother, she wouldn't be sitting here taking in the sunshine, watching her friends enjoy a game of baseball; something simple that had been taken for granted many years ago.

The men sat around the field, some on the ground, others on the benches. They were laughing and enjoying themselves. Beer was passed around, along with homemade wine and hard spirits brought from tribe Monroe's hamlet. The players were dirty and tired, yet happy. It was decided that they needed to do this often. Luc sat on the ground, his back against his woman. Elise laid her hand on his shoulder. From the outside it was a simple, insignificant gesture. For the two lovers, it was much more. It was a promise of love between them. It was a hint at a passionate night together and of unlimited avenues of ecstasy. A simple touch spoke volumes; electricity pulsed through them with the slightest movement.

The group ate dinner, talking and laughing, the conversation moving from topic to topic. Sierra helped Elise and Bridgette with the wine and beer for the men. The General was sitting between Marcus and Monroe, with Jack in front of him. Elise could not hear their conversation from where she was standing, but constantly made eye contact with Luc. She could not deny her passion for him, nor her love. She imagined that it was in fact written all over her face, like some lovesick teenager eager for her first taste of love.

She felt herself fortunate to have been found by this clan. She imagined Monroe felt the same. She could see in his expression and the way he talked to the trio; he was like a father talking with his sons. Elise turned to Sierra, "Did your father want the match between you and Marcus?"

Sierra's expression changed a fraction as she answered Elise, "You Woodsmen are bold."

Elise laughed, "Yes, I guess we are. I didn't mean to pry; I was just being curious. I'm sorry. I can just tell that he likes the cousins, and I figured that he wanted the match."

Sierra smiled. "I better get used to the boldness of this clan, especially since I'm going to be one of you soon." She paused, then smiled, "It's okay. I'm shy. The only person I really speak my mind with is my father. And you are right; he likes the cousins very much. However, the choice was mine and mine alone. I desired Marcus since the first time the Woodsmen came to raid. I was only a young girl, but I knew someday that he would be my husband."

Elise liked her answer. Not that she expected anything in particular, but her answer was romantic. She had always been a romantic; she couldn't help herself. Some people were more realistic, but the way she figured it, you only have one life, so shoot for the moon, and maybe, just maybe, you will catch a falling star.

After dinner, the group sat around a bonfire, drinking beer, and more homemade alcohol from the Monroe's. The group seemed to have endless things to talk about, farming, horses, the distilled spirits and how easy it was to make. The group's conversation turned to talk of warring tribes. The General told Monroe's group about their prisoner. They talked about how he came to be on the clan's compound and how their scavenge had gone wrong.

Monroe told the group that they had only been raided by Clan Woodsmen. Before they each came to their little farm, it was a different story. Each man or woman had their own trials before joining Tribe Monroe. The General nodded his head as he listened to Monroe; the story was similar to their own. Each person had their own survival stories.

The group shared Jack and Elise's story and how they had all come to be together. The Monroe's were enthralled in the telling of the tale, as if they were listening to a play. They were all surprised at how it had unfolded into the prisoner being on the compound.

The fire blazed on, but both groups grew tired from a long day. Luc and Elise, followed by Jack and Marcus, led the Monroe's to the yurts and bunk house they had built especially for the barbeque. The Monroe's were impressed by the hospitality and were proud to be spending their time at the compound with Clan Woodsmen. Monroe and his daughter had a yurt to themselves, and with everyone comfortable and all beds accounted for, they all said their goodnights. Luc and Elise walked back to the main house. Jack and Marcus made their way back to the bonfire. The two men had no reason to rush to their beds. Their rooms were a solitary reminder of their single status.

Luc and Elise retired to their room. The two lovers climbed into bed exhausted. They chatted about their day; it had been fantastic, better than they had imagined or hoped for. They joked about something funny that had taken place during the game. Elise told him that he had looked sexy when it was his turn to bat. She told him about how she liked Monroe and felt safe with him. The two tribes interacted as if they were one, and thanks to Monroe, they would be, through Sierra and Marcus. They talked about Sierra and Marcus and wondered how that might turn out. They seemed like opposites, one shy and cautious, the other unafraid and uninhibited. They both wondered if the two would embrace their differences and thrive or rebel against each other like a wave crashing against a boulder.

Elise voiced her thoughts aloud wondering if Marcus would be a tender husband that a young Sierra needed in order to grow and blossom into the woman she deserves to be.

Luc assured Elise that when a man was a soldier, he became a different man, but most of them did; they had to. He explained to her that a man must become the harder, more intimidating side of himself, the hunter, the conqueror, the beast. Unfortunately, some men could not turn off that side of himself once he tapped into it.

She understood that; her brothers were much the same way. She felt that Luc could be both, where her brother Jack was more soldier than lover.

She could only hope that Marcus was more like Luc than Jack. Luc had more tolerance and understanding for emotional feminine ways than her brother. Jack would not tolerate her tantrums, even as a child. Only time would give them the answers they pondered. Their conversations died and Luc rolled over to blow out their single candle. Elise had other things in mind for them.

She ran her hand along his back. She kissed his neck and ear. She whispered dirty things that all men like to hear; she purred them into his ear like a temptress. Elise pulled her cotton night shirt over her head and straddled him. She liked her soldier between her legs. She felt like a conqueror herself, being on top of the mighty General. She grabbed his hands in a bold attempt to inflame his passion. She placed them on her chest and moved with him. The room was dark, but she could see his smile. She could fell his heat and smell his masculine aroma of arousal. She took him in her hand and brought his hard lust to full arousal pushing him inside of her. She rode him hard until they both climaxed together. She rolled off him, and he pulled her into his arms.

He kissed her neck, whispering, "I love you," in her ear. "I can't wait to marry you tomorrow, my love."

Elise smiled. She answered him, "I love you. I can't wait either."

He pulled her tighter to him and Elise fell asleep with the promise that tomorrow was going to be an even more spectacular day than today.

CHAPTER 19

Elise jumped out of bed excitedly; this was going to be a wonderful day. She had conquered the General. Today they would be husband and wife. She was madly in love with the man that she needed from the beginning. She wasn't naive enough to think that life was rainbows and butterflies, but if there was love, true love, you could work anything out. Anything.

Elise walked into the dining hall and found the men sitting around enjoying coffee. She walked up to them and Luc stood up. He kissed her on the cheek and brushed her hair from her face with his hand. She smiled at him; she could see the passion in his face as he leaned in to whisper something French in her ear. She had started picking up bits and pieces and understood one word, 'mine.' She felt electricity shoot through her veins, feeling as if he too, was excited about their marriage. She loved the way he smelled, masculine and clean with a hint of outdoor lumberjack.

The men all said their good mornings as she excused herself to find Bridgette. She found Sierra and Bridgette talking in the kitchen. Elise knew the day would be long. They had multiple games planned for early in the day before a late brunch. They scheduled a twilight wedding ceremony and feast to finish off their day.

Bridgette smiled at Elise, "Good morning, sunshine."

Elise giggled. "Morning ladies. What are y'all up to? Do you need any help?"

Sierra gave Elise a wave and jumped off her stool. The two women walked over to Elise and told her they needed her help. The trio walked to the material room.

Sierra and Bridgette walked ahead of her; they didn't talk or stop to make sure she followed. They seemed to be bent on some mission and shared a secret only the two of them knew.

The women walked into the room. The window was already open, indicating that they had been there that morning.

A light breeze filtered in, but the room was warm, foretelling of a hot day to come.

"Close your eyes, Elise."

Elise gave Bridgette a funny look, making her and Sierra laugh.

"Please," Sierra added next.

Elise did as she was asked. A moment later, the ladies asked her to open her eyes. Elise opened her eyes to the pair holding out two objects. Brigette was holding a beautiful day dress with see-through long sleeves and multiple silk trains. Its main body was a light yellow and the sleeves were a soft warm buttercream. The train was two shades of gold. The dress was lovely. Sierra held out a flower crown. It had multiple colored flowers and ribbon in gold, yellow, and cream streaming from it. Elise knew right away the pair had made a set for her wedding. She was breathless as she whispered her thanks and a tear ran down her cheek. The pair walked to her and threw their arms around her. They held each other like sisters for what seemed an eternity. Finally, Bridgette broke the serenity by asking Elise to try it on to make sure it fit. Elise shut the door and pulled off her dress. The items fit perfectly; she knew they would. If Bridgette was anything, she was a perfectionist with a needle and thread. She was a skilled and talented seamstress with an eye for beauty.

The day had indeed been hot. Elise had to make several trips to her room to wet a cloth from her pitcher. The cool water had helped ease some of her discomfort. She felt tired and needed a rest after the contest with the crossbows. It turned from a competition to more of a training exercise. The Woodsmen had lined up multiple targets of different sizes and shapes. The contest had been no contest, so they decided to make it fun for everyone. It became evident early on that Monroe's men were no match for the Woodsmen.

Marcus and Sierra spent most of their time together, he showed her how to use the crossbow accurately. She seemed to pick it up with ease. The General neither lingered, nor concentrated on one person, dividing his attention easily amongst the men that wanted to learn.

Monroe stood back and watched with Elise. He would make some joke or quip from time to time, always keeping Elise at ease. Robert came to watch and help. His wound seemed to be healing well. It gave him little trouble, probably because the man was stubborn as a bull. He seemed more irritable than usual.

Elise's curiosity won; she finally brought the subject up with Bridgette, "He seems to be healing well enough." Elise pointed at Robert.

Bridgette snickered, "Yeah, well, his attitude is seriously lacking. He's acting like a bear."

Elise smiled at her friend, "I didn't notice a difference." The two women laughed. "What's going on with him? His injury seems to be doing better?"

Bridgette shrugged her shoulders, "I'm not sure. He isn't sharing. The cousins would know, but your guess is as good as mine."

Elise thought about their conversation. She finished her cooling regimen, then went to the rocker by the window. She could see and hear the fun going on. She still felt a part of it even though she wasn't out in it. Although the breeze was lacking, and she was uncomfortable, she closed her eyes to rest.

The two groups ate and played minor games like horseshoes and bean bag toss, something fun and moderately competitive to pass the afternoon. Luc left his company multiple times in search of Elise, always being told by Bridgette that she was resting. He enjoyed the camaraderie of both groups and drank beer, but he missed Elise being beside him. He felt that the afternoon dragged on.

He finally dismissed himself to get ready for the wedding ceremony. He wanted it to be special for Elise. He knew things like this were important to women. He had communicated his wishes to Bridgette, she understood and was actually two steps ahead of him. Everyone eventually went their separate ways to clean up and rest before the ceremony and fun afterwards.

Bridgette knocked on the door and entered to find Elise bathing. She had her hair pinned in a bun and was washing her arms with a cloth. Bridgette understood why The General had fallen in love with her friend. She was an image of beauty, stunning and exotic.

"It's time to get ready. Look what I have for you." Bridgette laid the dress and crown on the bed, then came to her and opened a small box. "I saved these for special occasions. I haven't worn makeup in forever." She laid the small box on the counter.

Elise was shocked. She hadn't seen makeup, let alone wear any, in a very long time. She was surprised and grateful that her friend would share her treasure with her. Bridgette told Elise she could use whatever she wanted and left the room. Elise finished her bath, then went through the treasure box and laid out multiple items.

Elise brushed her hair and pulled on her beautiful golden crown of flowers. She took one last look in the mirror. The dress and crown alone were stunning but being able to add a little extra to her face made everything pop. She felt like a star. She was excited and exuded an aura of anticipation.

Bridgette came into the room to get Elise. She stopped dead in her tracks; Elise was beyond glorious. She radiated exotic magnetism. Her eyes were beautiful but lined in kohl she looked like an Egyptian princess. She was heart stopping.

The General was ready and waiting for his woman. Luc stood talking with Marcus and Monroe. He asked Jack to wait for Elise by the house. Luc felt that even though this was an informal affair, it still needed to be perfect. He wanted to have the best that he could give her, that anyone could give her.

The sun was setting. His formal uniform was built for the cooler climates. He wasn't uncomfortable, soldiers would never admit to such an elevated emotion, but he wasn't exactly comfortable. For Elise, he could be patient.

He handed the wooden rings back to Monroe. He was thankful once again for him. Monroe was more than willing to perform the ceremony for them and knew that he would make it memorable.

Elise was surprised to see Jack waiting for her. He looked so handsome. She knew right away that he was going to deliver her to the General. Bridgette and Sierra picked wildflowers for Elise to carry. She felt nervous, but not sure why. She had no reason to feel anything but excitement. She was also thrilled that a man like Luc wanted her.

She was stunned the moment the group came into view, then everything faded but The General. He was standing so proud and tall in his military uniform. He was clean cut and shaven. His beard was gone, revealing the gorgeous man underneath. He was a stunning creature with his beard and unruly hair, but clean cut and shaven, he looked the role of an officer, not just soldier and warrior. He was magnificent. His eyes were entrapping, and Elise felt lightning running through her.

Bridgette came into view, signaling the brother and sister were on their way. Luc held his breath for a fraction of a second. Lightning went through his veins as he once again zinged with Elise. Her eyes were a smoldering promise of passion and a good life. Her eyes. Those beautiful green eyes seemed to reach into his soul. The kohl surrounding them made them more intense and stunning. She looked beautiful in her yellow dress. He felt pride and knew that he was envied.

The couple stood facing each other and holding hands. Monroe talked about faith, family, endurance, tolerance, and most importantly, love and respect for each other. He even told a few stories of his own and made a few jokes. The ceremony lasted a half hour or so and ended with a prayer. Finally, the participants shared their vows.

Monroe looked at Luc. "Do you Luc Christopher Trembley, General and head leader of Clan Woodsman, take this woman, Elise Marie Jensen, as your wife, before God and both Tribes?

Luc smiled, "I do."

Monroe held out the wooden ring and Elise was shocked. Monroe winked at her, "I hope it fits." Elise giggled. The ring slid on with ease. Monroe faced Elise. "Elise, do you take Luc Christopher Trembley as your husband, before God and both tribes?"

Elise smiled up at Luc. "I do."

Monroe handed the second ring to Elise and she slid it on his finger. "I now pronounce you husband and wife. For goodness' sake, Luc, kiss your wife." The couple kissed and the crowd cheered.

Everyone enjoyed the evening. There was food, games, and a lot of drinking. The two tribes hung out late into the night. The bonfire grew smaller and smaller, and the sun had almost risen by the time everyone found their beds.

Elise and Luc were cuddled in bed together for the first time as husband and wife. They sneaked out of the festivities to enjoy each other in their most intimate way. Luc was laying over Elise, kissing her and enjoying the feel of her underneath him when shouts from the yard startled them both. Luc jumped out of bed and ran to his window.

Elise sat up with the blanket covering her. "What is it Luc? What's wrong?"

Luc ran to his dresser and threw on a pair of jeans and his boots. He shouted at her as he was running out of the bedroom door, "Get dressed! The barn is on fire!"

Elise jumped out bed. She threw on a pair of shorts and a t-shirt. Men were running from different directions. Elise watched as Luc ran into the barn, already ingulfed in flames. Horses ran out, then nothing. The flames got higher and heat became more intense. Marcus ran inside. Moments later, he ran out helping Luc with one arm around his shoulders. There was a long-jagged cut along Luc's leg where something that had fallen must have cut him. Elise ran to him as men were trying to put out the flames.

There was minimal water from the holding tanks to use. The barn began smoldering, and nothing was going to stop it from consuming itself.

Elise was holding a cloth to stop the bleeding from Luc's leg. Marcus heard shouts and was running toward the shed. A truck burst out of the shed opening. Elise could not see the driver. Men were shouting and hollering. Chaos was erupting around them as men were running in the direction of the shed. Elise could here shots being fired, then the sounds of something crashing. Robert pulled Luc up and Elise and Robert helped him back to the big house. They deposited him into a chair in the formal dining room. Bridgette brought fresh water and bandages for Elise. The cut was deeper than she had suspected. Bridgette brought her some of the strong alcohol, along with a needle and thread.

Luc took several swigs of the strong brew and Robert held him to the chair as Elise poured the rest on his leg. She cleaned his leg with the fresh water and cloth. Luc was swearing in French making Robert laugh. They spoke to each other in what seemed like a heated argument. Robert let him go, grabbed the alcohol, and shoved it in his hand. Luc once again took a swig, then tossed it on the table. Sweat started to pour from his head. Robert once again held him to the chair and indicated to Elise to finish his leg.

Elise had just finished sewing up his leg when Marcus came in. He was angry. She could tell by his stride and his expression; his entire demeanor spoke of mayhem. He walked up to the trio and sat down. His face was dirty and smudged. Soot mixed with sweat. He ran his hands threw his hair. "Luc it was that son of a bitch, Trevor."

Luc sat there, no emotion on his face what-so-ever. He nodded his head. "Did you kill him?"

Marcus looked away. He didn't answer. Elise noticed the twitch in Luc's jaw and the change in his eyes; the General was present. "Spit it out, Marcus." He said it quietly, his tone was a disguise of the turmoil raging inside of him. "Spit it out!" he roared at him.

Marcus stood up and looked at him. "He took that bastard in the cage with him."

Luc nodded his head in understanding. "Who was on guard?" he asked Marcus.

"It was Brent."

The General stared at Marcus waiting for him to continue.

"He's okay. He got hit in the head, but he's going to live."

Luc nodded at his cousin, turning his head to look at Elise. She was sitting beside him, listening, and taking in the scene.

"Your cousin just saved your life and that is how you thank him."

She stood up angry at herself for getting angry at Luc. She looked down at her hands. They were covered in blood, and immediately, she was sorry. The nausea began. She ran from the hall until she was alone in her room. She washed the blood from her hands and splashed water on her face. She felt shaky. Her hands and legs were trembling from adrenaline or fear, she wasn't sure which, perhaps both. She was spent, both emotionally and physically. The room felt like it was spinning. She walked toward the window and put her hand on the rocker to sit. Suddenly, her world went black.

Sierra was standing in the doorway as she watched Elise rush from the hall. She saw the chaos in yard and fields surrounding the big house. She wasn't sure what was going on. The scene in the house wasn't much different. Angry shouts of French and English came from the dining hall. She could see the cousins arguing. Robert grabbed Marcus and flung him away from The General. Their words were harsh and disjointed. Sierra heard a noise and suddenly the arguing stopped. It sounded like glass breaking as if something had fallen.

Luc stood up and winced in pain as his hurt leg throbbed and denied him the action he sought. He said something to Marcus, and the cousin rushed out. Robert grabbed Luc and helped him walk down the hall into his section of rooms. Sierra followed at a distance, unsure of how these angry men might react to her intrusion.

Sierra was very young when the world fell apart. This world they all lived in was all she knew. She had been told stories of the turmoil, pain, and heartache that had led to this time. The diseases decimated the population, then the food shortages, that's when the riots ensued. The war had come when the country was at its weakest. Families were divided. People were starving. She had heard of the stress and mental disparities that occurred. The stress took its toll and drove some to madness. She wondered if that was why the survivors today were hard and unyielding.

Luc hated being assisted like some damn baby. He'd been to war; he'd been in fire fights. What brings him down? Some son of a bitch, weasel dick asshole, that set his barn on fire. He'd kill that bastard when he got his hands on him. That was a promise. Robert helped him down his hall. When he walked through the door, the scene around him turned his blood cold. Marcus was kneeling over Elise. The table had flipped over knocking the hurricane lantern to the floor.

Marcus turned around, "She's okay. She's going to have a few nasty bruises. She must have fainted."

"Somebody get Bridgette in here. Marcus go get Jack and pick me up in front of the house. We're going after that bastard."

Elise slowly opened her eyes. Her body felt broken, like thousands of shards of glass. She moved slowly, Marcus' face came into view and she jumped. He was not who she expected to see.

Marcus touched her hand, "Don't move. You must have fainted."

She looked around. "Luc?"

"I'm here, Chérie."

Elise pulled herself into a sitting position as her body screamed in pain. She absently rubbed her arm, taking in the scene around her. Marcus threw her arm over his shoulder and lifted her up off the floor. He walked over, depositing her on the bed. Luc sat next to her rubbing her arm. The bruises had already started to form.

"I'm sorry."

Luc laughed. "For what my pet?"

She smiled shyly at him.

He kissed her head, then turned to Marcus, "Did you hear me?"

Marcus stared at him for a fraction of a second. "You're not going anywhere, dumbass. I'll take Jack and a few men. I don't feel like babysitting." With that sharp remark he walked out the door.

Robert started to laugh. Luc started shouting at them in French making Robert laugh more.

Bridgette came rushing into the room. "Sierra came and got me. Oh my, Elise, are you okay?"

She walked over to the pitcher getting a cool cloth. Bridgette fussed over Elise while Luc sat there angry that he couldn't go with his men. His anger fueled with every second.

Monroe came into the couple's room and found them sitting together. Luc's leg was propped up and Elise was resting her head on his shoulder. "Aren't you two a fine pair?"

Luc nodded his head; he was in no mood but respected Monroe too much to be caustic.

"I see," Monroe laughed. "Do you have anything to help you get around until your leg heals?"

"No, unfortunately."

Monroe nodded. "I'll make myself useful then and see what I can do." He turned and started towards the door.

"Monroe," Luc called after him and the old man turned, "thank you."

He smiled at Luc. "Don't thank me yet, General."

Luc gave him a crooked smile and Monroe continued on his way.

Elise and Luc laid together for some of the afternoon. The window was opened allowing a slight breeze. The clouds had darkened and taken on an ominous shade. The sun disappeared. Luc felt the atmosphere was mimicking his current mood. He didn't have any visitors after Monroe and awaited news from the compound. He knew that Jack and Marcus would report to him when they returned, but he was getting impatient.

He was not accustomed to sitting around and watching others work. He had been hurt before but not to the point where he was immobile. He felt raw and exposed and somewhat vulnerable. He made sure his pistol was next to him before Robert went on his way.

It seemed like an eternity before Monroe came back with make-shift wooden crutches. Elise had long since left him in the room alone. His mood had not improved. It seemed the darker the sky, the darker his mood.

Robert came in to assist Monroe. They got Luc up and handed him the crutches. The athlete and soldier in him did not need the assist up nor the time to get accustomed to them. With the crutches, he was able to maneuver about with ease. He thanked Monroe once again for his help. Robert and Monroe followed Luc out of the house and into yard.

"Where is everyone?"

Robert realized he didn't know about the broken gate. Apparently, Marcus had not revealed that bit of misfortune that would have set him to his breaking point. Luc did not know how vulnerable they actually were at that moment.

"Most of the men are down at the gate."

Luc stop walking, then half turned to Robert, the realization all over his face.

"That rat bastard, son of a whore! Stealing our vehicle isn't enough, he's got tear up our gate?"

They continued walking. Monroe knew by his tone and the twitch in his jaw just how angry the General really was.

Luc and a few of his original men walked to Brent's yurt. Jene answered the door. She had been fussing over her husband. He seemed moderately irate and somewhat stressed. When the door opened showing who had come to visit, Brent jumped out of the chair he was sitting in. When he started to speak, Luc put one hand up silencing him. He didn't want an apology and he certainly didn't want any excuses.

"I came to make sure you were okay."

Brent took in his commanding officer with his eyes. "What the hell happened to you?"

Luc gestured for Brent to join him and the men outside. Brent walked out, lit a smoke, and told them his side of the story. Luc listened, nodded his head, then walked away. The men briefly consoled Brent and explained the crutched and current disposition of their General.

Elise looked down at her hand. She hadn't had a chance to really look at her ring. It was beautiful and fit perfectly. She was happy despite the mayhem that transpired since their union. She knew that most men would not have taken extra steps to make things perfect; however, her husband had. He made everything as traditional as possible. She realized that he was beyond thoughtful.

She grabbed water and a light lunch and headed back to their room. Elise walked in and noticed Luc was gone. She went to the table and laid down the tray of food. Bridgette had already cleaned up the mess. She must remember to thank her. She stared out the window and noticed Luc, Robert, and Monroe walking toward the compound gate.

No words were spoken as the men continued walking. A different turmoil was raging in each one and each issue was as unique as the men themselves. Monroe's mind drifted to another time and place long ago. Time was running out to tell Sierra the truth. He procrastinated telling her, but something in his soul told him that the hourglass was reaching the end of its sand.

Robert was not worried about his clan. He felt the men would run as far as possible. Cowards like those two wouldn't come back. They didn't even stay and fight. Instead, his mind was fixed on a shapely figure that warmed his bed from time to time.

Luc was a different story. He felt the weight of the world bearing down on his shoulders. He imagined his home, their compound, was safe. He was cautious and careful but had let his guard down and let the enemy in with open arms. Shame on him. His gut told him that this was far from over.

CLAN WOODSMEN: THE GENERAL'S REFUGE   A.C. GILLIES

Chapter 20

The rain started. The sky lit up repeatedly with lightning and thunder boomed in the distance. The men sat in the dining hall. The sound of rain pelted the roof while both tribes talked and debated. Jack and Marcus had yet to return. Luc was anxious on the inside. The General on the outside was callous in his remarks, his tone clipped and unyielding. He was angry at himself. He was angry that he hadn't been able to go with Marcus. Where were they? A small part of him felt that he'd been distracted since Elise came to be with them. He would never place something like that on her shoulders. She was a welcome distraction. He loved Elise. He was thankful for her.

Elise walked around filling drinks, helping the other women with this and that. She lit the lanterns and kept herself occupied. As her husband's mood took a darker note, her mind drifted to a place she couldn't help. She wondered if he was feeling remorse about their union. Was he angry at her? She didn't want to believe it, but she had spent a lifetime second guessing herself. Why should now be any different?

The storm was raging on when the door blew open and Jack and Marcus rushed inside. They were wet and dirty. Luc stood up and made his way to them. He stood looking at Marcus, not saying a word. Everyone watched unsure how the scene would play out. The two men took off their boots leaving them at the door. Marcus and Luc didn't say two words. Luc turned and walked away. Jack and Marcus sat down across from each other. They were quiet and reserved. Everyone held their questions. Marcus ran his hand through his hair. Sierra noticed his distress. Unsure if he would like the company, she stayed away, wishing she could help.

Marcus was angry they couldn't find that weasel dick and the degenerate escapee. He knew Luc was disappointed; he hated disappointing him. He had looked up to Luc since they were children.

Marcus was tired and dirty, but all he wanted was to keep looking. Jack finally convinced him to come back to the compound. He and Jack had become friends. He understood Jack, but Jack did not understand Luc. Luc would not tolerate failure and incompetence; however, he wasn't a total hard-ass. He understood impossible outcomes and was tolerant and appreciated best efforts. Marcus could not stand the disappointed look on his face. That look was worse than any words he could have said to them at that moment.

Elise walked up to the pair bringing them a cloth to dry what they could of themselves. Bridgette followed carrying food. Sierra found her opportunity and brought them beer. She sat next to Marcus, hoping for a word, a look, anything. She got nothing from him. She was too young to understand the workings of a man. When a man had an unfinished task, he could think of nothing else.

Elise placed her hand on her brother's shoulder, "Can I ask?"

Jack replied, "You can ask, but the truth is nothing happened. We looked all day. We tried different routes. Nothing. We were a good quarter hour behind those chickenshits. We would have needed a miracle to find them."

Elise asked the question all three women wanted to know, the question the men already knew the answer to without even consulting the man himself. "Why is Luc so angry."

"Seriously?" Marcus looked incredulous.

Elise looked down, shamefaced that she didn't know the answer.

Jack decided to relieve her mind. "E, it's because it never should have happened." Elise cocked her to the side, not understanding.

Marcus took over. "We," he moved his figure between himself and Jack, "meaning his men, should never have been caught off guard. We should have noticed Trevor right away. He should never have been near the shed. Someone should have seen him setting the barn on fire. Someone should have shot his ass before they reached the gate, etc. It's all about failure, Elise."

Elise woke to the sound of her husband strolling around the room. The lighting flashed in the sky somewhere in the distance. The storm raged on, not only on the outside, but she could feel the tension radiating from Luc.

He noticed that she watched him. "I'm sorry that I woke you."

She yawned. "No, I'm fine." She got out of bed and walked over to him. He was looking out into the black night. She put her hand on his shoulder. "Do you want to talk about it?" She whispered to him.

"No." One word.

Her pride stung. He had been open with her this far in their relationship, always communicating when he was bothered by something. She turned to walk away, then decided that if he was going to be an ass, so was she. "You're being a selfish bastard."

He turned around to face her. "What did you say to me."

"You heard me."

He reached out, grabbing her by her night gown. She flinched, thinking she had gone too far. He pulled her roughly to him. One of the crutches fell to the ground. "What did you say?" Her heart was pounding.

She smiled at him. "I said you're being a selfish BASTARD." She screamed the last word at him. He crushed her body next to him. He kissed her brutally, she reveled in his kiss matching his passion.

The two lovers were kissing passionately when the door burst open and Jack rushed in. "I'll kill you if," his last word hung in the air, his sentenced suspended in time, as he saw the two lovers embraced.

"Get out Jack and shut the fucking door."

Jack smiled, saluted, and slammed the door. He opened it again. He couldn't help himself, "People are trying to sleep. Why don't you tame that wild heathen you call a wife?"

Elise screamed at her brother, "Shut the fucking door Jack!"

For the first time that day, the trio laughed, lifting their souls.

Elise walked behind Luc into the dining hall. They were late to rise, having had a restless night. Jack was sitting next to Monroe. When he saw Luc, he gave him a crooked, all-knowing smile. Elise shook her head at her trouble-making brother. She headed to the kitchen to get coffee and see if her help was needed. She returned to the three men making light conversation. Luc's temperament and all over disposition had improved. He needed an outlet for his anger. He used his passion constructively, turning his negative energy into something positive for both him and Elise. His better mood benefited them as well as the clan.

Marcus came into the hall minutes after looking rough around the edges. His hair was disheveled. His eyes were blood shot and red. He still smelled of hard liquor. Unfortunately, he had not used his night constructively. Monroe eyed him hoping he had made a good decision in giving his daughter to this man.

Marcus noticed Luc's allover attitude change. He gave him a lopsided smile that told Luc everything he needed to know.

"It's okay Marcus. None of what happened yesterday was your fault. It was mine, and mine alone. We will fix everything and keep our eyes open and our backs covered for the day those chickenshits come back with reinforcements. I should have put a bullet in that bastard's head and buried him out past the gates. As for Trevor, I should have watched him closer."

Marcus shook his head in the negative. "You selfish bastard, I'm not going to let you take all the credit for yesterday's mayhem."

Robert walked in, "You're both selfish bastards." The group all laughed knowing that the tension was over.

Monroe decided that now was as good as any other time to talk with the cousins. "I was thinking that my people better head home. You have enough to deal with. If it's okay with your clan, I would like for Sierra and myself to stay here with you for a time? My men have also decided that they will come to help you rebuild your barn or assist with anything else that needs to be done."

Luc responded to him, "You, your daughter, and your people are welcome to stay here any time. I figured with Marcus and Sierra being engaged, they would need this time to get to know one another, however, you need not burden your people, this is not your problem."

Monroe answered him, "I know it's not my problem, but we are family, so actually, it does kind of make it my problem."

Luc smiled, and nodded his head in one single gesture of thanks.

The day was long as Elise followed Luc around the compound. The couple was never alone, and she rarely spoke, it seemed someone else always occupied his time or conversation. He asked her to assist him in inventorying the chaos of the compound. They needed to account for what had been lost, damaged or stolen. They started right after he finished his morning coffee.

Marcus, Jack, and Monroe were with them as they made their way to the compound's main gate. Luc shook his head at the damage that one person could make. He had to mentally calm himself from getting angry time and again. The damage was a waste, and waste always made him angry.

Men had already started mending the gate yesterday before the storm came. The same men got an early start and were working when the group arrived. The gate had been completely damaged. They were framing up the hole with rough wood. The guards on watch yelled down to Luc to let him know they saw no signs of trouble. One guard apologized for not being able to stop the mutilation of the gate. Luc gave him a nod in understanding.

Monroe and Jack disappeared for a time, leaving only Marcus and the couple to look over the ashes and rubble that was once the horse barn. Luc asked Elise to make a list of things that would have to be replaced. In addition to the supplies needed to care for and feed the horses, he considered the items needed to ride them: saddles, blankets, bridles, etc.

Most of the horse fence attached to the barn was left undamaged. The horses were grazing in the open fields for the time being. They seemed unhurt and unaware of their present homeless state. Thankfully, it was summer and there was plenty of time to rebuild before it became cold enough to worry over the loss.

They walked to the yurt that belonged to Trevor. Robert joined the trio as they were walking through the field. Robert and Marcus were allowed inside with Luc. The men had asked Elise to wait for them outside. She imagined it was more for privacy than security. The men took a brief look around. They spotted nothing out of the ordinary. They turned over his cot. Nothing was revealed, no answers forthcoming. Luc looked around the yurt, daring something to jump to his attention.

"I want to burn this yurt." Luc's statement was more to himself than his comrades. Neither replied. They knew Luc, if he was going to do it, he would, no matter what anyone else had to say. Time would tell.

Monroe and Jack rejoined the group. They made their way to the shed. Elise had not been near the shed since the day her brother was brought to the compound. A vison of her vomiting made her flush with embarrassment. Marcus held the door open as each man went inside. Elise watched the door close. A fraction of time passed, then Jack opened the door gesturing for her to follow. The men looked around at the minimal damage done to the shed.

"I'm surprised that chickenshit didn't tear this place apart," Luc said to his group with disgust dripping off his words.

"No time." Robert replied. Everyone looked at Robert. He continued, "Think about it. He was sneaking around, set the barn on fire. He knew he had to get past Brent, get the prisoner, and get gone before we could catch him. No time."

Marcus went to the weapon case; everything was intact. The only thing missing from the shed was the detainee and one of the vehicles. There was minimal damage, and nothing to replace. Monroe looked around taking in the different dynamics of the shed: workplace, armory, storage, prison, infirmary. Everything you needed for survival.

Monroe spoke to Luc, "This shed is impressive."

Luc told him the story of how he came to find the compound. Monroe was surprised that someone had built such a worthy place, then deserted it, never to return.

After a thorough inspection, the men were satisfied enough to leave the shed. The men requested a private word, so Elise excused herself to seek out Bridgette. As she walked to the main house, her legs became like lead, and the sudden need to rest assaulted her.

Elise sat by the window. The sun had gone down. Twilight hid the darkening of the clouds signaling another night of storms. The breeze blew in moving her hair lightly around her face. She was tired. Her day had been long. She hadn't felt nausea in days and hoped that part of her pregnancy had passed. She drifted off to sleep thinking about her baby and their future.

Luc and his men built another fire. They sat around drinking and talking. They had important things to discuss. They had lost a lot in the last few days. Another scavenge would be needed. Without their riding gear, how would they hunt? They had only lost one vehicle, but the loss of the vehicle wasn't as devastating as the loss of their wagon. They used the wagon for hunting. When the riding gear and wagon went up in flames, so did their primary means of support. They could live without a lot, but they could not do without their ability to provide for their clan.

Monroe sat on his cot watching his daughter sleep. He had a heavy heart. He wondered about Marcus and hoped that his drinking was a rare occasion and not something he used as a crutch to get through life. If that was the case, his daughter would be in for a rough life, full of heartache and disappointment. He hoped that Marcus would be a responsible and fair husband.

His mind took him to a time when he was a young husband. He remembered the heartache he put his bride through when he played his immature male games, running around chasing skirts, and drinking until dawn. His mind drifted back to the darkness inside the yurt. He knew that he needed to talk with his daughter before his time ran out. He needed to get some things off his chest, so that his soul may rest.

Luc talked with his men about going on a hunting party. Jack agreed. Marcus did not.

Marcus tried to get everyone to see reason, "If we wait, they will come to us."

Luc was angry, maybe too angry to see reason. "I don't want to sit around here, like some duck waiting to be shot out of the water. I say we go and find them and take them out on our terms."

Jack wanted blood, "Those bastards killed my brother. I'm with Luc. I say we go after them."

Robert spoke next, "With your leg, what the hell are you going to do? You need to heal. What happens if they come back and we are out looking for them? What happens to your wife, and the other women left here? Do you think they will ask them to wash clothes and fix them food? Use your head. You will get revenge, just not today, and not tomorrow."

Marcus looked at Luc waiting for a response.

"I'm thinking," he told his cousin.

Typical reaction from his cousin, avoidance when he didn't want to deal with it. Marcus shook his head. Robert laughed. Brent took a puff on his cigarette.

The men sat round arguing. Luc knew the truth. He begrudgingly acknowledged the reality of the situation. He didn't want to accept it, but Robert's logic was undeniable. He didn't want to see reason, not at that particular moment in time. His leg was wounded, but his pride is what hurt. He was a soldier and a damn good one. He couldn't listen to the bullshit any longer. He got up and walked back to the main house. He'd be damned if he had to sit there listening to the men tell him what he couldn't do. He needed something, anything to give him a diversion. He walked to the library hoping to find something to occupy his time. He glanced around the room but felt too antsy to read. He sat on the chair, propped up his leg, and closed his eyes. He sat in the dark room with his eyes closed, listening to the silence, listening to his breathing, listening to anything but what his mind had to say.

Chapter 21

The days turned into weeks, and the weeks into months. Life on the compound returned to normal, but no longer complacent about security. Luc doubled the guards on the wall and had men patrol the compound grounds at night. Luc's leg healed giving him no trouble. He was a fighter and his stubborn pride made him work harder, longer and better, not just to rehab his injury but in everything he did.

The Monroe's had kept their promise and came to help repair the barn. Smaller hunting parties went out, leaving more men on the grounds. The Monroe's brought them much needed items for their horses. Luc and Marcus even started riding their horses without the conveniences of a saddle. They trained themselves to go bareback so nothing would hold them back in the future. The men trained harder and fought each other in tougher, more grueling hand-to-hand combat training. Luc knew deep in his soul that they would be dealing with that clan once again.

The more the days passed, the more he loved Elise, but the more distant he became. Elise did not understand what she had done. In his mind, he had let her get too close to him. He wasn't sure that he'd survive if he lost her. He tried hardening his heart where she was concerned. He convinced himself that was best. He lied to himself, denying them both some peace and needed comfort before the storm.

Elise went about her chores. This day was no different than the last few had been, or the ones before that. She couldn't understand why Luc always choose to stay out of the house until dark, come to his bed so late, and leave before the sun came up. He spent his time with his men and Monroe. It was painfully evident that he was keeping his distance from her now.

Elise began to be envious of the attention that Marcus freely gave Sierra, not that she wanted Marcus nor his attention. Their relationship was just a reminder of what she used to have with Luc. It showed her that Luc was keeping himself from her intentionally, or so it seemed.

Elise started to show while simultaneously the leaves started changing colors. This would be her third season at the compound with Clan Woodsmen. For her, it seemed like a lifetime. She missed the way Luc would seek her out. She missed the way he would kiss her passionately and the love they would make. He seemed to want anything but affection from her. He stopped allowing her to assist his bath. He wasn't ugly to her, just callous. He seemed to have the weight of the world on his shoulders. His mind always preoccupied. He hadn't touched her or even attempted to since the night Jack barged in.

Elise was hanging laundry when Jack came out to check on her. "How are you feeling little sister?"

She smiled, touched her tummy lovingly and replied to him, "Fine. As fine as anyone could be."

Jack smiled at her; he turned his attention to the field where the men worked on hand to hand combat.

She nodded in that direction. "Why aren't you out there?"

He didn't look at her when he answered, "I'm going with Luc and Marcus on a hunting party."

"Funny, Luc didn't say anything. I'm pretty sure we have enough meat. You guys went out a couple days ago." He turned his attention back to her. The look in his eyes made her stomach do flips. She felt nauseous. He didn't have to answer. She knew where they were going and why.

"Don't look at me like that E."

She looked down at the ground. "He couldn't come tell me."

Jack lifted her face up with his thumb and index finger, "Don't put me in the middle. I'm telling you. That's good enough."

Typical man to dismiss her as not being important enough. Elise turned her back on her brother; she didn't want him to see her tears. She heard him sigh, then turn and walk away. She watched Jack walk into the field with the other men. He walked up to Luc, said something, then he turned to Marcus. The men started walking out of her sight in the direction of the shed.

Elise watched the men in field for a few more minutes. Brent continued the combat training. The men all seemed at ease and familiar with the different techniques. She studied them, watching their moves, hoping that she could remember if the need should ever arise. She finished hanging her items, growing more and more agitated with each garment.

She knew the moment they left the compound; the roar of the engine signaled their departure. She decided she would wait up for Luc tonight. She was sick of his shit. She was going to get to the bottom of whatever was going on. Elise felt she'd been getting the silent treatment long enough.

Elise walked to the garden where she was met by Monroe. "What's troubling you, dear?"

She looked at him a moment, then answered. "I'm not sure. Luc is angry. I can't figure it out. I can't fix it. I don't understand. He won't talk to me. He's changing and I don't know what to do about it."

Monroe put his hand on her shoulder. "Walk with me, Elise. My old bones need it."

She had enjoyed their small walk. He let her talk and bare her soul. He would nod or say something encouraging, but mostly he kept quiet. She could see in his eyes and expression that his mind was working on her problem, yet he never revealed the solution. She felt better. After their brief walk, they turned their attention to the garden. The Monroe's had given them a few things to try and they seemed to be working. Monroe spent the rest of his evening helping Elise in the garden. The two of them passed the time telling stories of the past. They discussed things they had once believed in and cherished that sadly no longer held any merit in their world.

Elise washed her hair, then scrubbed her body. Her baths had become something she needed and cherished. They soothed her body after a long day. She no longer needed naps to fight off the exhaustion. She had energy to spare and helped wherever she could. She helped Bridgette mostly but always tried to find time to help in the garden. Elise finished her bath and crawled into bed leaving only a single candle lit. Elise closed her eyes trying only to rest them. She tried to stay awake long enough for Luc to return. However, exhaustion took over, replacing her troubled thoughts with troubled dreams.

Marcus and Luc took turns being the night watchman. Marcus closed his eyes listening to the sounds around him. Luc stared out into the dark night; his mood equally as dark. Jack opened the door of the Jeep, walked over to a nearby tree, and took a whiz. The men hid themselves far off the road, surrounded by trees. They brought sleeping bags and equipment to camp out. They decided the locked Jeep was a safer alternative.

Neither cousin made a comment as Jack came back, repositioned his pillow, closed his eyes, and proceeded to bitch about their current living arrangement, "Hell, I'd have to say this is one of the most uncomfortable places I've ever had to bed down. During the war, I was in a jungle in South America, so that's saying something."

Luc smiled at Jack. "I'd rather be in the jungle than the desert. Spent six months in the Sahara outside of Morocco. Sand in your eyes, sand in your food, sand in places sand should never be, my friend. I'd prefer not to go back, ever."

"When was this? Were you two together?" Jack curiously asked the cousins.

Marcus answered him, "We were together after OCS (officer candidate school), then we got promoted, then separated. I never went to Africa. I was doing recon down in Mexico at that time. Got in a bar fight, being drunk one too many times, got my rank taken away and put back into Luc's platoon when the war started."

Jack figured now was a good time to ask, "Were you really a General?"

"I got promoted to Major the same day I learned we were at war. After eighteen months, I went from Major to Colonel. Six months later, I was promoted to General. My group moved from camp to camp. I was a General for fourteen months, six days, and about ten hours. General was my nickname as a child. I was special forces; I wasn't out hunting a title. During the war, it just fell on me."

The three men told their own stories of the war. They each had things they would rather forget yet knew they never would.

The men were gone for most of the day seeing nothing, finding the same. They went in the direction the men on the gate had told them. Marcus and Jack showed Luc the direction they had gone before. They didn't go near the store but took a route that would lead them to it. Their hope to find their missing truck, something, anything, had proven to be pure fantasy.

Luc took off his wooden ring playing with it between his fingers. He got lost in the memory of those green eyes that he loved more than anything. He took a deep breath remembering the way she tasted. He pictured and reminisced about her smile, the way her hand felt in his hand while he was making love to her. He smiled thinking about how passionate she could be, how she could entice him with just a look or touch, how her eyes would betray her mind.

Jack's irritating voice interrupted his soft musing. "You regret marrying my sister?" His voice was quiet, dripping with sarcasm.

Luc turned around to look at Jack. "What the hell would give you that idea?"

Jack shrugged his shoulders. "Hell, I don't know. Maybe because you're being a pecker head?"

Luc opened the door of the Jeep and got out. He slammed the door behind himself. Marcus opened one eye, watched Luc walk away, then laughed. Jack smiled.

Elise woke the next morning, alone. She got dressed, cleaned up her room, then headed for breakfast. Elise was greeted by the sight of Robert sharing a cup of coffee with Monroe. She smiled at Monroe, then made her way to the kitchen to find Bridgette. As they chatted, Elise found out that the trio had not returned.

She spent the next few days trying to keep busy but constantly watching for the group to get back. Each night she left a candle burning; each morning she woke up a little more disappointed. She missed her husband. She missed her brother. But mostly, she missed her General.

Elise woke to the sound of rain. The wind was whipping the window back and forth. Lightning flashed in the distance. She made her way to the window, secured it in place, then stood for a moment looking out. It was dark still, and the moon was high. She didn't know what she was looking for. She was unsure of the time. She couldn't sleep and pacing around the room gave her no comfort. She sat at the window rocking and looking out into the darkness. She wondered where the men were and how they were doing.

She thought about her husband. Her mind drifted, taking her from her husband to her lover, her General. She thought about how erotic their first night had been and the way he had kissed her. Her mind took her to another time when they had made love like animals, hard and fast, tearing at each other, like their fierceness, was needed, even depended on for survival.

Elise loved his passion. She reveled in it. She enjoyed how he could be different lovers in one body. The feel of his lips brushing lightly against her skin. Her feminine cavern became moist with the need for him, not Luc, the General. She closed her eyes. She manifested him in her mind and could almost feel the touch of his fingers sliding over and in her body. Her back arched with the desire to be filled. She ran her hand down her neck, but it lacked the strong masculine touch she craved. She was hot with lust and longing, her passion throbbed and pulsed through her yearning body. She knew she couldn't sleep. Instead, she walked out into the cold rain hoping for some form of appeasement.

The storm subsided. The gentle rain hit her face like a thousand kisses from heaven. She smiled. Elise felt new and fresh as she played in the rain like a child. The rain washed her clean and gave her a new perspective on life. She didn't feel burdened at that moment. The rain accomplished a great feat. She felt like she did a decade ago, before the world had turned to shit.

Luc, Jack, and Marcus took many routes, all void of any signs of danger. They stumbled upon another clan but kept their distance. They had no way of knowing what kind of people they were. The group did not instigate a fight, nor did they show fear. The group was small; no women or children were visible. The group was clean. No weapons could be seen. They did not seem to pose a threat to the trio. The men kept their distance just the same. They had been gone for six days, and finally decided the store was a dead end.

They went in the direction they remembered the group had taken the day Robert was shot. Nothing. There were too many variables and roads, too many places they had never gone. Without backup, more men, and more time, they would be at a disadvantage. The men were tired of sleeping in the Jeep and decided to head home to the compound.

The sun was just rising as the men sat at the table drinking coffee. Monroe was surprised to see them sitting there.

Marcus spoke first, "Monroe."

Jack and Luc nodded their heads in greeting. Monroe laughed, "Morning boys."

Luc gave him a lopsided smile; Monroe and his need to call them "boys". It didn't bother Luc. He knew it was a term of endearment, not a putdown coming from Monroe. It felt funny just the same.

Marcus took control of the conversation, "I would like a private word with you, Monroe. If that's okay, sometime today, preferably as soon as possible."

Monroe nodded his head at Marcus in reply. The men made small talk, filling in Monroe about their last few days.

Luc dismissed himself from the group. He was hoping to see his lovely Elise. He went to their room. The bed was empty, but it had not been made. It was clear that she had been in it at some point. Alarm bells went off in Luc. He started looking in the obvious places, but when he didn't find her, he became frantic.

Luc's brisk walk told Marcus something was up. He stood up and asked his cousin. "What's up, Luc?"

Luc replied to him, "I can't find Elise."

Jack stood up. "What the hell did you say to her before we left."

Luc stood there for a moment, then replied quietly, "Nothing."

Jack shrugged his shoulders giving Luc a face that told Luc everything he needed to know without him having to open his mouth.

Luc shook his head. "Shut up Jack."

He left the men to find Bridgette. Bridgette would know where Elise might be. Bridgette was surprised to see the men back.

"Where is she?" Luc half shouted at her. Bridgette shook her head in confusion; she didn't have a clue what he was talking about. "Where is Elise, Bridgette?"

She looked at him stunned. "What do you mean? In bed I would guess."

She could see the storm in his eyes, the twitch in his jaw. "Would I be here, if that's was where she was?" He stormed out the room leaving Bridgette confused and upset.

Elise yawned. She jumped up looking around confused. For a moment, she had forgotten where she had last been. She smiled as she started to remember, she had enjoyed the rain and the feeling of freedom. She had gone to check on her horse. As she brushed her horse, she felt warm and content. Finally, relaxed, she curled up and fell asleep in the barn.

She could see the rays of sunshine coming in through the windows. She stood up, brushed herself off, then headed to the main house. Elise was shocked to see her brother and Marcus talking with Monroe. They were deep in conversation when they heard the door open.

Jack laughed, "Somebody's in trouble."

Elise walked over to them. She yawned, stretched, then pulled hay out of her hair. "What are you talking about Jack? When did you guys get back?"

He smiled at her, revealing nothing. Luc picked that moment to walk in. She turned to him and smiled. She could see the rage in his face. He walked up to her, grabbing her shoulders, shook her. "Where the hell have you been?"

She was shocked and upset that he would treat her this way in front of others. She just stared at him.

He shook her again. "Answer me."

She had never been courageous, but now she was pissed off. "Get your damns hands off of me, General."

He dropped his hands to his side. They stood there facing each other like some Wild West showdown. Her chest moved up and down while the adrenaline pulsed through her body. Their eyes told each other they weren't playing games.

Elise walked away with her head held high. She was proud of herself. She hadn't done anything wrong, and she didn't deserve to be treated like that, especially not in front of others. Luc looked around himself. The first thing he noticed was the disappointment written all over Monroe. The second was the fact that Jack was standing up his eyes shooting daggers at him. The third was Marcus standing by with a murderous expression on his face. Why was there always mutiny where that woman was concerned? Angry, Luc walked out of the house.

Marcus took a deep breath. He hated being put in that position. If their lover's quarrel would have escalated to where Jack felt the need to intervene, he would have to take Jack out. No matter if Luc is right or wrong, Marcus did, had always, and would always, have Luc's back.

Jack looked at Marcus. "Seriously?"

Marcus shrugged his shoulders and replied. "Jack, they need to work it out without us in the middle."

Jack gave Marcus a dirty look, then he too walked out of the house. Monroe looked up at Marcus. Marcus shook his head then sat back down. Monroe respected the cousins. However, he didn't like the way the General was treating Elise. She deserved better and one day he would regret it. Monroe took a deep breath; he knew all about regret.

CHAPTER 22

Luc took a walk. He knew he was being a dick. What was wrong with him? He ran his hand threw his hair. He kicked at the ground with his boot. From the inside, a battle raged within his mind. From the outside, he looked like a spoiled child. He knew he could not handle the loss of another wife and child; he knew it would kill him if he lost his Elise. She was his soul mate, his life. He kept walking and realized that life was too short. He realized he was making everyone miserable for an unseen future that no one could control.

Luc walked around the compound. He started by checking the water supply, then looked for anything he could do to stay away from the main house. He thought about how sexy Elise had been in her night gown. He saw the hay in her hair and got jealous and aroused simultaneously. He was being jealous; there was no other way to describe it. His mind kept drifting to the barn, he couldn't help himself. He knew no other man would dare touch what was his. He'd kill any man that touched her, and everyone knew it. They hadn't been intimate in months. He didn't want to pressure her while she was so delicate. Her body had started changing weeks ago and he didn't want her to feel obligated to please him. He wanted her willing and wanting. She made no move to join them, so he did not ask.

Elise found Luc feeding the horses. "I've been looking for you all morning."
He turned around to look at her. Her body was silhouetted with the light spilling in around her. He returned his attention back to his task. He wanted a truce. He wanted to move on, but the smartass in him couldn't let it go. "Yeah, sounds like we have something in common."

She took a deep breath, anger building inside of her. "What is your problem? Why are you being such an ass?"

He snickered at her.

She continued, "I'm sick of your shit." Elise started to cry. "What did I do? Why don't you want me anymore?"

He turned around and walked over to her. "Where were you?" She blinked; tears streamed down her cheek, "What?"

He shook his head, "Answer me, I want the truth. Who were you with?"

She looked at him, the realization of what he was thinking finally dawning on her. Jealous bastard. She answered him, "I couldn't sleep last night. I came into the barn to see my horse. I fell asleep."

He snickered at her, "Bullshit."

She took a deep breath. "You don't have to believe me, but it's the truth. You really think a man wants me like this? You certainly don't." She turned her back to him to walk out.

He grabbed her, spinning her back to him. He crushed her roughly, pulling her against himself.

She was upset, tears running down her cheeks. "I love you, Luc."

He kissed her passionately, and she threw her arms around his shoulders. He tore off her nightgown, hungry to take what was his. She matched his passion ripping his shirt open. He took her on the floor in the barn; anyone could have walked in on them. At that moment, he didn't care, he had a need to fill. A need that she could only give him.

Kissing his body, she told him how badly she wanted to please him. Her need was as strong as his. They made love like waves crashing on the shore. He rolled over, pulling her on top of him. She rode him like a warrior ridding his stallion into battle. Elise climaxed, pushing Luc over the edge. Sweaty and spent, they lay in the hay together. Their emotions were raw, their nerves were at ease.

Elise and Luc laughed as they pulled the hay out of each other's hair. She took in a long breath of his rugged masculine scent, running her hand over the rough muscles of his abdomen. She whispered, "I love you" as she kissed him below his naval. He smiled. He lusted after his wife; not many men could say the same.

"Why have you been so distant." She purred at him with her head laying on his rock-hard abs.

"I'm sorry Elise. I don't have an excuse. I'm just..." He didn't finish. He left his sentence hanging in the void.

She looked up at him, "What?" She wanted to know. Even if the answer hurt, she needed to know.

He shook his head. "Damn it, Elise, I'm afraid."

She was shocked by his answer; she rolled her eyes at him. "Afraid of what? What are you talking about?"

He sighed and ran a hand through his hair. He took a deep breath and answered her, "I'm afraid of burying another wife and child."

The realization hit her like a ton of bricks. "Oh. Luc, please don't worry. I'm not going anywhere. We aren't going anywhere. I love you. I can't bare you keeping me out. I just can't bare it."

Luc kissed her softly. "I know my love, neither can I. I'm sorry."

The couple walked out of the barn hand in hand. No one was aware of their barn tryst. Elise smiled beguilingly at Luc; she blew him a kiss then walked back to the main house. Bridgette ran to Elise as soon as she closed the door.

"Where have you been? Have you heard?" Elise shook her head in the negative, Bridgette continued. "Marcus and Sierra will marry two days from now."

Elise smiled, then responded to her friend. "How nice. We need to help her get ready."

Bridgette agreed and the two ladies went in search of Sierra to congratulate her and start planning.

The two clans prepared for the event by once again becoming one. Sierra asked her father to make her a special gazebo for the ceremony. The men started early that morning. The gazebo would be rustic cut wood with hanging candlelight jars. Sierra had liked Elise and Luc's evening wedding and wanted the same. Since it was fall, she wanted branches and vines instead of flowers. Monroe had one of his men bring Sierra's wedding dress from the hamlet. She had been given her mother's dress long ago and knew one day she too would wear it.

Men went hunting most of the day and brought back what would be a hearty feast.

The last two days had gone by quickly, especially for the three ladies. Sierra's dress needed minor alterations taking away precious time needed for other things. The afternoon sun started its downward trek indicating to the women that the appointed time was approaching. Elise fixed Sierra's hair and added minor highlights of makeup to the already stunning face of the young beauty.

Sierra surprised Elise and Bridgette with a question. "I'm afraid. What do I do?"

Elise didn't understand her question, "What do you mean?"

Sierra looked down at her hands sitting in her lap. She was embarrassed already with the first question; she didn't really want to elaborate. "Well, I, well I mean, what do I do in bed?"

Elise was somewhat surprised, as open as Monroe was, he had not explained to his daughter about the wedding night. Elise glanced at Bridgette, then back at Sierra. "Well, when a man and woman love each other, they make love."

Sierra looked at Elise with irritation written all over her face. "I know the basic's, Elise. What I meant was. Umm, Marcus may desire to marry me, but how do I make him love me? How do I make him want me?"

Elise had forgotten how innocent Sierra really was. She was young, maybe too young. "Passion is something you cannot explain. It is something you feel. You tell him with every kiss that you want to please him. You show him in your actions that you are his. Does that make sense?"

Sierra nodded her head implying that she understood. She lied to Elise. She had no idea what she was talking about. She would just have to wait and see.

Sierra put on her dress and waited for her father. Elise thought she looked like a mythical princess. She glowed with the love and excitement she felt for Marcus. She was finally getting what she had always hoped for. She was getting her soldier. Monroe came in and started crying as he looked at his baby. She was going to be another man's wife in such a short time, yet she would always be his baby.

His heart ached with the want to keep her to himself just a little longer.

Elise and Bridgette left the two so that they may be alone before the ceremony. The two ladies made their way to the waiting clans. Elise took her seat with Luc. He smiled and kissed her lightly on the lips as he took her hand in his. Marcus was standing on the newly built gazebo. It was dark rustic wood with many jars lighting up the vines and branches that hung from it. Marcus was handsome standing in his uniform waiting for his bride. Like Luc had for their wedding, Marcus was clean cut and shaven. The cousins were a dynamic pair, especially in their uniforms.

Everyone watched as Monroe and his daughter came into view. She was stunning. Marcus and Sierra complimented each other equally. Both were handsome, tall, and striking. Elise and Luc held onto each other as the bride and groom made the promise to love and cherish each other as husband and wife. Monroe gave the couple a gift, two rings from his own marriage with his beautiful wife that he loved and missed dearly. When the couple kissed as husband and wife, the crowd cheered.

The groups once again enjoyed food, and wine and stayed up late into the night celebrating. Elise kissed her husband goodnight letting him know she couldn't stay up any longer. Luc assured his wife by kissing her cheek and whispering softly in her ear, "I won't be far behind you my love." He gave her chills, and she couldn't wait until the time came when they could once again make love.

Marcus pulled Sierra into his room. He lit a candle, then proceeded to light them a fire. Sierra took in her surroundings. His room, no, their room. The room was basic with minimal clutter. She remained by the door as she tried to familiarize herself with her new accommodations.

Marcus realized that she must be a little nervous, "Please. Come in. Sit down. This is ours now."

He walked over to her and took her hands in his. He leaned over and kissed her lightly on her cheek. She smiled at him. He nodded to the bed, walking over to it. He sat down, then patted the spot next to himself.

Feeling unsure of herself, she moved sluggishly to sit next to him.

"I'm not going to hurt you, Sierra." He assured her softly, his tone a masculine, seductive timbre showing his need. "I want you. I've wanted you since the moment we met."

He kissed her neck sending shivers down her body. He got off the bed, pulling her up to stand with him. He wanted her to get out her dress. Ruining her mother's dress in his haste would not go well for him in the future. He slipped his hand along her neck, then unzipped her dress.

"Slip out of your dress for me. Let me watch you. I want to see every inch of your body."

Sierra was shy. Feeling naughty, she started at her shoulders. His eyes took a more seductive look indicating his arousal. She watched him. She noticed his reaction, giving her more bravado. She moved the dress to a nearby chair. She stood with her back to him, letting him look at her. Her shyness was gone. She stood proud like a Greek statuette. She turned her head so that he could view her profile.

His need brought him to her; he pressed himself against her back. Running his fingers through her long blond hair, he tangled them until he had a firm grip and pulled. He kissed her neck, then took his hand to the base of her throat and ran his hand along her collar bone, stopping at one of her soft rosy peaks. She arched her back against him, letting him know that she was ready for him.
She wanted to touch him but was too afraid. She didn't know if he would want that.

He laid on top of her as she stretched out on the bed. He stayed between her legs, kissing her face and neck. He wrapped her legs around him, needing some form of touch from her. He took his time exploring her body. He concentrated on her rosy peaks. She had no idea that she could be so wanton, her peaks sensitive, she yearned for more.

Marcus could no longer take the foreplay. He entered his bride, startling her. He pressed himself deep into her barrier. He hadn't asked but should have known. He kissed away her tears. He continued slower, more aware of her need to understand their joining. He took her hand and placed it on his body to show her that he needed to be touched as much as she did. He whispered French words softly in her ear. She smiled, she understood.

Elise woke the next morning feeling refreshed and ready to face her day. Unlike most mornings, this one she did not wake up alone. Luc was sleeping hard by her side. She had been too tired to wait up for him last night. She had no clue when he came to bed, so she let him sleep and went to the dining hall alone. She was greeted by Jack and Monroe sipping their morning coffee.

"Good morning, little sister."

"Morning Jack. Good morning, Monroe." She walked past the duo and into the kitchen.

Monroe smiled at Jack, "She seems happy this morning."

Jack nodded. Maybe Luc had finally stopped being a pecker head. He would never say something like that to Monroe, so he held his silence.

He was surprised when Monroe made another comment, "Looks like Luc finally figured out his ass from his elbow."

Jack smiled, maybe he did, he thought to himself.

Monroe decided that today was the day to go back to his home. His daughter was married, and she would need this time to settle in with her new people. He planned to visit often, but still felt torn. He wondered if his home would feel like home without his daughter there. He may need to rethink what piece of land he considered his sanctuary.

Monroe said his goodbye's and left with his people. Sierra asked him to stay, but he explained to her that he had to go. He promised her that he would be back soon and would visit often. They had a brief moment to themselves, but he could not bring himself to tell her his burden. As he watched Clan Woodsmen's compound fade behind him, his heart felt a great sadness. His regret was immense. He needed to tell his daughter the truth. He just couldn't bring himself to do it.

CHAPTER 23

The trees had long since lost their leaves. Snow began to fall. It was hardly the first snow since winter had started, but the dark sky promised it would be a lasting one. Luc pulled Elise closer to himself. They stood next to the blazing fireplace. Her time was nearing, and she had to constantly adjusted herself for comfort. Luc smiled down at his wife. He absently touched her protruding stomach, hoping to feel movement from his child.

As Elise neared the birth, she couldn't help but be wary. She was afraid something would go wrong. She was semi-terrified of the birthing itself. She remembered the pain from her first child. At that time, she had the assistance of her doctor, nurses and even drugs. Even with all that, the pain had been almost unbearable. Her body felt like it was going to rip itself in two. This time would be different, much different, harder. She thought about her daughter and Luc's son. She wondered if this was a hard time for him as well. She tried not to think about it. She tried not to dwell in the past. It hurt too much, and heartbreak from the past had no bearing on their future.

Elise sat in her rocker next to the fire. She was sewing something thing for the baby. She knew her time was coming regardless if she was prepared. The child would come when he or she was ready. Elise made many things for her child. She was getting good at sewing. She had been with Clan Woodsman for almost a year and she felt content. She rubbed the cloth. It was soft cotton and would make a fine nightgown for a baby. She was careful to keep her garments gender neutral.

Her mind drifted to a place and time long ago, when her brothers had walked in bringing male gifts only to find out that her baby was going to be a girl. They had seemed disappointed at the time. They changed their minds when her daughter was born, and they held the tiny infant in their arms.

Sierra came in to check on her, bringing her something to eat. Sierra, on the other hand, did not feel the same contentment with Clan Woodsmen. She missed her father when he was home. He promised to visit and did so often, but she felt melancholy, yearning for what was comfortable. Sierra tried to hide her feelings. She never revealed the depth of her sorrow, but her husband knew. Marcus did not know how to make his wife passionate towards him. He was a passionate man, much like Luc. His wife's formally cold heart did little to help the couple. She loved him, he felt that was true, but why couldn't he melt her heart?

Sierra put the tray of food down for Elise, "How are you feeling today?"

Elise smiled at her friend, "I'm good. Thank you for bringing me something to eat. I'm starving."

Sierra watched Elise labor out of the rocker and walk to the table. She stood looking out the window. "Are you going to sit?" Sierra was curious, not understanding why Elise preferred to stand.

Elise turned back around to look at her friend, then replied, "It's too hard to go up and down. I've been sitting for a bit, so I think I will try and stand for a while."

Sierra nodded her head, "I am going to take a walk, would you like to join me?"

Elise was tired but nodded her head in agreement. She knew she needed to walk to help with the birthing. She tried making herself do it every day. It was just too easy to become lazy, especially in the winter months.

Elise and Sierra bundled up and decided to search out their husbands as an excuse. The cousins were in the barn when their wives joined them. The men were surprised to see them, especially since it was so cold out.

"I don't want you going far. I actually don't want you out at all, Elise."

"I know Luc, it's just a short walk. Besides, it's good for the baby."

He smiled, leaned over and kissed his wife. She loved the smell of him. He smelled like wood, sweat, and all male. She gave him a seductive look, and he grinned. He knew what promises that look held. Even though she was pregnant, she had not become lax in her duties as a wife. She knew how to please him and did so often.

The ladies finished their walk. Sierra walked with Elise back to her room, then sat down with her at the fireplace. They talked about the baby. Sierra asked so many questions that Elise became suspicious enough to ask her a question. "Are you pregnant?"

Sierra looked down at her hands, "Yes, I think so anyways."

"When was your last monthly?"

Sierra thought about it for a moment, "A month or so. I'm not sure. I've had it where I've skipped a month before."

Elise shook her head. Most women have had those issues from time to time. "Why do you think you are pregnant?"

"Well, I'm feeling a little crappy."

Elise knew there could be many symptoms; sometimes it was just PMS. "Do your breast hurt?"

Sierra nodded her head briskly. "Oh, wow, yes, something unbelievable."

Elise shook her head, "You may be pregnant." Elise was feeling tired, "I'm sorry Sierra, I need to rest." Sierra nodded her head, she held out her hand for her friend. After helping Elise out of her rocker and into bed, she turned to leave.

"Elise."

Elise opened her eyes, looking at Sierra. She responded, "Yes?"

"Please don't say anything."

Elise smiled, "Don't worry Sierra; my lips are sealed."

Elise woke from her nap with a tightening in her abdomen. It felt light and moderately uncomfortable. She knew it was time for her baby to come. She didn't panic; she just laid there resting. She recalled that her labor before had lasted hours, so she knew she needed all the strength she could get. She closed her eyes and tried to go back to sleep.

The more the day went on, the more intense her pains became. Realizing she need to get someone before it was too late, she tried to get out of bed, but she fell to the floor as a contraction hit her. She cried out in pain.

Jack rushed into her room, finding her on the floor. He grabbed her up into his arms and put her back on the bed.

"It's time, Jack. The baby is coming." She cried out in pain as once again another contraction hit her.

"Damn it, E. They are right on top of each other. Why didn't you get someone sooner? I'll be right back."

He left her alone and went to get help. Another pain hit her, and she wondered if she was going to be able to handle it this time around.

Jack let Bridgette know what was going on, then went in search of Luc. He found him in the shed, elbow deep in the engine of one of the Jeeps. Luc waved in greeting, showing Jack his greasy hands.

"You better clean up, the baby's coming."

Luc jumped out of the engine hitting his head on his light. "Jack, let her know I'm coming. Please."

Jack knocked on the bedroom door before entering. He had no wish to see his sister's gina, no matter how beautiful and natural giving life was. Bridgette answered the door and Jack rushed through what he wanted to say, having no desire to stick around.

"Is she okay?"

Bridgette nodded.

"Luc is on his way. He's got to clean up first."

Bridgette nodded again, then put her finger up indicating she needed him to wait. She closed the door, then returned with a towel, washcloth, bar of soap, and what looked like a change of clothing. Jack took the items he had been given and met Luc coming in. Luc realized when he saw Jack that he was meant to clean up before he came to his room. At that moment, Elise cried out in pain. Both men paled, unsure of what to do.

Marcus came back to the house and upon hearing Elise in pain, he went straight to his room. He found his wife face down in the pillows, with her hands over her ears. She could hear how much pain Elise was in and knew that she would feel the same a few short months later. Marcus lay on the bed. He rubbed her back trying to sooth her, unsure of why she was so affected by the sounds.

Bridgette used a cloth to clean away the sweat from Elise. She was exhausted from the effort and the pain. She kept asking Bridgette for Luc and she kept assuring her that he was coming. Bridgette did not know what to do. She had never assisted in the birthing before. She needed Jene. She rung out the washcloth, then repeated it again and again. Finally, Luc showed up. He pulled the thin sheet from his wife. The sheet was soaked from blood and sweat. He knew that he was going to have to be the one to bring his own child into this world.

"Luc, I'm going to go get Jene."

Luc looked at Bridgette. "There is no time. We have to help her now. You can do this."

Elise screamed out in pain. He could see his child's head. "Stop screaming, next time push. You have to push."

Another contraction came and Elise screamed out.

"Damn it, Elise, you have to push!" Elise pushed as hard as she could; she held her scream until she thought she was going to pass out. Luc grabbed the baby's head and pulled as Elise pushed. The baby finally came out and Luc looked down at his son.

"You did it, Elise. It's a boy. He's a fine-looking boy."

Elise smiled, then closed her eyes. Luc cut the cord and handed his son to Bridgette. "Clean him up, then get out. She's lost a lot of blood."

Bridgette did as she was asked, she closed the door quietly as she took the baby with her.

Luc cleaned up Elise, then the bed. He checked on her constantly, to make sure she was breathing. He knew the best thing to do was to let her rest. He sat in the rocker watching her sleep. He was awoken with the sound of Jack entering the room carrying his son.

Jack walked over to Luc, whispering to him, "How is she?"

Luc looked over at his wife. "She's okay. She needs the rest."

Jack handed Luc his son, "That's a good-looking kid. Man, you guys did a good job. I took him from Bridgette as soon as she walked out with him. I figured that I've had him long enough."

Luc smiled up at Jack as he put his hand on his shoulder. Jack left them, turning back to see Luc holding his son up and admiring him.

The baby crying woke Luc and Elise. She pulled him closer to herself to nurse. Luc kissed his wife and lovingly admired the pair. "I love you, Elise."

She sleepily responded to her husband, "I love you back, Luc."

"What are we going to name him?"

Elise answered her husband with more of a question than a statement, "Kyle, after my brother?"

Luc nodded his head, "I like it, Ma Chérie."

Luc wouldn't allow Elise out of bed for days. She even took her meals in bed. She felt like a prisoner, but the more she complained the more he would insist. She knew she needed to heal, but she felt that he was taking it to the extreme. People came to see the young family. They wanted to congratulate the new parents and see the baby. Elise was thankful for Bridgette. She stayed by her side helping with everything. She knew that seeing her baby born would seal a bond between them forever. Jack was proud that the couple had named their baby after his brother. He missed his brother and he knew Elise must feel the same.

A few weeks had gone by since the birth of their son. Life was getting back to normal. Luc no longer fussed over his wife. He went back to being a leader and a soldier, leaving the house to the women. Elise was still recovering but gaining her strength with each day. Elise threw a log on the fire to keep the chill from the room.

Kyle was asleep swaddled in a blanket on the bed. Rose laid in a bed close to the fire; she yawned and stretched, content to be warm. Elise walked to the window. She stretched and looked out into the cold grey sky. The last snow had not disappeared when this one started to fall. She could see some of the men outside practicing with one another. Others were riding their horses for exercise. She liked to watch her husband ride his horse. They looked powerful as one, man and beast; they were a vibrant and commanding pair.

Elise heard commotion in the yard as Luc rode past her window in a full gallop. She walked outside. She could see a man from Monroe's at the gate. She did not understand what was going on.

Luc rode back to main house, leaving his horse in the open courtyard. He jumped down, rushing over to Elise. He grabbed her shoulders. "Get inside. Stay with the baby. Someone raided Tribe Monroe. His hamlet is on fire. I have to get my men and go."

Elise was shocked, "Be careful, Luc."

He kissed her passionately, "I will my love." He turned, jumped on his horse, and rushed to find the men he would be taking.

Luc was worried about leaving his compound, but he had no choice; he had to help his friend. He left most of his men behind, taking only Jack, Robert, and Brent. He needed Marcus to stay behind. Marcus was pissed, but Luc didn't want anyone else to be responsible for his wife and child.

The four riders pushed their horses. They could see smoke in the distance. A strong burning smell assaulted their senses; it was a combination of wood and earth. Luc was not prepared for the scene that he came upon. Everything had been burned. Bodies were lying everywhere. The men jumped off their horses. They started checking the bodies for signs of life.

Jack hollered for Luc. Monroe was on the ground covered in blood. He had a gash across his forehead and along his side. He was barely conscious; he mumbled something to the men that they could not decipher. Luc started caring for Monroe as Jack moved on to look for signs of life among the bodies littering their surroundings.

With a sad heart, Robert and Brent had already started making a uniform line of men needing to be buried. These people had become their friends.

Marcus asked everyone to get inside the main house. He had an uneasy feeling is gut. He had Bridgette and Elise make sure that all the windows and all entryways were barred tight, except the main entrance. The crowd was loud with speculation. People were talking, children were running around, and babies were crying.

Elise sat in a corner trying to comfort her infant, but the chaos around him seemed to keep him on edge.

Marcus walked over to Elise, "I'm sorry, but I need you close by, I need to keep eyes on you. Luc would kill me if something were to happen to you."

She understood, but she didn't respond. She didn't have to; her look told him that she would not fight him.

"I'll grab you a chair. Why don't you come into the storeroom? Maybe it will be quieter. I just don't want you in your room."

Marcus paced around the halls of the main house. He constantly checked on Elise and Kyle. He moved her rocker into the storeroom and the duo napped unaffected by the turmoil raging inside of him. He stood at the entrance watching them sleep. Elise must have felt his eyes because hers opened softly, she noticed Marcus. She smiled and gave him a light wave. He took in the scene, then walked away.

He wondered what he was doing wrong as a husband. He wished his young wife had half the passion Elise held for his cousin. He could see it in the way Elise looked at Luc and the way she touched him. He could feel the energy between them when they were together. Marcus walked to a window staring out into the ending day. The sun was close to setting, yet the men had not returned.

Sierra walked around asking if anyone needed anything. She watched her husband pacing and wondered if there was anything she could do. She felt helpless. She wanted to help ease his mind but didn't know what to do to or what to say. Someone had told her stories of soldiers when she young. Men like him didn't need simple emotions from women. They were hard and took what they wanted. They didn't want a woman falling all over them. She remembered what she had been told and tried to be what she thought a warrior would need. She walked over to where he stood staring out into the sky. She moved her hand to place it on his back, then put it back down. She wanted to touch him, but she couldn't handle rejection or an unkind word from him. She turned and walked away wondering if he even knew she had been there.

Marcus turned and watched his wife walk away. Why didn't she say anything? Why didn't she let him in? He didn't have time to ponder when the sound of something exploding ricocheted in his ears.

His group looked around in disbelief and terror. Marcus snatched up his rifle sitting by the door and rushed out. Elise stood up; the sound had startled her too. She ran into the dining hall putting Kyle into Sierra's arms. She rushed down the hall and into her room. She grabbed the knife that was hidden under Luc's pillow and hid it in her dress. Elise rushed back into the dining hall just as Marcus reentered.

He crouched down and pulled Elise lower. "Get everyone down! We are being attacked!" He rushed through his statement, then ran out the door.

Marcus half hid behind the wall of the compound with his rife aimed. The outer wall had been destroyed. He watched as a dozen or so riders came through the destruction that had once been their outer salvation. Marcus popped off a couple rounds and the riders stopped. A shot hit the wall just above Marcus, causing him to hide farther into the corner. He had to control his breathing. He took several sharp breaths. More shots could be heard. Marcus could tell by the multiple rounds they were coming from both enemy and friendly fire.

He calmed his breathing and psyched himself up for a run. He needed to find a better position. He crouched and ran for the cover of the horse barn.

A sharp ringing blast assaulted the air around Marcus, as pieces of wood and debris rained down all around him. Marcus' training instinctively told him a grenade had been lobed in his general direction. The barn was virtually shredded. He could see a horse lying on his side, his breathing labored. Marcus shook his head as he made a split-second decision. He knew what he had to do. He aimed his rifle at the wounded horse.

Shots hit the grass around him. He aimed and took out a rider galloping toward him. Another rider was shot from his perch next to his assaulter. Shots were being fired from all directions. Marcus could see other riders trying to burn down the buildings and yurts. He could see the smokehouse in flames.

One of his men ran to him, "These sons of bitches are destroying everything."

Marcus didn't need to be told; he could see it. He aimed his rifle taking another rider off of his horse. His comrade aimed, but before he could take his shot, he laid dead next to Marcus.

A truck pulled into the courtyard. Marcus watched as an RPG launched into the main compound. He stood as shots hit the ground around him. He aimed and took out the enemy that had just taken out one of the outer walls of the main compound. A shot rang in the air as Marcus fell to the ground. He sat up, checking his arms and chest, nothing. The pain in his leg started as he looked down. He'd been shot.

Elise was laying on the ground. There was a buzzing sound in her head. The sounds around her were muffled, almost an echo from far away. She looked around at the debris everywhere. What had just happened? People were looking around; it was like war in slow motion. Immediately, she got up, looking around for her son. She couldn't see him or Sierra. She became frantic; her screams seemed muffled.

Sierra appeared down the hall by the storeroom carrying her son. She indicated that she had been hiding in there. Elise pushed her back in and yelled for her to stay, then slammed the door.

The four riders could hear the havoc being unleashed on their home. Three riders pushed their horses forward with no thought to the fourth man burdened by the dying Monroe. They pushed forward until their compound could be seen. Luc now understood that the burning of Monroe's hamlet had been a trojan horse to separate and annihilate his clan. Luc and Jack reached the wall before Robert. They jumped off their horses, they grabbed their rifles as they hit the ground. They spoke quickly to each other. Luc took his rifle, aimed and looked around the wall; he covered Jack as he ran to the opposite side of a hole that had once been a solid barrier from the outside world.

By the time, the two men ran for it, Robert joined them laying down fire. Bullets were coming from all directions. They had to find cover behind debris, or anything to escape a shot. Luc ran up to the truck containing the assault rifle and RPG. Jack covered him as Luc jumped into the truck bed, startling the inhabitant. The men fought for a moment in hand-to-hand combat. Luc was the stronger man, always keeping his strength and stamina. He pulled his knife from his side, and in one quick stoke, he snuffed out the life of the lesser man.

With the truck secure and no longer a threat, the three men joined their comrades. Jack and Luc raced from cover to cover, destroying the interlopers. Luc spotted Marcus. Marcus was face down in a military crawl position, with his stomach on the ground, his forearms and only one knee doing all the work; his expression alone told Luc what he needed to know. His movements were labored. Luc knew he was wounded.

Robert yelled to the two men, "Cover me, I'm going for Marcus."

Robert raced out and grabbed Marcus as shots rained down around them. Robert pulled Marcus over to the truck and immediately applied pressure to his leg. Luc watched as Robert pulled out his knife and started cutting Marcus' pant leg.

Luc knew he was in good hands. He turned his attention back to Jack. "We need to get inside the main house. Cover me. When I reach the corner, I will lay down cover. Go to the opposite side of the wall. Try and get in a back way."

Jack shook his head, "I think we should stay together."

"No, I think our best chance is to split up. Damn it, Jack, just fucking cover me." He didn't give Jack a chance to respond. Luc took off, leaving Jack no alternative but to watch his friend's back.

Elise could hear the sounds of shot after shot coming from the outside. Everyone was afraid; hunkered down, they all just waited. She watched as the main door was thrown open. Two men rushed in, slamming the door behind themselves. She recognized one of the men right away. It was that chicken-shit, Trevor. The two men noticed her, then spoke to each other quietly.

Without breaking eye contact, the duo walked over to her. The taller, older version of Trevor walked up to her gripping her hair in his hand and yanking her to her feet. Elise screamed out in pain. One of the older Woodsmen stood up, then sat back down as a gun was aimed at his chest.

Trevor spoke to the man, "Yeah that's her. That's his whore."

"Good. He will be at our mercy." He grabbed Elise's face with his free hand, squeezing another cry from her. "You ready to watch him die?"

Elise spit in his face. He slapped her hard across the face, then he pushed her to ground. As soon as she hit the ground, he kicked her.

"He will kill you both." She said as she wiped the blood from her mouth, smearing it across her cheek and hand.

"Stop hurting her, Logan. She won't be any use to us."

"Shut your mouth Trevor. Do something useful before I decide to end your miserable existence."

Trevor walked away. He stood and looked out the closest window. He could see and hear the chaos in the yard. He moved around the room looking out each window. He could see men in all directions. He watched as his clansmen were struck down, man after man. He grew uneasy wondering if they would make it out alive. He turned his back away from the window. He walked over to Elise and yanked her up by her arm. "Get me something to drink, bitch."

Elise narrowed her eyes at him. "You bastard! What do you think the General is going to do after you betrayed him? Welcome you and your friend? The General is going to cut your heart out."

Trevor pointed to the man, "Logan is my brother, the leader of my clan. After today, I will be leader of your clan, and you, Elise, will be mine."

"I will never be yours."

"We will see."

Elise walked to the storeroom and grabbed bottles of wine. She put her finger up to her mouth indicating to Sierra to be quite and stay hidden. She walked up to Trevor handing him the bottles. Logan walked over to them.

He sneered at Elise. "You know your place. You will beg me to leave you alone long before I tire of you."

"Logan, she is mine. This clan is mine."

Logan backhanded his little brother, "Nothing is yours, Trevor, nothing."

The door burst open, and they all turned in that direction. Luc recognized Trevor and his companion immediately. Luc pointed his assault rifle at the man who was once his prisoner, the man Trevor released. He didn't bother closing the door. The man pulled Elise in front of himself and used her as a shield.

"Nice to see you again, you chicken shit. I get to finish what I started months ago. I should have put a bullet in you while you were locked in my shed."

Logan laughed at Luc. He sneered at him, "That is what is wrong with you. You aren't vicious enough. You should have killed me when you had the chance. Now I'm going to kill you."

"Don't worry, I won't hesitate again."

Luc turned his attention to Trevor, he aimed, one shot. The man hit the floor.

Logan gripped Elise's hair tighter causing her to scream out in pain. "I'm going to make you watch her die, then I'm going to kill you."

Elise pulled the knife from her dress. She gripped the handle and thrust it into Logan. She heard him cry out in pain as she was shoved sideways. She hit the floor with speed. Glass shattered around her as two shots rent the air simultaneously. She covered her ears as she lay on the ground.

CHAPTER 24

Luc rushed to Elise. He grabbed her up and pulled her into his arms, "Are you okay, Ma Chérie?"

She was shaken but unhurt. "I'm okay." She looked out the window; her brother stood there, his rifle stilled aimed, looking at his sister and brother-in-law embrace.

Jack walked around the side of the compound. He wanted to make sure everything was secure. He walked around debris and saw nothing but destruction. He made his way to Marcus. Robert was still taking care of him when Jack offered his assistance. The two men picked up Marcus and headed back to what had been the main house.

Luc kissed Elise over and over. They looked around the chaos that once been their dining hall. People were hurt and many would need attention. Jack and Robert were bringing Marcus in through the door. She suddenly remembered Sierra. The couple headed to the storeroom to get their baby and help Marcus's bride.

Elise opened the door quietly. She whispered, "Sierra." No response. "Sierra?"

"Yes."

"It's okay. It's safe to come out."

Sierra's face was pale. She came out of her hiding spot and handed the still sleeping Kyle to his parents. She seemed lost and frightened. She rushed to Marcus as the men were bringing him into the open doorway. She felt helpless; she didn't know what to do.

Jene noticed that Brent was missing and starting crying and calling his name. Luc rushed over to her. "Jene, shhh, Jene. He is fine. He is with Monroe."

Sierra followed the men carrying Marcus to his side of the house. His room was undamaged. Bridgette began gathering cloth and had one of the men get water and start a fire outside. The kitchen was destroyed, leaving nothing of use.

Elise followed Luc as he went inside Marcus' room, he stopped Elise from coming in. He put a hand up indicating for her to wait for him outside. Elise felt like she waited forever. When Luc came out, the General was present. He was a hard-outer shell. He did not speak to her, nor did he look to see if she followed. Instead, he took for granted that she would. They walked to their end of the house. What had once been, was now gone. Rubble and debris replaced structure and security. Elise's cat ran between their legs and out of the way. She was grateful that her cat was unhurt.

"Luc, what are we going to do?"

He turned to her. "I don't know, Elise."

He ran his hands through his hair and took a deep breath. "We need to go and help the others. Can you stay inside and do that, please?"

He walked away without waiting for a response. Her baby started to cry, so she went to the storeroom for privacy. She sat down; tears streamed down her face as she started to nurse.

Luc went to the outer wall. He motioned for Brent that it was all safe to enter. He got back on his horse and pulled Monroe into the compound. The men had made a make-shift stretcher that the horse could pull. Brent stopped in front of the main door. He unstrapped his burden, then let his horse wander. He took in the scene around him. He was angry, hurt, but most of all saddened. Jene rushed out to her husband seeing him just beyond the doorway. She helped him get Monroe inside. Brent kissed his wife, then went back into the yard to start burying bodies, friend and foe.

The sun had already set, and the men were barely getting started. The women stayed in the main compound caring for the hurt. The men on the outside were sickened by what had transpired. Luc and Jack picked up a body and were carrying it to a pile to be buried.

Luc shook his head. "I should have listened to you. I should not have hesitated to kill that bastard while he was in our custody."

Jack responded, "I'm not an I-told-you-so kind of guy. Let's just clean this shit up."

The men were dead tired as they looked over the life-less bodies of their comrades. They realized that there were only six left of the original group. They dug enough holes for their men, leaving a large mass grave for their enemy. Twice today, on two different pieces of land, they would be burying friends because of one man's decision not to end a wasted life. Luc felt the weight of his decision on his shoulders. He internalized it. His men had a different view. All this death and destruction was because of the greed of one selfish bastard that didn't honor the sanctity of life.

The moon was bright giving the men the light they needed to complete their task. Luc needed a break; he needed his wife. He washed himself, then entered the main house. He walked, amongst his people still occupying the dining hall. He did not find her. He walked down the hall to Marcus' room. He did not knock, but just entered without thought. Sierra was sitting next to him. Marcus was sleeping. He was hot; he seemed fevered and restless.

Luc threw the covers off Marcus. "Get some water. Can't you see he's burning up? Do something."

"I'm sorry. I do not know what to do."

"Sitting there isn't helping anyone. Get Bridgette. Get Elise." He paused then shouted the last at her, "Get someone. NOW!"

Sierra rushed out. She looked for someone, anyone, to help. She found Elise coming out of the storeroom with her baby. She rushed over to her. "Please, come help the General, Marcus is burning up."

Elise nodded her head. She walked over to Jene, to give her Kyle. She went to find Bridgette, getting fresh water and cloth. The two women rushed to help Marcus.

Sierra watched the women rush away. She noticed her father laying on a cot in a corner. She walked over to him and fell to the ground beside him. She grabbed his hand and started crying. "Father, I'm sorry I didn't come to you sooner."

"Don't cry my daughter. You must be strong. Listen to me." He coughed; his breathing labored. He paused, "I must tell you something."

Sierra wiped the moisture from her face, "Okay Father."

A tear rolled down Monroe's face. "I should have told you this long ago, but I couldn't. I think you will hate me after I tell you my tale."

"No, I could never hate you."

"Long ago, when I was a younger man, I was starving and angry. I came upon a cabin. I went inside thinking it was deserted. I started ransacking the place for food. A man came in and caught me. He had a gun and we fought. A stray bullet shot a woman I didn't even know was there. After seeing his wife fall, the man became enraged and we fought, fought to the death. I had been a soldier. I was strong. The man died at my feet."

"It wasn't your fault. That could happen to anyone. Please, Father, don't cry."

Monroe wiped a tear from his face, then continued. "I stood looking down at the couple, sad and afraid, when a noise startled me. It was a baby crying. You, Sierra, were that baby."

Sierra snuffed a cry out with her hand, "It doesn't matter, you are my father. I love you."

Monroe cried in earnest, "I love you, Sierra. After that day, I vowed that I would never take another life." With that statement, Monroe drew his final breath, leaving a crying Sierra laying across his body.

Luc was sleeping in a chair next to Marcus. He hadn't left his side throughout the night. Sierra walked in with Bridgette. Sierra and Luc eyed each other but made no comments. Their eyes told the story. "Where is my wife?"

Bridgette was the one to answer him. "I believe she fell asleep with the baby in her old room. It was undamaged."

"Can you two please see to Marcus until I can return." It was a statement, not a question. He accepted no refusal.

"That is why we are here after all," Sierra replied to him briskly. She had little sleep. Her day had been a nightmare and her night even worse. She felt lost in sea of emotional turmoil.

Luc eyed her, saying nothing. The slight movement of his jaw was the only revelation to his thoughts. He turned and left the room. He walked down the hall and opened the door quietly. Elise and his son were sound asleep on the bed. He remembered the night he made love to her in that bed. He could feel her passion; he loved and embraced it. He thought about how smug he had been thinking that his fortress was virtually impenetrable. He closed the door and went in search of his men.

The bodies had all been buried. The surviving men searched the grounds looking for anything useful. As Luc walked out into the courtyard, his men started to gather and make their way to their General. Jack was the first to arrive. "Looks like a shit show in the light of day."

Luc ignored his comment, changing the subject. "You get any sleep?"

"Nope, you?"

"Some, not much, but some. I stayed with Marcus all night."

"Is he awake? How's he feeling?"

"He had fever all night, but slept through it. He's asleep right now, has been all night, he has yet to wake up. I haven't talked to him since Robert drowned him in alcohol, pulled the bullet, and cauterized his wound."

Jack shook his head, "Damn."

Robert and Brent walked up to the pair. They talked for a few minutes, then made their way to the shed. It was undamaged. Being so far in the field, the enemy had little time to destroy it. The horses that survived were grazing in the fields with the four they took on their mission to Monroe's.

Luc told his group that Monroe died sometime in the night. He wanted to take Monroe and bury him at home. He thought that would be what he would want. The men got the beast ready. They stopped at the big house, loaded Monroe, then searched out his daughter.

Tears streamed down Sierra's face as they rode into the hamlet. She looked around at the ashes that had once been her home. No one came to greet her. The General had brought her father home to be buried. She cried as the men dug the hole then laid the old man inside. A few words were spoken, but she could hear nothing but the sadness from her own inner voice.

Luc and his remaining men gathered around Marcus, who was still in his bed. He pushed past his fever, yet he still felt weak. Three days had passed, and his men had many questions.

Luc spoke first, "I'm sorry Marcus. We all know you are not feeling well, but we must discuss something."

Marcus gave them a crooked smile, then nodded his head, "I'm not going anywhere boys; spit it out."

Luc again was the first to comment, "Our compound suffered too much damage. It would take a lifetime to repair. Some men think we need to move on."

Marcus became more intent as he realized that this was no ordinary visitation.

Robert commented next, "I say we move on and find something better."

Jack shook his head, "There is nothing better. I say we repair what we have."

Brent agreed, "I don't want to uproot my family. I say we stay."

Robert wanted his position understood. "We have used all the resources close to us. We are too vulnerable. We need to go somewhere deserted. We need to become the nomads we once were."

Marcus looked at Luc. For once, his expression told him nothing, revealed nothing, and showed that, for once, he must ask the question, "How do you feel, Luc?"

Luc took a deep breath, "I do not know Marcus. I just do not know. We could go, then someday we could return."

Marcus took a deep breath, "I'm sorry I need to rest."

The men understood and left him, but the conversation was unfinished. The men could not leave it alone. A decision had to be made. They walked out into the fields and began once again. They talked and debated for what seemed hours. Finally, they made their decision. It was final. They walked back to the main house to tell their clan what they decided.

CHAPTER 25

Luc pulled Elise to himself. He kissed her passionately, taking in her smell. He loved her eyes, her face, he loved everything about his wife. He let her go, then walked around to the driver's side of the vehicle.

Elise sat down in the front seat of the Jeep. Kyle was strapped in a sling surrounding her body. Marcus and Sierra jumped in the back. She blew a kiss to her brother, Jack. He would be driving the second Jeep with Brent and his family. Robert and Bridgette would be in the beast with the others. A few of the men were on horses. They had the route and knew when and where to rendezvous.

Elise took one last look around her home, their home, a safe haven that had brought love back into her life. They were leaving behind a place they had all come to love, cherish, and feel comfort in. She was sad to go but knew that what they left behind were only things, replaceable objects. She was taking with her all the things in life she could not live without, her baby, her husband, her brother; her family. She took a deep breath. She knew their journey would not be easy. She looked at her husband sitting next to her as they pulled out of the compound. She held his hand as she cradled her son.

The group of men had decided where they would go. The desert. Another unknown. The men felt that it would be their best shot at survival. They thought the desert would be a secluded haven for them, somewhere they could finally be at peace, somewhere they could be safe, somewhere no one else would be.

Elise looked down at her son. He was beautiful. Hopefully, this new place would be an oasis, a new refuge. She squeezed her husband's fingers. Together they would be okay. Together they would survive. Together they would love and live.

Their journey would be long; days, months even. They would have to scavenge and take what they needed along the way, hopefully without drawing much attention.

Luc's main priority was to protect his wife and son. He would do whatever was necessary to protect his family and his clan. Luc squeezed Elise's fingers back.

"This place was once my haven, my refuge. Now you have given me my true sanctuary. Wherever you go, I go. You are my home, my life, my love."

She smiled. They were one.

To be continued:

Book 2 Clan Woodsmen: Desert Heat

The second edition is seen through the eyes of many Woodsmen where their journey for survival leads them into the unforgiving desert.

The General, Marcus and Elise struggle through their relationships with each other, and their relationships between each other. They journey through the desert, desperately trying to hold on to who they are.

Sierra learns how she fits into her new clan. She journeys through mental issues and struggles with her losses. She opens up and blossoms into the wife Marcus needs. She once again starts to paint as a means to cope, using the desert as her inspiration.

A fiery new addition to the clan, a desert beauty named Isabel, tries to settle her inner unrest between being a warrior, or a lover. With the help of Jack, she discovers that she can be both.

Through all of their struggles, through hunger and fear, they strive to maintain their humanity and faith using their strengths as one. They don't allow the betrayals of the past, to shape their relationship with the future.

Made in the USA
Columbia, SC
19 May 2021

38231315R00136